# GUARDIANS OF DHARMA

## The Hidden Resonance

BOOK 1



ASHISH GOYAL

Clever Fox® PUBLISHING

Chennai • Bangalore

CLEVER FOX PUBLISHING
Chennai, India

Published by CLEVER FOX PUBLISHING 2025

ISBN: 978-93-6707-499-2

# CONTENTS

# PREFACE

*I* am not an author.

I am a reader, a listener, and an imaginator — someone who builds entire world in the mind while reading or hearing a story.

This book is rooted in the love and guidance of my parents, Asha and Rajkumar, who inspired me to explore our scriptures and nurtured my curiosity for the Sanatan path. In this vast banyan of knowledge, I have touched only a few leaves, but they showed me where the roots lie.

My real inspiration came from my children, Raghav and Navya. In today's fast-paced, reel-driven world, long tales often lose their patience. So I began telling them short stories — weaving Sanatan truths into everyday moments — and without realising it, I had been writing this book in my heart for the last 5–7 years.

To my wife, Smita, who has always stood beside me in every dream and every madness; to my niece and nephew, Prisha and Manas, and to my sister, Shripriya — my lifelong supporter and one of my fiercest critics.

To my friends and colleagues, who read patiently, questioned honestly, and helped shape these pages. And to my daughter — my toughest critic — who guided me to write in the style you now hold in your hands, even if she still believes it could be better.

I bow in gratitude to every legendary personality appearing in this book. Each one has touched my soul somewhere, and I have taken the creative liberty to weave them into this work with respect and love.

My thanks also goes to the quiet companions of this journey — the first light of dawn, the midnight silence, the moments I borrowed from time, the pen and paper that carried my words, and the modern tools — Google, Microsoft, AI, my reMarkable, my iPad, my laptop — that helped me gather and shape them. Above all, to the Creator of the Universe, who gave me the grace to create.

This book is dedicated to young readers, to Gen Z, and to parents who wish to plant the seed of Sanatan culture in their homes and hearts. If this work inspires even a single reader to pause, reflect, and take pride in our heritage, I will feel accomplished.

As this is my debut, I ask forgiveness for any errors — factual or in spirit — and for any moment where I may not have met your reading quest.

May these pages not just be read, but felt — like echoes of an ancient song in a modern heart.
May every young seeker find in them a spark of courage, a thread of belonging, and a reminder that dharma is never far away.

And so, with folded hands, I leave you with this blessing…

रक्षकाः धर्मनादं च पालयन्तु सदाऽधुना ।

रक्षकाः सत्यदीपं च प्रदीपयन्तु नित्यम् ॥

***May the Guardians protect every resonance of Dharma.***
***May the Guardians enkindle the eternal flame of Truth.***

Those who wish to reach me may write to: ashishgoyal_jpr2001@yahoo.co.in

***Ashish***

*To continue this journey with me visit:*
**www.guardiansofdharma.com**

# SECTION ONE

# THE AWAKENING

## Chapter 1

# WHISPERS IN THE MIST

*"Strange," Navya whispered. "The winds feel...*
*different tonight."*

The moon hung low, like a half-shut eye watching from the sky. Pine trees rustled softly as if trading secrets with the wind. Far off, an owl's lonely call pierced the stillness that had settled over Saraswati Valley Academy.

Navya stood by the tall arched window of her dorm room, her silhouette framed in moonlight. Her eyes traced the hills in the distance — dark, hushed outlines that bordered the valley like ancient sentinels. The forests beyond seemed to breathe — not just with wind, but with something older. Something watching.

Unseen by the rest of the world, something had stirred.

Two floors below, Prisha sat cross-legged on her bed, the moonlight brushing the open pages of her old copy of the *Shrimad Bhagavatam*. A quiet ritual she had inherited from her grandfather — one that lived on in whispers and verses.

Her fingers glided across the delicate script as her lips formed the ancient mantra:

**"Om Namo Bhagavate Vasudevaya**
**Saccidanandarūpaya**
**Viśvotpattyadihetave..."**

***"I bow to Lord Vasudeva, whose form is eternal, full of knowledge and bliss; who is the cause of the universe's creation, sustenance, and dissolution."***

She closed her eyes and whispered the meaning aloud. The words hummed like a soft pulse beneath her skin, as if the verse itself remembered something she did not. How could something so old feel so... alive?

A light knock pulled her back.

Navya stepped in.

"Can't sleep?" Prisha asked, already knowing.

Navya shrugged. "Neither can you. Reading your favourite grandpa scriptures again?"

Her voice teased, but her eyes lingered on the glowing page. For all her sarcasm, even Navya felt the pull of the words — though she rarely admitted it.

"They speak to me," Prisha said quietly. "Sometimes I feel like... they're waiting."

Navya leaned against the bedpost, arms folded. "Strange night, isn't it? The forest feels... awake."

The silence that followed wasn't empty. It was full. Full of unspoken questions, quiet stirrings, and a thread — invisible but taut — that connected them to something just beyond their reach.

**Earlier that morning...**

Saraswati Valley Academy sat like a crown carved from stone, nestled deep in the green folds of Uttarakhand's hills, a few quiet kilometres outside Dehradun.

Built in the late 19th century by Sir Harold Statham — a British officer enchanted by Indian philosophy — the school had grown into a rare blend of old-world charm and modern excellence. His vision? To build a place where science, art, culture, and the ancient wisdom of India could breathe together.

A long driveway lined with Sal trees led to a sandstone building crowned by a tall white clocktower. Classrooms branched out like wings, and beyond them, past a lotus pond, the hostels sat like sleepy guardians of teenage dreams.

It was late autumn. The mornings carried the crisp perfume of pine and wildflowers. Evenings cloaked the valley in fog soft as old wool.

Inside the school's grand auditorium, excitement bubbled like soda fizz.

"... and first place in Class 11 goes to — *Baani Gandhi!*"

Principal Bhargava's calm, resonant voice echoed across the room.

Polite applause followed as Baani, graceful as ever, walked up to receive her medal. Sharp-witted, soft-spoken, and humble to the core — even the quieter students nodded in approval.

Prisha and Navya clapped too, exchanging a private smile.

Two rows behind, Agastya's arms folded across his chest, his jaw tight. Ishaan, Simran, and Kabir — his usual orbit — exchanged dramatic eye-rolls.

"And now," the principal continued, "Special recognition for innovation in the Tech Club goes to — *Manas Agarwal!*"

A ripple of laughter followed as Manas stood, hair in wild disarray, looking as though he had just been struck by lightning. Which, knowing Manas, wasn't entirely off.

Professor Aalekh — the ever-jovial PE instructor — leaned towards Raghav.

"Your friend's brain might short-circuit one day," he chuckled.

"As long as he doesn't fry mine," Raghav replied.

Aalekh laughed. "That's the spirit, young man!"

**Later, in the Mess Hall...**

The scent of hot parathas and tomato soup hung in the air. Wooden benches creaked under laughing students as the hall filled with clatter, chaos, and ketchup debates.

Mrs. Smita — queen of the kitchen and mess supervisor extraordinaire — patrolled like a general in a flowery apron.

"Navya! Eat your vegetables. You skipped breakfast, too!"

"Aunty," Navya groaned, "you sound worse than my mom."

"That's a compliment," Mrs. Smita replied, pointing her ladle like a weapon of affection.

Prisha giggled. "Navya, one day you'll *miss* this food."

Navya rolled her eyes. "Maybe... but *today* isn't that day."

**In the Library...**

By evening, the library whispered a different kind of peace. Old books breathed softly under golden lamplight. A grandfather clock ticked like a patient sage.

Mrs. Pragya, the librarian, noticed Prisha flipping through a book.

"You've found my favourite guest," she said warmly.

"It feels... alive," Prisha replied.

"It is," Mrs. Pragya smiled. "Knowledge never dies. Scriptures don't just sit. They wait — for the right hearts to awaken them."

Navya, standing nearby, muttered, “Still looks like just another heavy book with difficult words.”

Mrs. Pragya chuckled. “Even the wildest rivers begin as a hidden spring. You, too, will find your stream, Navya.”

Neither of them knew then — how true those words would be.

**Back to the Mess...**

Standing by the window once more, Navya whispered, “Do you ever feel like something’s... calling us?”

Prisha gently closed the *Bhagavatam*. Her fingers lingered on the cover, tracing the embossed script.

“I do. But I don’t know what it means… yet.”

Outside, the wind whispered through the valley. The hills stood quiet, old, listening.

And deep within the forest — past where eyes could see and reason could follow — something ancient stirred.

The Guardians of Dharma were beginning to awaken.

---

*सच्चिदानन्दरूपाय विश्वोत्पत्त्यादिहेतवे ।*
*तापत्रय विनाशाय श्रीकृष्णाय वयं नमः ॥*

*Meaning*

***We bow to Lord Shri Krishna,***
***who is of the nature of existence, consciousness, and bliss;***
***who is the cause of the universe’s creation and dissolution;***
***and who removes the threefold sufferings of life.***

*(Bhagavatam: Canto 1, Chapter 1, Shloka 1)*

---

SARASWATI
VALLEY ACADEMY

# Chapter 2

# THE FOREST BECKONS

It began like any other school day at Saraswati Valley Academy — the usual bustle of uniforms, bells, and announcements. But beneath it all, something was shifting.

Winter's breath had begun to whisper across the hills. Dew clung to windowpanes like tiny secrets, and the pine trees outside rustled in an unspoken rhythm. Students pulled their navy-blue sweaters closer as the morning assembly began under a bright-blue sky.

Prisha Jain stood quietly in line, eyes half-lost in thought. Next to her, Navya Agrawal tapped her foot — impatient, as always.

Principal Bhargava delivered his usual Monday mantra on "discipline and dignity," while Professor Aalekh, the PE instructor, yawned discreetly beside him.

Navya leaned in and whispered, "If he says 'value-based education' one more time, I'll pass out standing."

Prisha stifled a giggle.

"Silence in the line, girls!" came the sharp voice of Ms. Ankita, the science teacher with eyes like X-rays and bangles that never dared to jingle.

The assembly ended. Classes began.

**Period Two: History with Mrs. Menon**

If Ms. Ankita was steel, Mrs. Menon was silk. Her soft sari and gentle sandalwood perfume brought a hush to the room. Today, she spoke with quiet warmth.

"Children, do you know why the Indus Valley Civilization is still talked about today?"

Baani Gandhi's hand shot up. "Because it's so old? Like, it's one of the very first cities in the world?"

Mrs. Menon nodded. "That's right, Baani. But it's not just the age—it's what those people did with their time. They built cities with running water, planned streets, and even had a form of writing we still can't fully read. Their solutions to everyday problems are still inspiring."

Prisha added, "Did they really live so differently from us?"

Mrs. Menon smiled at her. "In some ways, yes—no smartphones, no internet. But in other ways, not so different. They cared about their homes, their families, and how to live together peacefully. Some of their inventions—like drainage systems—were ahead of their time, and we use those ideas even now."

Navya groaned. "But why does it matter in the 21st century?"

Mrs. Menon's smile was steady. "Because knowing how people adapted and innovated in the past helps us solve problems today. It's about learning from the world's first city-builders, not just reading about them."

For a moment—even if she'd never admit it—Navya felt almost curious. Prisha looked out the window, still thoughtful.

**Post-Lunch Silence**

After a hearty lunch (with Mrs. Smita personally supervising Navya's salad), most students drifted into a food coma.

Not Prisha.

She slipped away to the library — her sanctuary. Behind tall shelves and the scent of ancient paper, she settled on a cushion beneath a carved window that opened towards the forest.

Outside, the trees swayed. The breeze sighed. A koel called.

Something inside her stirred.

Then — footsteps. Gentle, earthy.

It was Abdul chacha, the gardener, balancing a tray of potted herbs.

"Again dreaming of the jungle, beti?" he asked, placing a tulsi plant on the sill.

"I think the jungle dreams of me too, Abdul chacha."

He smiled, brushing the leaves with fingers worn by seasons.

"Maybe you were born under the stars of the *vanadevis* — the forest goddesses. Go. The trees wait for those who listen."

**Later That Evening...**

Navya stood near the herbal garden, scrolling through her smartwatch, pretending to be bored.

But her eyes kept drifting towards the woods.

Something about those purple-leafed creepers she'd seen two days ago still tugged at her.

She didn't hear Prisha approach.

"You're going into the forest?" Prisha asked softly.

Navya jumped. "Wha—? No! I mean... maybe."

They stared at each other for a second.

Then both laughed.

They didn't need to explain it. Both had felt the same pull — that silent call echoing from the trees.

**That Night**

Stars shimmered like silver seeds scattered across the velvet sky.

In two separate dorm rooms, two girls opened their windows at the same time — unknowingly connected.

They breathed in the air.

And for a heartbeat longer than usual, they each felt it:

A hum beneath the soil.
A rhythm in the wind.
As if the forest had a heartbeat — and it had just begun to stir.

They didn't know yet...
But soon, this rhythm would become the song of their lives.

---

*स वै पुंसां परो धर्मो यतो भक्तिरधोक्षजे ।*
*अहैतुकी अपरतिहता या यात्मा सुप्रसीदति ॥*

*Meaning*

***The highest dharma for all humanity***
***is that which awakens pure, unmotivated,***
***and uninterrupted devotion***
***to the Supreme Lord —***
***for only such devotion can fully satisfy the soul.***

*(Bhagavatam: Canto 1, Chapter 2, Shloka 6)*

---

# Chapter 3

# WHISPERS BEHIND THE CURTAIN

**Three Weeks Before Winter Exams**

The exam bell rang loud and urgent, slicing through the soft Dehradun air. At Saraswati Valley Academy, winter had begun to tighten its grip — breaths fogged the air like tiny ghosts, and woollen mufflers wrapped tighter around anxious necks.

Inside the assembly courtyard, students stood in lines, half-awake but wholly nervous.

Principal Bhargava stepped to the podium.

"Children," he began, "final exams are not merely about marks, but about mindfulness. Let Saraswati—the goddess of wisdom—guide your thoughts."

Baani tugged her woollen cap lower. "Three weeks to academic doom," she muttered.

"Three weeks to Bhargava sir's motivational monologues," Prisha added.

"And counting," Navya yawned.

Professor Aalekh came forward.

"One announcement: This week, we begin emergency preparedness drills. Due to recent cyber threats and regional tensions, you'll also have advanced PE sessions. Mental and physical resilience is no longer optional — it's essential."

A murmur passed through the students.

"And," he added with a wink, "we may just discover the next Olympic champion."

Groans and fist pumps followed alike.

## Morning Garden Encounter

On her way to class, Prisha passed the herbal garden. Abdul chacha was tending to the rose bed, his fingers gently brushing the soil.

"Off to the forest again?" he asked without looking.

"Just the edge," she replied. "It's... calming."

Abdul turned, eyes warm but serious.

"Forests are like a sacred book, beti. They speak only to those who truly listen. But remember — even the purest verses have hidden warnings."

He stood, brushing off his kurta.

"The forest is good. But some paths mislead. Some roots entangle. Even trees forget their own way home."

Prisha hesitated.

"I'll be careful."

He smiled.

"Even if the world is ending and you hold a sapling — plant it. The world needs caretakers more than conquerors."

The words stayed with her — heavy, yet strangely hopeful.

## PE Drill Mayhem

The PE field had transformed into a bootcamp. Ropes, cones, tire paths — a war zone disguised as sport.

"Breathe like warriors, not snoring grandfathers!" Professor Aalekh roared.

Raghav collapsed beside Manas.

"I just saw my soul leave my body."

Manas checked his smartwatch prototype.

"You burned enough calories to earn a paratha."

Nearby, Agastya ran laps while Simran and Kabir trailed behind.

"Are we training for exams or war?" Simran puffed.

"Hopefully both," Kabir said. "Because this feels like doomsday."

After the drills, the kids flopped onto the field. Someone started beatboxing.

Raghav grinned and declared:

"GDP of this school = Gadgets, Drama, and Parathas!"

**Navya's Forest Waltz**

That evening, Navya slipped away. The pull of the forest had grown stronger — not loud, but rhythmic. Ancient.

She stepped deeper into the trees, and then... her body began to move.

A gentle sway. A spin. A sudden foot tap.

She hadn't planned to dance, but the forest played a tune only she could hear. Her body responded — gracefully, instinctively — like water finding its flow.

Her arms rose, her feet struck the earth. Kathak burst forth from within her — twirls like whirlpools, footwork like thunder. Her stories danced: Krishna's leela, moonlit Ras, divine play.

For one moment, the trees seemed to move with her. The air shimmered.

Then it stopped. Breathless, she stood still.

"That was... weirdly beautiful," she whispered.

Later that night, lying in bed, she muttered:

"Must be exhaustion. PE + Kathak = hallucination."

But deep down, she knew it wasn't.

**Prisha's Mystical Encounter**

Prisha had wandered deeper into the woods, drawn to a circle of ancient stones near a mossy pond.

As she approached, silence fell. The birds stopped singing. The air shimmered faintly.

She knelt, placing her hand on the soil.

A warm current surged through her — not painful, but powerful. Images burst into her mind: a battle, chanting sages, a slow-motion peacock feather.

And then, nothing. It was gone.

The light faded. Evening shadows crept in. She stood, shaken but unafraid.

**Tension at the Hostel**

Back at the dorms, Prisha returned late. Navya stood near the door, arms crossed.

"Where were you?! Do you even realize how worried people were?"

Prisha lowered her gaze.

"I had to lie to the juniors. What if a teacher noticed? What if something happened?"

Still no response.

Then Navya noticed: dirt on her hands, a tear in her sleeve, and eyes... not afraid, but distant.

"You're not hurt, are you?" Navya asked, softer now.

Prisha shook her head. "Just... lost track of time."

Navya sighed. "You're lucky I'm too tired to yell more."

A faint smile broke across Prisha's lips.

They sat in silence — not cold, not distant. Something fragile had begun to grow.

**Prisha's Dorm Monologue**

The dorm was silent. Outside, the trees rustled like they were whispering to the stars.

Prisha stared at the ceiling.

*Why didn't I turn back? What was that glow beneath the roots? It didn't feel like danger… it felt like home.*

Her fingers found the spine of her *Shrimad Bhagavatam.*

*The forest isn't just a place. It's a presence. Like it knows something I've forgotten.*

She thought about Navya. *She was angry… but she protected me.*

A thought bloomed — unsettling yet exciting:

*Something ancient is waking up. And it knows our names.*

---

कृष्णे स्वधामोपगते धर्मज्ञानादिभिः सह ।
कलौ नष्टदृशामेष पुराणार्कोऽधुनोदयः ॥

*Meaning*

***When Lord Krishna returned to His divine abode,***
***taking dharma and wisdom with Him,***
***this Purana (Shrimad Bhagavatam) arose like the sun to illuminate the dark age of Kali for those who have lost sight of truth.***

*(Bhagavatam: Canto 1, Chapter 3, Shloka 43)*

---

# Chapter 4

# RHYTHMS AND REFLECTIONS

**A Week Before Mid-Term Exams**

The sun peeked out from behind a gauzy curtain of clouds, casting mellow light over Saraswati Valley Academy. The mountains beyond stood cloaked in morning haze, and the trees around the campus whispered among themselves, already humming secrets of the coming spring.

Inside the library, the atmosphere was unusually charged. Most classrooms had spilled their students into the open reading halls and tree-shaded courtyards. Teachers flitted around like birds on a mission, whispering instructions, collecting doubts, and offering last-minute tips.

Navya sat cross-legged on the floor, books splayed in front of her. A low, irritated hum vibrated in her throat.

"My brain refuses to digest another word," she whispered.

"Try chewing it slowly this time. Not all knowledge is fast food." Prisha said from the chair beside her, flipping through her notebook.

Navya scowled. "I came here first. You only sat next to me because there was no other seat."

"And yet," Prisha said sweetly, "the universe brought us together."

They locked eyes. Navya rolled hers. Prisha smiled.

Around them, the murmur of students grew. Some were buried in their notes, some whispering formulas, others solving math problems mid-air. Every corridor was alive with the intensity only exams could bring.

On the southern field, Raghav paced, clutching his stomach.

"I want to fail! I want to fail!" he wailed loud enough for birds to fly off nearby trees.

Manas leaned against the pillar with arms crossed. "That's the opposite of what people normally want, GDP."

"Exactly!" Raghav announced. "Grade Detachment Phobia! GDP! I fear grades! It's genetic!"

"You mean pathetic," Agastya mumbled.

Baani giggled from behind a tree. "GDP—Grievously Dramatic Personality."

Manas added with a grin, "Or Giggle-Dispensing Prankster."

Their laughter was short-lived. A shrill whistle pierced the air. PE time.

**Drills and Drizzles**

Professor Aalekh stood with his arms crossed, eyes scanning the ragtag formation of sweaty, groaning students.

"Balance drills first. Then agility cones. Then the rope grid. Ten-second breaks in between. Life doesn't give you timeouts!"

Kabir muttered, "Life also doesn't make you run before an algebra test."

Simran elbowed him. "Shut up and jump."

Raghav stumbled over a cone and dramatically flopped to the ground. "Tell my story!" he gasped.

Aalekh raised an eyebrow. "I will. In my memoir: *The Boy Who Couldn't Skip.*"

Even Aarav chuckled.

By the end of the drill, students were splayed like sunflowers in dirt, exhausted and panting.

Prisha, wiping her forehead, whispered, "Remind me to invent an anti-sweat spell."

Navya groaned. "Remind me to run away before the next PE period."

**Encrypted Whispers**

Back in his dorm, Manas Agarwal stared at his laptop screen. His fingers flew across the keyboard, launching a custom diagnostic code into the school's network. He leaned closer, eyes scanning streams of encrypted logs.

Command prompt:

`>> run /Xgate.security/scan.portals -deep`

Lines of code flickered. At first, nothing.

Then—

`! ALERT: Unusual activity pattern detected on internal Node 77`

He leaned back. "Node 77… that's the library wing."

He expanded the signal trace. A small anomaly flickered again—tiny, too faint for regular software to detect. But his self-written watchdog script had caught it.

A subtle but consistent intrusion pattern.

His voice dropped to a murmur: "Someone's trying to probe the firewall again... but smarter this time. They're mimicking our own internal data packets."

His fingers moved swiftly, eyes ablaze with curiosity and calculation.

Command prompt:

`>> inject.traceroute + scramble.origin`

"Let's see who you are..."

A response blipped. Then vanished.

Another line appeared, glowing red.

`Nice catch, Manas. See you soon.`

He froze.

"What the..."

**In the Shade of Green**

Earlier that afternoon, Prisha had wandered towards the herbal garden. Abdul chacha was kneeling between rows of lemongrass and holy basil.

"Chacha," she said softly.

He looked up with a fond smile. "Ah, little breeze in a storm. Where to now?"

She hesitated. "I want to explore the forest edges a little. Just near the banyan curve. Won't go too far."

His eyes narrowed, not unkindly.

"Forest is like the soul," he said. "Welcoming… but deep. Go, but don't go blind. Paths twist. Some trees trick. Some call. Even a step too far can become a journey."

She wasn't sure she fully understood. But she smiled anyway.

He glanced up, his eyes momentarily thoughtful. "Once in my hometown, a young girl used to sit by a neem tree, reciting ancient shlokas better than any pandit. Her name was Anusuya."

Prisha tilted her head. "What happened to her?"

"She found a path few dare to walk." He smiled. "But that's a story for another time."

**Unseen Rhythms**

Navya had taken a different route into the woods. The air smelled of petrichor, moss, and old secrets.

She paused near a clearing ringed by sal trees.

And then—something happened.

A strange wind danced through the leaves, lifting the edges of her scarf. Her ankles moved on their own. Just a little at first.

A spin.
A pause.

Then a rhythmic tapping, her feet finding the taal without thought. Her hands rose, her wrists moving with liquid grace. She was dancing — not to any song she knew, but to something pulsing in the earth itself.

Her kathak turned playful, devotional.

She was no longer alone.

Leaves rustled in joy. Trees leaned slightly. The clearing shimmered with something ancient.

Later, walking back, heart still pounding, she thought:

Did the forest dance with me? Or am I just exhausted from PE?

She shook her head. "Navya, stop being dramatic."

But she didn't entirely believe herself.

**Vrindavan's Eternal Night**

In a realm beyond time, in the spiritual heart of existence — Vrindavan — Lord Krishna played His flute. The flute played not from lips but from the cosmos itself, and the earth danced in rhythm.

The night stretched endlessly, woven with moonlight and divine fragrance. Gopis appeared, drawn by the melody — souls dancing towards their beloved.

Under kadamba trees, feet moved like whispers.

An eternal rasa. A cosmic rhythm.

As Krishna danced among them, time stilled. Galaxies paused. The moon forgot to rise that night, choosing instead to hang motionless, watching in awe.

This was no performance.

Each gopi saw Krishna before her. Each heartbeat was answered. Each step mirrored.

It was love — in its purest, most surrendering form. The dance of the divine with the devotee.

And somewhere, far in a modern forest, a girl had echoed that dance without knowing why.

**The Unspoken Rift**

Later that night, Navya stormed down the corridor of the dormitories, her eyes burning.

She caught Prisha just as she entered the stairwell. "You disappeared. Again."

Prisha avoided her eyes. "I needed some quiet."

"Quiet? Everyone was looking for you! What if someone reported it?"

"I didn't go far."

"You didn't even tell me!"

There was a long silence. Then Navya softened as she noticed the scratches on Prisha's hands and the weariness in her eyes.

"I'm not mad," she said quietly. "Just… worried."

Prisha nodded. "I won't do it again."

They didn't speak more. But that night, something shifted.

In her bed, Prisha stared at the ceiling.

Why do I feel like the trees are whispering?

She reached under her pillow, her fingers brushing against her Bhagavatam.

And why does it feel like… something's coming?

शृण्वतां स्वकथाः कृष्णः पुण्यश्रवणकीर्तनः ।

हृद्यन्तःस्थो ह्यभद्राणि विदुनोति सुहृत्सताम् ॥

*Meaning*

***"Sri Krishna, who is the friend of the devoted, purifies the heart of anyone who hears about Him. His stories, when heard or sung, remove all inauspiciousness and reside in the heart as blessings."***

*(Bhagavatam: Canto 1, Chapter 2, Verse 17)*

# Chapter 5

# SEEDS OF DEPARTURE

*(One Month After the Mid-Terms)*

The bitter chill of winter had faded into memory, replaced by the soft warmth of North India's spring. Saraswati Valley Academy buzzed once again — laughter echoed off the hostel walls, cricket balls thudded across corridors, and the sweet, glorious freedom of post-exam life filled the air.

Pens had been flung. Questions forgotten. Children had returned to their true nature — whirlwinds of energy.

And yet, beneath the laughter, something subtle stirred.

**The Whisper of Change**

Near the biology lab, Navya and Manas clutched a cream envelope bearing the school seal. Inside was news that warmed and confused them: their parents — Meera and Ayan Agarwal, celebrated botanists — were coming to visit.

They didn't know all the details yet. But there was talk of a sabbatical.

**In the principal's office, the meeting was warm but weighty.**

Principal Bhargava, tall and soft-spoken, leaned back as Meera explained:

"We've long wanted to spend more time with our children. Our work has taken us all over the world. But they're growing so fast. This time, we thought... maybe we can merge our worlds."

Ayan added, "We have a research project in Similipal. We'd like to take them with us — and continue their learning through a blend of online tools and direct teaching."

Principal Bhargava steepled his fingers, thoughtful.

"You are serving the nation through science. And your children are exceptional. If you submit a formal plan and the education committee approves, they may go with you."

As they spoke, a small figure darted across the courtyard. A boy chased butterflies, arms flapping like wings.

It was Raghav.

He skidded to a stop, spotted the visitors, and grinned.

"Good afternoon, Uncle-Aunty!"

Meera blinked — something about him tugged at her heart.

Just then, Navya and Manas entered. Meera ruffled Raghav's hair.

"I love this boy already," she laughed.

"You don't love me?" Manas pouted.

She smiled and pulled him close.

"You're a part of me, beta. But he... he has some kind of divinity mischief in his smile."

And just as if on cue, Raghav came darting back again, shouting:

"GDP alert! Grade-Devastation Pending!"

The room burst into laughter.

**Parallel Tale: Yashoda and the Butter Thief**

In the heart of Vrindavan, beneath the cool shade of a tamala tree, Yashoda watched her little Kanha sleep. His cheeks were round, his lashes long, and in his tiny fist rested a stolen lump of butter.

Earlier that day, she'd chased him around the courtyard, waving a churning stick, laughing between scolds.

"Kanha! You little thief!"

Now, watching him sleep, her heart softened. Her scolding had melted into song.

She hummed a lullaby — ancient, sacred, full of love.

The gopis outside paused to listen. The wind slowed. Even the tulsi leaves leaned in.

"May this love protect you, my child," she whispered.

And far away, in another land, Raghav smiled in his sleep.

**New Roots**

Back in school, a soft buzz spread.

"A Sanskrit scholar is joining," someone whispered.

In the herb garden, Abdul chacha leaned towards Prisha and said:

"Her name is Anusuya. When she was young, she could recite all 700 shlokas of the Gita without pause. I watched her grow. Now, she walks paths most never dare."

He said no more.

**New Admission**

Mid-term admissions were rare — but not impossible.

A boy named Gaurav joined the Class where Raghav studied.

He was quiet, eyes observant, more drawn to trees than to people. Much like Prisha.

They hadn't spoken yet. But something about him felt... familiar.

**Meeting Under the Gulmohar**

That evening, Meera and Ayan walked with their children beneath the gulmohar trees, the red blossoms rustling above.

Raghav raced past again — arms full of petals and a packet of chips.

"I just decoded the chip-to-crumb ratio. It's GDP — *Gross Disappointment Percent!*"

They all burst out laughing.

"He's like a walking punchline," Manas said.

Meera watched him disappear down the path.

Something in her heart tugged again.

**Reflections of a Soul**

That night, Raghav lay in bed, phone pressed to his ear, words tumbling out in a rush—8 pm was minutes away, and after that, calls were strictly off-limits. His parents were laughing on the other end as he squeezed in every story he could: tales of Gaurav, butterflies, and a kind aunty who ruffled his hair.

"I even made the librarian smile today!" he blurted, proud and breathless.

When the clock chimed eight and silence settled over the dorm, Raghav whispered into the dark:

Why do I make people smile… when I sometimes feel so alone?

Why did that aunty look at me like I was hers?

Why does the word 'butter' feel so warm today?

एवं सन्दर्शयन् भक्तिं नयानैर्हृत्सु पाण्डवाः।
स्वानां जनानां श्रेयः स्याद्दर्शयन् बालचेष्टितम्॥

*Meaning*
***Through innocent childlike acts,***
***Krishna reveals the deepest devotion,***
***capturing hearts and bestowing divine blessings.***
***Even in play, He leads His people to the highest good.***

*(Bhagavatam: Canto 10, Chapter 11, Shloka 7)*

***In Krishna's early leelas, even something as ordinary as churning butter becomes a canvas for divine play.***

*The gopis' efforts, Yashoda's love, and Krishna's mischief — all reflect that pure love can make the mundane sacred.*

*Just as Yashoda adores Krishna, not knowing He is the Lord of the cosmos,* ***Meera's spontaneous affection for Raghav*** *emerges from a deeper soul connection.*

***Sometimes, the heart knows what the mind cannot explain.***

# Chapter 6

# ECHOES BEFORE DEPARTURE

It was the kind of evening where the light lingered a little longer on windowsills. The air at Saraswati Valley Academy had grown softer — not lazy, but hushed.

Exams were over. And yet, the world hadn't quite snapped back to joy. Not yet. The children, the teachers, even the trees seemed to wait. For something. For what would come next.

That was when Prisha shifted rooms.

A quiet request during exams — quietly approved, quietly moved. Her old dorm had felt too noisy for revision. Navya's room had an empty bed. And so, without fanfare, all four girls now shared a roof.

The dorm buzzed with a warm, evolving energy —
Aaranya, practical and sarcastic.
Simran, snack-lover and endlessly curious.
Navya, deep in her plant world.
And Prisha, quiet but quietly blooming.

**In the Dorm — Similipal and a Sisterhood**

One evening, Navya asked casually, "So Prisha… this Similipal — it's your home, right?"

Prisha looked up from her sketchbook. "Yeah. I was born there."

"Where exactly is it?"

"Odisha," she replied with a soft smile. "Forests, waterfalls, red soil… and mist that walks like a person."

She hesitated, then added,

"My parents run a luxury resort. Not just rooms — cottages hidden in trees, glass suites that open into jungle. We had chefs from four cities... guests from five continents."

Simran blinked.

"Like... actual tourists? Fancy rooms?"

Prisha grinned.

"It was wild luxury. Candlelit dinners under banyans. Tribal music by bonfires. A spa between sal trees."

Aaranya sat up.

"That doesn't sound like a forest. That sounds like a dream."

"It was both," Prisha whispered.

**Classroom Breezes — A Real School Day**

The next day, school felt... normal. No quest. No mystery. Just full timetables.

In English, they read a poem on rivers and roots. Navya raised her hand to compare the river to Similipal's streams. The teacher blinked — pleasantly surprised. Simran elbowed her under the desk.

In Math, Raghav tried to draw a perfect circle freehand.

"This is geometry, not modern art," the teacher sighed. "Modern art pays more," he muttered. Manas snorted.

In Social Studies, Manas debated AI in education.

"Digital privacy laws aren't designed for students using AI-integrated learning," he argued. "Manas," the teacher said, "this is an Indian Constitution class. Not your tech startup pitch."

But the spark had returned.
The school was alive again — not just a backdrop for mystery, but a place where friendships quietly grew.

**Garden Path — Manas & Abdul Chacha**

Later that day, Manas paced near the greenhouse, tablet in hand.

"Cross-indexing rainfall zones with soil density, wind flow calibration..."

"You're talking to the hibiscus again," Abdul chacha smiled, trimming marigolds.

Manas blinked.

"Sorry, chacha. I'm trying to debug Similipal's weather simulation. The carbon readings don't match the rain cycle."

"Rain doesn't follow algorithms," Abdul said gently. "It falls where the earth is thirsty."

Manas looked up.

"That's poetic."

"That's farming," chacha replied.

**Canteen Chaos — A GDP Saga**

At lunch, Raghav plopped into his seat with his usual flair.

"I've renamed Navya's obsession."

Simran raised an eyebrow.

"Go on."

"A GDP Saga."

"GDP?" Aaranya asked.

"Greenery-Devotion Phenomenon. Or maybe... Gigantic Discussion on Plants. I'm still refining the branding."

Prisha rolled her eyes.

"What's next? GST — Green Sapling Tracker?"

"Hey, I run a certified Giggle Distribution Protocol," Raghav beamed. "Tax-free joy."

Navya smiled despite herself.

Raghav and Prisha — as siblings — had a rhythm of their own.

**The Music Room — Fusion in Thought**

That evening, Raghav sat at his keyboard, his fingers drifting between two worlds—a few notes from Beethoven's Moonlight Sonata, then a slow, searching shift into Raag Yaman. The tune wasn't perfect, but it was honest. He played with his eyes half-closed, letting the music swirl around him.

Manas came in, dropping his bag on the floor. "Hey Raghav, what's this Simlipal? Is it as wild as Navya speaking?"

Manas flopped onto the chair beside him. "What's so special? I mean… is it a real place, or just a fancy vacation spot?"

Raghav's smile softened. "Simlipal's as real as it gets. Forests so thick you can't see the sky. Rivers that disappear in the mist. My childhood is there—climbing trees, chasing monkeys, listening to the rain on tin roofs."

Manas listened, eyes wide. "I never knew you were such a poet, bro."

Raghav laughed. "I'm just a homesick kid with a keyboard, that's all."

In the quiet that followed, Navya, sitting by the window, traced circles on the glass with her finger. She hadn't seen Simlipal. She didn't feel its pull like Prisha did. But the name set in her chest like a hum – *unplayed*, but present.

**Bhagwatam Parallel | The Story of Dhruva**

That night, Prisha sat with her *Shrimad Bhagavatam*, blanket around her.

In the kingdom of Uttanapada, a little prince named **Dhruva** had been pushed aside by his stepmother when he tried to sit on his father's lap.

"You are not worthy," she said.
"Go worship Vishnu if you want a place."

He ran to his mother, **Suniti**. She didn't blame. She simply said,

"If even your father's love feels far… seek the One who holds all love."

So Dhruva — just five years old — walked into the forest.

There, he met **Sage Narada**.

Narada tested him:

"This path is hard, little one. Go home."

But Dhruva said,

"I am small... but my wish is not."

Narada smiled and gave him the mantra:
***"Om Namo Bhagavate Vasudevaya."***

For six months, Dhruva meditated.
No food.
No movement.
Only stillness.

Even the wind paused for him.

And then… **Lord Vishnu appeared.**

"What do you seek, Dhruva?"

He bowed.

"I wanted a throne. But now… I only want You."

Vishnu blessed him —
A kingdom on earth while alive…
And after death, a throne in the sky.

**Dhruva Tara — the North Star.**

**Modern Day Parallel**

Prisha closed the book, heart full.

She wasn't chasing a throne.
But she was chasing a pull — unseen, unexplained, unshakable.

She looked across the room.
Navya was asleep, a half-drawn leaf in her notes.

And Prisha whispered:

"Not all forests are wild.
Some are just waiting for you to come home."

---

ॐ नमो भगवते वासुदेवाय

*Meaning:*

***I bow to Lord Vasudeva — the Supreme Being,***
***who lives within all beings***
***and is the source of all peace, strength, and knowledge.***

*(Bhagavatam: Canto 4, Chapter 8, Shloka 54)*
*(This is the mantra given to Dhruva by Narada Muni.)*

---

# Chapter 7

# THE WEIGHT OF WHAT COMES NEXT

**The Pinboard of Possibilities**

The morning after final exams arrived like a sigh — not tired, not joyous, but that odd kind of breath you take when something is ending... and something else is beginning.

In the main corridor, the school's central pinboard had been updated:

- Holiday travel forms to be submitted by Monday.
- Sabbatical permission for Navya Agarwal and Manas Agarwal — approved.

Just like that, it was official. The corridor buzzed with whispers — of home, of results, of departures. Murmurs floated through the halls like drifting pollen.

**Asha Ma'am Arrives**

Vice Principal Asha, tall and observant, called Navya and Manas to her office. She sipped warm lemon tea as she spoke.

"Your parents' sabbatical schooling proposal has been approved. You'll begin hybrid learning soon — as long as your academic performance stays consistent."

Navya nodded slowly.

"As long as there's Wi-Fi in the forest, we're good," Manas added.

Asha smiled.

"There's wisdom in trees. Just be sure to download it with your heart too."

She looked out the window.

"Principal Bhargava has taken a short leave. Visiting his daughter in Europe. I'll be handling approvals for now."

**Dorm Vibes — Nighttime Conversations**

That night in the dorm, Simran folded her clothes.

"Can you believe it's almost vacation time?"

"Feels weird," Aaranya said. "This term flew by."

"I'll be in the city. My cousin's wedding — dance practices, mehndi, pure chaos," Simran grinned.

Navya glanced at Prisha.

"You're going home, right?"

"Similipal. Finally," Prisha nodded — and for the first time in weeks, she laughed. Not a polite smile. A bright, bubbling laugh that made Simran grin and Aaranya look up.

Simran tossed a pillow.

"Still can't believe your house is basically a forest spa."

Prisha smiled, gazing out the window.

"It's more than that. There's... something else waiting there... My childhood... My room..."

**The First Echo — A Tile in the Mess**

The next afternoon, Navya and Prisha helped Smita Ma'am in the mess hall — part of their post-exam community duties.

While moving a sack of rice near the back wall, Navya slipped slightly.

Click.

A tile shifted.

Beneath it lay dust, and a glint — a small, smooth metallic disc, unlike any CD or chip they'd seen before. No label. Just a faint ridge and an engraved triangle.

Later, when Manas saw it, he muttered:

"I don't even know what kind of port this fits into..."

Abdul chacha passed by, paused, and caught a glimpse. His eyes darkened.

"Some things were sealed for a reason," he murmured.

And walked away.

Manas slid the disc into his bag.

**Classroom Echoes — Teachers and Threads**

In English, Rajani Ma'am read a poem comparing rivers to stories.

"Rivers change their path," she said, "but still flow towards the ocean. Just like truth."

Prisha scribbled: *Similipal is the ocean. Something is pulling me there.*

In Hindi, Arvind Sir asked them to compose dohas.

Raghav's read:

"Na likhu main pathshala,
GDP meri bala."

"What is this GDP?" Arvind asked.

"Giggle Distribution Protocol, sir."

"You need a protocol for common sense," the teacher muttered.

**Staff Room Murmurs**

In the rare silence of the staff room, the teachers took their tea.

Rajani Ma'am stirred hers.

"That Manas boy — sharp, but his brain runs on code."

"And Raghav?" Arvind Sir chuckled. "His brain runs on jokes."

Mrs. Menon smiled.

"But Prisha… there's something deeper this term. Her essays have changed."

Ankita added,

"And the new boy, Gaurav. Observant. Quiet. But always… there when something strange happens."

**Raghav and the Room of Sound**

That evening, Raghav sat at his keyboard. No antics. No experiments.

He played the forgotten tune he'd found in the library last week — a sheet no one remembered placing.

Beethoven flowed into folk. Western and Indian melodies stitched together.

And for a moment… the room flickered.

Not the lights. The air.

It shimmered.

**The Bhagavatam Parallel |** The Humbling of King Bali – **18$^{th}$ Avatar - Vamana**

Bali was no ordinary king.

Grandson of Prahlada, son of Virochana, ruler of the asuras — he was noble, powerful… and slowly, proud.

To conquer all three worlds, Bali began a maha-yajna, a great Vedic fire ritual.

The devas could not stop him — not with force. So they turned to Lord Vishnu, who descended as the eighteenth avatar: Vamana — a radiant dwarf Brahmin, small in form, vast in spirit.

He arrived at Bali's yajna.

"What do you desire?" asked the king.

"Three steps of land," Vamana replied.

Bali laughed.

"That's all? Take more!"

"Three steps will suffice."

With sacred water, the promise was sealed.

Then — Vamana grew.

Enormous. Cosmic.

> One step covered the Earth.
>
> The second, the heavens.
>
> And then…

"Where shall I place my third?" He asked.

Bali understood. He bowed.

"Place it on me."

Vamana stepped on Bali's head — not to punish, but to bless. He sent Bali to Patala — the netherworld — not in exile, but as its king.

And He promised: in another era, Bali would become the next Indra, ruler of the heavens.

In another version of the tale, Lakshmi tied a rakhi on Bali's wrist, making him her eternal brother.

A bond not of war, but surrender.

**Modern Day Parallel**

Prisha closed the *Bhagavatam*, her fingers warm on the page.

Three steps.
Three echoes.

> The tile in the mess.
>
> The shimmer in the air.
>
> The feeling in her bones.

Like Bali, she was learning:

*Some things must be bowed to. Not solved. Not owned. Just understood.*

She looked at the disc in Manas's bag.

"Some truths walk in small forms," she whispered.
"But their steps… shake the world."

---

त्रीन् पदान् मे निदर्शे याचितो दैत्य-दानवैः।
पद्भ्यां मे पृथिवी व्याप्ता द्वितीयेन दिवं विभो॥

*Meaning:*

***"With My first step, I covered the Earth.***
***With the second, the heavens.***
***O mighty king, where shall I place My third?"***

*(Bhagavatam: Canto 8, Chapter 20, Shloka 25)*

---

## Chapter 8

# DIGITAL SHADOWS AND WHISPERED MAPS

The monsoon had not arrived, but something electric was in the air. Saraswati Valley Academy felt like it was holding its breath. A layer of tension, so slight it might have been imagined, settled on the tree-lined corridors and humming computer labs.

**Results & Reflections**

The results were finally out.

Students gathered around the notice boards in small, buzzing groups. Some laughed in relief, others stared at their marksheets a bit too long.

Raghav scratched his head. "Hindi — disaster. Math and English — heroic comeback."

Prisha nudged him, "You passed. Don't complain."

Simran grinned, "Top in biology. Worst in drawing. My cactus still looks like a pineapple."

Gaurav, the new boy, quietly received his average scores — the rule for mid-term joiners. He didn't mind. It was fair.

Augustya and Kabir came rushing through the crowd, elbowing their way to the front.

"I bet I failed History," Kabir muttered.

"Then why are you running?" Augustya grinned.

Navya simply folded her sheet. "Promoted. That's enough for today."

They were all moving up. A new grade. A new chapter.

And just before vacation began, a new academic session was quietly declared open.

### In the Library Vault

Manas had skipped his last class — not for mischief, but for a mission.

Hidden behind the newer racks of encyclopedias and rare nature journals was a rusted cabinet locked by a forgotten latch. It wasn't really locked — just stuck, like it didn't want to be opened. But curiosity, Manas had learned, was a master key.

Inside were books older than the academy itself. Atlases with rivers that no longer existed. Almanacs from the pre-independence era. And in between them, wrapped in cotton cloth, a folded, aging **map** with notes in both English and Sanskrit.

He frowned. It wasn't any ordinary map. It showed the school grounds — but also places that didn't exist anymore. A stone archway where the new basketball court stood. An underground room near the northern wall. And three words scribbled faintly: ***Veena Vidhya Vani.***

The phrase hummed in his mind like a chant.

### The Map, the Disc and the Pulse

Back in the dorm, Manas locked his door. Raghav had gone to the music room. The others were out too. Perfect.

He placed the disc and the old map side by side under his reading lamp, examining the faint inscriptions. It didn't look like any tech he'd ever seen—no obvious port, no metallic contacts, no power button. Still, Manas was undeterred.

He pulled out his phone and a small tool kit. Using his custom-built magnifier, he scanned the map's edge, searching for patterns, etchings, maybe even hidden QR codes. The scanner app flickered. Static. Then, for a split second, odd symbols danced across his screen—nothing in any modern script.

He tapped at his laptop, running the images through a code-breaker he'd designed for fun. The screen blinked:

**CODE RECOGNIZED**
**RUNNING PROTOCOL: MANVANTARA-1**

What followed was a mess of ancient symbols, rotating mandalas, data packets named after yugas, and an encrypted module labelled **NAKSHATRA-LOCK**.

But it was the word **Manvantara** that made Manas pause.

"What even is a Manvantara?" he muttered.

He opened a subroutine in his code and ran a search through the Sanskrit text archives he had stored months ago.

**Output:**

**Time According to the Shrimad Bhagavatam**

*Based on Canto 3, Chapter 11 – "Calculation of Time, from the Atom"*

| Bhagavatam Unit | Modern Equivalent |
|---|---|
| Anu (atom) | Smallest particle |
| Trasarenu | 3 Anu |
| Truti | 3 Trasarenu (≈ 1/16,875 sec) |
| Vedha | 2 Truti (≈ 1/8,437 sec) |
| Lava | 3 Vedha (≈ 1/2,812 sec) |
| Nimesha | 3 Lava (≈ 0.4 seconds) |
| Kshana | 3 Nimesha (≈ 1.2 seconds) |
| Kastha | 5 Kshana (≈ 6 seconds) |
| Laghu | 15 Kastha (≈ 1.5 minutes) |
| Nadika / Danda | 15 Laghu (≈ 22.5 minutes) |
| 1 Muhurta | 2 Nadikas (≈ 45 minutes) |
| 1 Day-Night | 30 Muhurtas (≈ 24 hours) |
| Human Year | 360 Days |
| 1 Deva Year | 360 Human Years |
| 1 Maha Yuga | 4.32 million Human Years |
| 1 Kali Yuga | 432,000 Years |
| 1 Dvapara Yuga | 864,000 Years |
| 1 Treta Yuga | 1,296,000 Years |
| 1 Satya Yuga | 1,728,000 Years |
| 71 Maha Yugas | 1 Manvantara (≈ 306.72 million years) |
| 14 Manvantaras | 1 Kalpa (≈ 4.3 billion years – 1 day of Brahma) |
| 100 Brahma Years | 1 Lifetime of Brahma (≈ 311 trillion human years) |

**Current Kaliyuga Year (2025 CE)**: *5127*

Manas blinked at the screen.

"So… time begins from atoms? And we're in the 5127th year of just the last quarter of a single Maha Yuga?"

The numbers were too big. But somewhere in that vastness… the word **Manvantara** clicked.

Maybe the map, the disc and perhaps this school didn't just hold code. Maybe it held cycles.

And secrets.

### Mess Hall Murmurs

Vacation plans were now the official gossip of the mess.

"I'm going to Nainital," Aaranya announced dramatically. "Boating, momos, and no classes."

Simran smirked. "I'm going for my cousin's wedding in Jaipur. Loads of noise, glitter, and rasgullas.". It smells like old magic."

Navya said softly, "We'll be in Similipal. A research trip."

"More like a jungle retreat," Raghav muttered. "With real GDP."

"What GDP now?" Prisha asked, giggling.

"Greenery Discovery Party," he grinned. "Or Ghar-wapsi of Devoted Plants."

Laughter followed. But Manas wasn't laughing. He was sketching the symbols he saw on the disc.

### Bhagavatam Parallel | 14th Avatar - Matsya and the Flood of Knowledge

That night, Prisha sat near the window, her journal open. The Bhagavatam rested beside her like a trusted elder.

She began to read: In ancient times, King Satyavrata ruled with justice. One day, as he was offering water to the gods, a tiny fish swam into his cupped hands.

"Don't return me to the river," the fish pleaded. "Larger fish will devour me."

Moved, the king placed it in a pot. But it grew. He moved it to a pond. It grew again. A lake. Then the ocean. Still, it grew.

The fish was **Matsya**, the fourteenth avatar of Vishnu.

Matsya warned Satyavrata of a coming deluge and instructed him to build a boat. When the great flood came, the boat carried sages, seeds, and scriptures.

With the serpent Vasuki as a rope and the mountain as anchor, Matsya guided them through chaos.

He revealed secrets of time, dharma, and creation itself.

"All knowledge must survive," he said, "so the world may begin again."

**Modern Day Parallel**

Manas wasn't guiding a boat. But maybe... he had found the flood.

And the strange disc in his bag? A fish with secrets.

The code had whispered something. Not destruction.

Preservation.

---

एकदा कर्मनिर्मुक्तो राजा सत्यव्रतो महीम्।
कृतस्नानोदकश्शान्तश् च जपन् आसीन्मुहुर्मुहुः॥

*Meaning:*
***"One day, King Satyavrata, freed from duties, sat peacefully, chanting by the water after a holy bath."***

*(Bhagavatam: Canto 8, Chapter 24, Shloka 8)*

---

# *Chapter 9*

# THE CHANT AND THE CIPHER

**Sanskrit Class — A Normal Beginning**

It was a regular weekday afternoon when the senior students — including Prisha, Navya, and a few others — walked into their Sanskrit class. The room was neat and simple, with clean white walls, soft sunlight filtering in, and blackboards scribbled with sentences from earlier sessions.

A woman stood at the front — calm, poised, wearing a pale cotton saree and no visible makeup. Only a small rudraksha mala peeked from her wrist.

"Good afternoon. I'm Anusuya," she said. "Let's begin."

She didn't sound mystical. She sounded like any other teacher. Yet, the room felt just a little quieter.

A few moments into the class, she smiled gently.
"Can anyone speak a single line, phrase, shloka — even a few Sanskrit words?"

Some looked away awkwardly. Others pretended to write.
Then Prisha raised her hand.
*"Om namo bhagavate vasudevaya,"* she said softly.

As she spoke, her hand rested absentmindedly on her bag — the one where the disc had been kept since morning.
Raghav had given it to her after breakfast.
*"Take it today,"* he'd said casually. *"It was giving my keyboard weird vibes."*

Anusuya nodded at Prisha's recitation. "Beautiful," she said, and moved on.

## A Clue in the Bag

That evening, Prisha sat on her bed, pulling out books for homework. Her fingers brushed against the strange disc.

She turned it over in her hands, studying the surface under the lamplight. But there was nothing—no markings, no letters, no shine. If anything had ever been carved, it was long since blurred by years of dust and touch. The metal looked old, almost battered, like it had traveled through too many hands, too many seasons.

She ran her thumb along the edge. Was it designed this way, or had time simply erased its secrets?

The disc felt heavier than it should, cool against her skin, holding stories that refused to show themselves. No glow. No vibration. Just silence and the weight of a mystery.

Prisha set it gently on the table, not knowing that somewhere, in its hidden depths, a secret waited for the right moment—and the right touch—to awaken.

## Corridor Whispers — Pulkit and Anusuya

The next day, the corridors buzzed with footsteps and laughter as students moved between classes.

Near the staircase, a new presence caught the eye—a man in simple, well-worn clothes, with an air of quiet energy. Some students whispered, "Who's that?" but no one lingered long enough for answers.

Anusuya was already there, greeting him with a respectful nod. She handed him a stitched, weathered manuscript. "You might find something interesting here," she murmured in low Sanskrit.

Pulkit Roy smiled, voice gentle. "Sanskrit makes everything simpler, doesn't it?" he replied, as if sharing a private joke with Anusuya.

Just then, Prisha approached, her bag slung nervously over her shoulder.

"Sir, Manas said you wanted to take a look at this," she said quietly, pulling the strange disc from her bag.

Pulkit's eyebrows lifted in open curiosity. He accepted the disc with care, turning it over in his hands. "Now this… is something you don't see every day," he said, real wonder in his voice.

"For testing?" Prisha asked, still a little hesitant.

He nodded, reassuring. "Exactly. And I'll let you both know what I find."

## The School Life Rolls On

Classes continued.

In English, Rajani ma'am gave a creative prompt: *"Write from the perspective of a tree."*

Navya wrote dramatically:

"I have stood for centuries — holding secrets, squirrels, and storms."

In Hindi, Arvind sir gave a translation exercise. Raghav tried converting it into a playful rap — only to be scolded. *"Yeh kavita nahi hai, Raghav!"*

He grinned anyway.

Meanwhile, Kabir and Augustya were discussing their plans for the cultural project, wondering if they could interview a few tribal musicians during the break.

In the next room, Gaurav sat doodling spirals and shapes. He loved patterns — his father was a renowned decipherer of ancient symbols, and he'd grown up surrounded by codes and carvings. For him, it was just instinctive.

## Operation Firewall

The sun dipped low outside the tech lab as Manas knocked gently on the glass door. Pulkit Roy looked up from his monitor and waved him in.

"Any leads?" Manas asked, dropping his bag beside the desk.

Pulkit gestured to the screen. Lines of code flashed in rapid sequence.

"I've isolated the breach path. The attackers didn't try to crash the system. They were… searching."

"Searching for what?"

"That's the puzzle," Pulkit said, rubbing his forehead. "They bypassed security checkpoints without corrupting data. Almost like they were combing through specific files."

"Student data?" Manas guessed.

"Possibly. Or internal archives. But they were meticulous — no obvious damage, just silent tracing."

He opened a folder Manas hadn't seen before — filled with unfamiliar code strings, some in basic scripts, others with odd syntax.

"Looks like someone tried layering something over our systems. Not a virus. More like a mask — to hide or retrieve information."

Manas leaned forward. "So not destruction… retrieval."

Pulkit nodded slowly. "Exactly. Almost like someone was trying to find a buried file. Or test the school's defenses without tripping alarms."

There was a pause.

Manas hesitated, then said, "Actually… a few days back, I noticed something weird when I was scanning the network with my own program. Someone tried probing the firewall—felt like they were poking around. I managed to block the intrusion, but right after, I got this message on my screen: 'Nice catch, Manas. See you soon.'"

He looked at Pulkit, eyes narrowed. "Is that linked to what's happening now?"

Pulkit grinned, raising his hands in mock surrender. "Guilty. That was me testing your skills. Just making sure our network's in good hands—and you passed."

Manas rolled his eyes, but couldn't help grinning. "You could've just asked for a demo, sir."

Pulkit chuckled and reached into a side drawer, pulling out something wrapped in cloth.

"The disc Prisha gave me," he said. "Strange timing, right?"

Manas blinked. "You've started analyzing it?"

"Not yet. I want to scan it through multi-spectral layers—structural composition, magnetic resonance, anything. It doesn't look digital, but… neither did early computation stones in ancient systems."

Manas smirked. "You think it's some kind of data key?"

"I think it's worth checking. It might hold language or sound codes—maybe even symbolic encryption."

Pulkit shut the folder. "We'll continue tomorrow. But for now, keep this between us. No one outside this room."

Manas nodded, eyes shining. "Operation GDP is just getting started."

**Lunch Break Conversations**

The next day, the four friends sat in the garden under their usual neem tree.

Manas opened his laptop. "Pulkit sir and I are trying to decode the disc. He's planning to run it through a spectrum analyzer—see if we can uncover anything hidden beneath the surface. It might even be linked to the cyberattack. Or something bigger."

Navya pulled out her phone. "Simlipal's thirty hours away *by train* from Dehradun!"

Manas groaned. "I'll be an old man by then."

Raghav rolled his eyes. "Simlipal is home, bro. You don't need Google Maps to get there."

Prisha grinned. "I'll talk to our parents. Maybe you can stay with us."

Kabir and Gaurav walked past. Kabir shouted, "Hey! Don't forget the science fair prep!"

Gaurav added, "And someone tell Rajani ma'am that a tree can't talk in Latin!"

They all laughed.

Everything felt light — and yet, just under the surface, something was shifting.

**Bhagavatam Parallel | 19th Avatar - Parashurama: The Warrior Sage**

That night, Prisha opened her diary page where she copied the summary of the story she had read in the morning. Long ago, in an age when kings turned cruel and power had begun to rot, there arose a fierce flame of dharma — Parashurama, the nineteenth avatar of Vishnu.

Born to Sage Jamadagni and Renuka, Parashurama was both Brahmin and warrior. When asked by his father to behead his own mother as a test of obedience, he did so without hesitation. Impressed, Jamadagni granted him a boon, and Renuka was restored to life.

But the fire within Parashurama had already been lit.

When a violent king murdered his father, Parashurama picked up his axe — and vowed to rid the earth of corrupt Kshatriyas. He fought twenty-one battles to restore balance and protect righteousness.

He carried both Lord Shiva's bow and Lord Vishnu's bow — symbols of immense power. One of these would one day be used to test a young prince named Rama.

When his mission was done, Parashurama didn't die. He vanished into the mountains and is said to live even now — the only Vishnu avatar who still walks the earth, waiting for the rise of dharma again.

**Modern Day Parallel**

Manas stared at the code on his screen. His brows furrowed.
He wasn't just trying to fix a hack anymore.

He was chasing patterns. Truth. Injustice.

Trying to bring clarity — not just to a system, but to the silence that followed it.

In his own way…

He, too, was learning to wield an invisible axe.

---

श्रीभगवानुवाच
ज्ञानं परम् गुह्यं मे यद्विज्ञानसमन्वितम् ।
स रहस्यं तदङ्गं च गृहाण गदितं मया ॥

*Meaning:*
***"O dear one, I shall now tell you the most confidential knowledge, along with its realization and the secret of secrets. Listen with care."***

*(Bhagavatam: Canto 11, Chapter 2, Shloka 34)*

---

# Chapter 10

# THE LAYERS BENEATH

**Spectrum Scanner**

Pulkit Roy adjusted the dials of the school's rarely-used multi-spectrum analyzer — a sleek machine with glowing panels and a curved scanner arch. Manas stood beside him, arms folded, eyes sharp.

"You think this is actually going to work?" Manas asked.

Pulkit didn't look up. "We're not looking for Wi-Fi or Bluetooth. We're scanning for structural memory — traces of resonance, heat patterns, anything odd."

He entered a command. The machine began humming. Waves of light passed slowly over the metallic disc as projections flickered onto the screen — temperature variations, magnetic pulses, internal outlines.

"There's something here," Pulkit murmured.

"What kind of something?"

Pulkit pointed. "This second layer — it's not just metal. Looks like an organic composite. Shell, maybe bone. And… it's not symmetrical inside. That's rare for an object this precisely shaped."

Manas leaned closer. "So... it's handmade?"

"Could be. But more fascinating — see this?" He zoomed in on a faint cavity. "There's a hollow chamber. Less than 2 millimetres. Etched with ridges. Too small for language. But maybe sound-based. Vibration-activated."

Manas's eyes lit up. "So it's not a disc. It's a lock."

Pulkit smiled. "And we just might have the key. Who knows it's a lock or a key or even something else, but whatever it is, it's a mystery as of now."

**Raag Ka-Ya-Ma-Ya**

That afternoon, in the music room, Prutha Ma'am tuned her tanpura as Raghav entered, still humming the melody from his dream.

She paused. "You've caught something ancient," she said gently. "Where did you learn it?"

Raghav hesitated. "I… didn't. I dreamed it."

She gasped softly. "These syllables—Ka, Ya, Ma, Ya… I've heard them somewhere before, but I can't quite remember where. I think… loosely… it's called a song of destruction—or maybe construction? I'm sorry, it's just on the tip of my tongue."

Prutha frowned, frustrated with herself. How could she forget something that felt so important? The answer hovered, maddeningly close, but refused to land.

She smiled softly. "Music remembers what the mind forgets, Raghav. That raag may help you more than you know."

**Threads Converge**

The next morning, the school's old computer lab buzzed with renewed energy.

Pulkit projected the disc's scan results onto a whiteboard. Manas scribbled notes beside him.

"This section of code," Pulkit said, "aligns with time stamps from the breach attempts."

Manas frowned. "Wait — you think the hacker was looking for this disc?"

"Not the disc itself, maybe, but something connected to it. Or something it leads to."

They fell silent for a moment. Pulkit tapped his pen on the table. "It's worth testing."

**Neem Tree Conversations**

That evening, the group sat under the old neem tree — Manas, Raghav, Prisha, Navya — joined by Kabir and Gaurav.

Manas looked tired but energised. "Pulkit sir thinks the disc might be linked to the hack. The internal timestamps from the scans match the breach log."

Navya frowned. "But why would anyone track a metal disc? It's not even digital."

Raghav tossed a neem leaf into the air. "Unless it's a very old kind of digital."

Gaurav, sketching quietly, added, "Or symbolic. My dad says the oldest computers were temples. Algorithms in stone."

Kabir laughed. "You say the weirdest cool things."

Prisha leaned back, her voice low. "We're close to something. I don't know what. But it's all tied together."

Manas smiled. "Operation GDP just got real."

**Bhagwatam Parallel | 9th Avatar – Prithu: Parallel of the Purifier**

That night, Prisha curled up in bed with the Bhagavatam open across her knees.

She found herself drawn to a new story — the tale of King Prithu.

Prithu was not born in the usual way. He was churned forth from the corpse of King Vena — a tyrant whose reign had drained the land dry.

The earth had stopped yielding crops. The sages cried out.

Prithu rose as their answer — a dharmic king born not of lineage, but of purpose.

When the earth resisted his call, he didn't rage. He reasoned.

He pursued her until she yielded in the form of a sacred cow. From her, he drew not milk — but life itself: agriculture, herbs, nourishment.

He charted rivers and coasts. Named continents. Balanced trade and nature. He ruled not with force, but harmony.

So profound was his purity that Lord Vishnu himself blessed him.

This wasn't just a king. He was the ninth avatar of Vishnu — *Prithu, the Purifier.*

**Manas's Realization**

Lights out. The others slept.

Manas sat alone with his laptop glowing softly on his lap. No typing. Just thinking.

Prithu hadn't fought to conquer.

He'd restored balance.

Not revenge. Not destruction. Order.

Manas murmured aloud, "Decode to restore. Not destroy."

He didn't know if the hacker felt the same — but he knew now how *he* wanted to respond.

पृथुस्तु भगवान् राज्ञां सर्वस्य जगतः पतिः।
अवतारो नरदेवस्य विष्णोर्यस्य महात्मनः॥

*Meaning:*

***"Prithu was truly a divine king, the protector of the world — the avatar of the great soul, Vishnu himself."***

*(Bhagavatam: Canto 4, Chapter 11, Shloka 27)*

# Chapter 11

# THE FIREWALL CRACKS

**Eyes That Watch — Vice Principal Asha**

The low hum of the lab broke beneath the sharp click of heels.

Vice Principal Asha entered, arms crossed, her eyes locked on the monitors where streams of code danced like unsolved riddles.

"This has gone far enough," she said quietly, turning to Pulkit Roy.

Pulkit, the visiting cyber-research mentor, gave a calm nod. He wasn't just any teacher — once the youngest director in the Department of Information Forensic Technology, he had built encryption models using ancient symbols. Now on sabbatical, he was helping Saraswati Valley Academy ride through a storm no textbook could describe.

Beside him, Manas tapped furiously on the keyboard. Anusuya and Prisha leaned in close, alert and observant. Raghav sat cross-legged with a notepad, quiet but tuned to every word.

Asha's voice softened. "I don't want panic. But I want answers. Fast. If this goes beyond school-level mischief, we escalate it. Understood?"

**The Digital Layer Beneath**

Pulkit perched on the lab stool, one leg folded, typing fast. Manas adjusted the scanner's frequency with surgical focus.

"We've passed the magnetic field layer," Manas murmured. "There's something faint… etched into the metal. Like old punch cards."

Pulkit zoomed in.

Anusuya leaned forward, adjusting her glasses. "These aren't just codes," she said. "Some characters resemble Grantha or early Nagarī. Look here — these patterns repeat. Almost like a mantra."

Manas blinked. "So it's not a virus... it's something older?"

She nodded. "And maybe sound-based. Or memory-linked."

Just then, Raghav murmured, "Sound...?"

Pulkit nodded. "At first, I thought it was a breach. Now, it feels like someone embedded a rhythm — a pattern that activates under exact conditions."

Prisha opened her notebook and showed a sketched replica of the disc. "What if the disc wasn't just a key... but a translator?"

Pulkit's eyes sparkled. "Exactly what I was thinking."

From the shadows, Asha's voice dropped: "Then we need to understand what it's trying to say."

**Raag Ka-Ya-Ma-Ya Returns**

Raghav finally broke his silence.

"I know it sounds odd, but… this raag, Ka-Ya-Ma-Ya, it just keeps coming to me. I'm not learning it from anyone—it's like it's already inside me, waiting to come out. Prutha Ma'am said those syllables felt important, maybe linked to some ancient song about creation or destruction, but she couldn't quite remember. It's mysterious… and it feels powerful."

Pulkit raised an eyebrow. "That's not odd at all. If this code mirrors ancient rhythm... your music might be the missing signal."

"You want me to sing to it?" Raghav asked, unsure.

Pulkit smirked. "Why not? Operation GDP's first musical experiment."

Manas mumbled, "Are we solving a cyberattack… or decoding a cosmic equation?"

**Firewall Breached — What They Found**

They connected a directional mic to the scanner.

Raghav closed his eyes and hummed the *Ka-Ya-Ma-Ya* raag, each syllable slow, steady, resonant.

At first, nothing.

Then — a blink on the scanner.

Not an alarm. Just a quiet shift.

A hidden archive unlocked.

On the screen appeared a file:

Ananta_001

Inside it: thousands of old data snippets — names, scripts, coordinates, timelines…

Then a second code layer surfaced — and even Pulkit sat back in shock.

Lines of school network directories. Archived logs. Internal security codes. Hidden folders with strange names.

One folder read:
ARCHIVE_12D // Simlipal_Herbal_Field_Lab

Pulkit read it aloud. "Why access an old research project?"

Manas frowned. "Wait — that's in one of my parents' papers. From Simlipal."

Prisha's eyes widened. "Their tribal herb mapping project?"

Pulkit exhaled slowly. "If this breach isn't about student data… someone's using the school's network as a gateway. To something much bigger."

Anusuya whispered, "This isn't a school database anymore."

Asha's voice was quiet, almost lost in thought. "Then the real question is... what is *Ananta*?"

**Whispered Threads**

Later that evening, the kids sat in the mess hall, their plates half-touched.

"We solved it… sort of," Manas said, stirring his dal. "But it feels like we've just opened the first door."

"What's *Ananta_001*?" Prisha asked softly. "And why now?"

Raghav tapped the table rhythmically. "It was my raag. The power of *Ka-Ya-Ma-Ya*," he grinned. "Brought to you by GDP — *Guaranteed Disc Power!*"

Navya rolled her eyes. "Maybe someone's testing us. Not just with firewalls — but with choices."

Manas looked up. "Choices?"

"To see if we're ready," she said, her voice calm. "Not for war. But for something older... something they never teach in schools."

They all exchanged glances — no answers, just the pulse of something larger, rising quietly around them.

**Bhagavatam Parallel | 17th Avatar - Narasimha**

That night, alone in the dorm lounge, Prisha turned to the Bhagavatam. Her eyes rested on a story that felt strangely familiar.

There was once a boy, Prahlada. A gentle soul, a devotee of Vishnu, born in the house of hatred.

His father, Hiranyakashipu, had earned near-invincibility. No god, beast, weapon, or moment could end him. No one could kill him inside or outside, by day or night.

He turned on his own son for worshipping Vishnu.

Prahlada kept chanting: *Om Namo Bhagavate Vasudevaya.*

And then… twilight.

A pillar cracked. From it leapt Narasimha — neither man nor beast, neither dusk nor night. No weapons. No rules broken.

He placed the tyrant on his thighs — not the earth. He used claws — not tools.

Justice roared through the silence.

**Modern Day Parallel**

In the dim lab glow, Manas stared at the code.

"They tried everything to keep us out," he whispered. "But it was one sound — one chant — that broke through."

Raghav smiled. "GDP wins again."

Pulkit tapped the console thoughtfully. "That breach wasn't random. Someone *wanted* this unlocked — just not too soon."

Anusuya added quietly, "Just like Narasimha. Hidden. Timed. Precise."

She looked at the glowing disc and said, more to herself than the others, "When systems fail… symbols rise."

---

नृसिंह परिरूपाय नमस्ते ते जगत्पते।
अजाय सत्त्वरूपाय नमः सुरासुरार्चित॥

*Meaning:*

***O Narasimha, embodiment beyond form — I bow to You, Lord of all worlds. You are unborn, pure essence, worshipped by both gods and demons.***

*(Bhagwatam: Canto 7, Chapter 9, Shloka 10)*

---

## Chapter 12

# THE JOURNEY BEGINS

**Loose Ends and Lock Codes**

The morning sun filtered gently through the lab's glass windows — but inside, it felt like a countdown had begun.

Manas was typing furiously, sweat forming along his brow. On the main screen, red bars pulsed rapidly, ticking down from five minutes.

Pulkit Roy, hunched beside him, scanned line after line of raw code, barking instructions. "Shift the firewall layer. Go to subnet three! They're tunneling in through a masked archive protocol!"

"I see it!" Manas replied. "They're not attacking — they're accessing. Deep. Like, system-core-deep."

Anusuya leaned forward, her eyes darting over a strange column of text flashing on the side monitor. "These are not just scripts... this is proto-Nagarī. Some kind of embedded command mantra!"

Pulkit didn't even look up. "Translate fast. If they reach the archive, we're done."

"Three minutes left," Manas called out.

Anusuya's fingers flew over a notepad.
"It says: unlock through resonance memory key… I think it's reacting to layered access."

"Try mapping it to the disc's sound pattern," Pulkit snapped.

Two minutes.

Pulkit opened a backdoor script, running a deep encryption override.
"We're not stopping them. We're racing them to encrypt first. Manas, trigger Archive Lockdown Mode!"

Manas did.

"Forty seconds!" he yelled.

Anusuya suddenly stood up.
"Done. Phrase decoded. Apply this line: *svar-vṛtta-ananta-pravesha* — access loop infinite break."

Pulkit grabbed it, inserted it into the final patch of code. He pressed Enter.

The monitors went black.

Then, after two long seconds, they lit up green.
ARCHIVE SUCCESSFULLY ENCRYPTED. BREACH BLOCKED.

Pulkit smiled faintly. "Which means we got here just in time."

Vice Principal Asha, standing at the back with folded arms, exhaled deeply.
"Then it's settled. Whatever they were trying to cover — it's archived now. I'll alert the board."

"Will it happen again?" Prisha asked quietly.

Anusuya replied, "Maybe. Maybe not. But not today. Today, you won."

Raghav leaned back, hands behind his head. "GDP, baby. Guaranteed Digital Protection."

Everyone groaned — but smiled.

**The Last Week and Laddoos**

Smita, the beloved mess supervisor, was in an unusually generous mood. With exams over and vacation ahead, she'd begun doting on the children like they were her own.

"Raghav Jain!" she called out in mock anger that evening, "You think I didn't see that extra laddoo vanish from the tray?"

He froze mid-bite, cheeks puffed like a squirrel.

"I was just... conducting quality control, Smita Ma'am," he said innocently.

"You mean GDP — *Ghar le jaane layak Dessert Protection*?" Manas joked.

Smita rolled her eyes and smacked Raghav lightly with her towel. Everyone burst into laughter.

**Suitcases and Goodbyes**

The dorms buzzed with activity. Suitcases were dragged out. Books were stacked. Socks were discovered in strange corners.

Navya carefully rolled her clothes and tucked her herbal notebook between them. Prisha wrote a small thank-you card to Anusuya, slipping it quietly into her desk drawer.

Some students clutched printed train tickets their parents had couriered.
Others waited for pickup messages. And a few — like Aaranya — sighed,
"My parents are coming next to next week. I'll be here for a while."

Outside, Abdul chacha helped lift heavy bags, his wrinkled smile never fading.
*"Take care of each other, beta,"* he said to the four friends. "And don't forget the soil you stand on."

Raghav saluted him with a grin. "Never, chacha."

**Reunions and Plans**

By afternoon, cars had started arriving.

Dr. Meera and Ayan Agrawal stepped out, waving as they spotted Manas and Navya.

Meera instantly enveloped Raghav in a hug. "You've grown taller again, na?"

"I think it's just my backpack," he mumbled shyly.

Minutes later, Parag and Priya Jain — Prisha and Raghav's parents — arrived too.
A sleek black SUV with their hotel's logo pulled up quietly.

Inside the common area, the two families sat down with coffee.

"So you'll be working in Simlipal this summer?" Parag asked.

"Yes," Ayan nodded. "Forest mapping and botanical research."

"Then we must host you," Priya smiled. "Let us handle your stay, logistics — everything."

Meera looked touched. "That's very kind of you. Actually, we may take a detour to Mumbai first. Just for a week. We'll come to Simlipal after."

"It's all settled then," Parag said. "We'll keep everything ready."

As they all stepped out into the quiet sunlit lawn near the school gate, Ayan turned to Parag with a thoughtful look.
"By the way… I've always meant to ask. Raghav and Prisha — they're a year apart from Navya and Manas, right? But they're all in the same class. How did that happen?"

Priya smiled, tucking a strand of hair behind her ear. "That was our choice. We delayed their formal schooling intentionally. We were living deep in the forest back then — Simlipal was still home, and we wanted them to spend those early years in the wild. Climbing trees, walking barefoot, talking to birds."

Parag added with a laugh,
"Not memorizing spellings and math tables before they could chase butterflies."

Meera's eyes lit up.
"That explains it! They've always had that grounded, natural curiosity."

"And that's why the bond between them is… different," Ayan nodded. "Makes so much sense now."

**Gratitude and Teachers**

Before departure, the kids made their rounds.

To Mrs. Menon — Navya and Prisha's history teacher — they offered chocolates and a card.
"Keep asking questions," she said, hugging them tightly.

To Mrs. Ankita — Raghav and Manas's Science teacher — they gave a small potted plant.
"You've all bloomed so beautifully," she whispered.

Vice Principal Asha gave them a rare smile.
"You've made this school proud. We'll miss your noise."

Then came a quiet corner near the Sanskrit room.

Anusuya and Pulkit stood side by side. "You've done well," Pulkit said.
"You've done more," Anusuya added softly, looking at each of them. "Now carry it with grace."

Prisha smiled. "We'll return stronger."

**Onwards**

The engines rumbled. Drivers packed suitcases.

Kids waved from windows. Friends clung for one last selfie. Some cried. Some laughed.

And as the wheels turned and the horizon stretched…

The four looked back at Saraswati Valley Academy one last time.

"Simlipal," Navya whispered.

"Finally," Prisha said.

And the train pulled ahead — not just towards home, but towards the next chapter.

**Bhagavatam Parallel | 11th Avatar - Mohini**

In the cosmic sea of milk — *Kshira Sagara* — a churning began unlike any other.

The devas and asuras had joined forces to extract the *amrit*, the nectar of immortality. Mountains turned, serpents twisted, and lifetimes passed with every churn.

Finally, the pot of nectar arose — glowing with divine energy. But before the devas could taste it, the asuras seized it with force and greed.

Panic spread. Despair clouded the heavens. All seemed lost.

Then, from that same divine sea, emerged a vision no one expected —

*Mohini.*

A woman radiant with charm, grace, and a mysterious calm.

None recognised her as Lord Vishnu.

With a smile, she approached the asuras. "Let me distribute the nectar," she offered sweetly.

Dazed by her beauty, the asuras agreed — without question.

Mohini moved among them, serving from the pot… but only to the devas.

Her elegance was a distraction; her intelligence, the real weapon.

By the time the asuras realised the trick, the nectar was gone — and the devas had regained their strength.

There was no battle. Just strategy. No fire. No war. Only timing, wit, and grace.

When dharma is threatened, the divine doesn't always roar. Sometimes, it simply smiles — and outwits darkness.

**Modern Day Parallel**

That same grace echoed in the Saraswati Valley lab.

As the countdown ticked, chaos loomed — five minutes from breach.

No swords. No firewalls. Just minds racing faster than time.

Pulkit's commands, Manas's fingers, Anusuya's decoding — each like a step of Mohini's dance.

And just before the final second…

They secured the archive. The school was safe. Not with power.

But with brilliance.

*श्रीभगवानुवाच*
*मायामनुष्यरूपेण परं संस्तभ्य तेजसा।*
*प्रविष्टोऽसुरदेहेषु प्रवृत्तिर्मेऽनुपश्यत।।*

*Meaning:*

***The Lord said: "I took the form of a human woman through divine illusion, radiating such brilliance that none could see through it. I entered the minds of the asuras — observe how I act through such subtle means."***

*(Bhagwatam: Canto 8, Chapter 12, Shloka 43)*

# SECTION TWO

# SIMLIPAL CALLING

## Chapter 13

# CITY BEFORE THE FOREST

**Day 1 – Rooftop Whispers**

The Mumbai sunset looked like a saffron prayer cloth fluttering across skyscrapers. On the rooftop garden of Triveni Society — an old but proud residential complex nestled in South Bombay, which they also called SoBo — a quiet jungle swayed. Not one planted for beauty, but one grown for memory.

Navya knelt beside a patch of silver-veined orchids, gently misting the soil with a copper spray bottle. Manas sat cross-legged nearby, trying (and failing) to launch a recycled paper drone.

"It's flying like a deflated papad," he muttered.
"Maybe it's looking for soil to crash into," Navya offered dryly.
"It's a botanical landing," he grinned.

Meera stepped onto the terrace carrying two steaming mugs of lemongrass tea. Ayan followed, setting down a wooden tray of seed envelopes.

"The drone's dead again?" Meera asked.
"I call it a GDP crash," Manas declared dramatically.
Navya raised an eyebrow. "GDP?"
"Gliding Dronic Prototype. Failed. Just like Raghav's Great
Dholak Power at the annual show."

Meera burst into laughter. “Oh, I remember that! He tried balancing a dholak on a suitcase handle while singing a classical song... slipped halfway and still finished on beat.”
“He claims he invented a new taal while falling,” Manas added.
“They should put that in music textbooks,” Navya said.
Meera smiled, then turned serious.

“About that,” Manas began, “why exactly Simlipal again? You’ve been everywhere — Madagascar, Patagonia, even the Arctic Circle. Why are we going back to a forest you’ve already mapped?”

The wind paused.
Meera exchanged a glance with Ayan before sitting on the garden bench. “Because something has changed,” she said quietly. “Something we need to verify.”
Navya looked up. “Changed how?”
Ayan answered, “The soil’s electromagnetic response pattern has shifted in certain patches. We noticed it on satellite data in three different forests. Simlipal is the only one where we’ve seen it before.”
Manas blinked. “Wait, you’re using satellite heat maps to study plant vibrations?”
Ayan laughed. “That’s the short version.”
Meera’s gaze drifted towards the horizon. “We’re not just studying forests. We’re studying… memory.”
“Whose memory?” Navya asked.
“The Earth’s,” Meera said, her voice softer than the wind.

Their parents had roamed the world — from Madagascar to the Arctic, from Amazon rainforests to Norwegian tundras — and yet it was a patch of jungle in Odisha that was calling them back.

**Day 2 – Rain, Albums & Echoes**

Rain painted the windows grey. Inside the Agrawal home, the living room was warm with sandalwood aroma and the rustle of old photo albums.

Manas had unearthed a thick leather-bound one labeled “Expeditions: Vol. 1” and was flipping through it like a spy.

“Operation Parental Secrets begins,” he declared. Navya rolled her eyes. “It’s not a conspiracy. It’s your childhood.”

Page after page, the world unfolded — Meera standing knee-deep in a swamp beside a tribal healer in Papua New Guinea. Ayan balancing on a frozen slope in Norway, cradling a pot of arctic moss.

A photo caught Navya’s eye: Meera and Ayan kneeling before a baobab tree in Madagascar, each holding one side of a wooden box carved with spirals.

"You've both gone so far," Navya said softly.
"To reach what was near," Meera replied.

She opened a side pouch from the album — and slid out a yellowing page. A palm-leaf manuscript rubbing. Circular patterns. Some symbols almost… breathing.

"We found this in the Southern Ghats," Ayan said. "Some of these symbols — we've now seen them in Simlipal."
Navya stared at the page. "What does it mean?"
"We're not sure," Meera said. "Not yet. But it's calling."

**Day 3 – Malls and Murmurs**

That afternoon, the four of them walked through the airy halls of Jio World Drive, SoBo's glimmering urban retreat — not for luxury, but for love. Simlipal was calling, and it was time to prepare.

Navya and Meera picked out a muted green raincoat for Prisha, a handwoven shawl for Priya, and a journal wrapped in banana fibre.

In a quiet moment, Ayan chose a deep forest-green kurta for Parag, nodding approvingly at the cut. "Simple. Useful. Suits him."

Then, in the corner of the music section, Meera's eyes fell on a bark-paper songbook. She flipped it open and smiled.

Inside, written in playful script, was a riddle-like Hindi poem:

*का का बोले काँच का पत्थर,*

*या या हँसा छुप गया अन्दर।*

*म मा बोला मिट्टी का जादू,*

*या या छवि छुपा रहे राजू!*

Meera laughed — a soft, warm sound that surprised even Navya.

"What?" Navya asked.
"Raghav would love this," Meera said, her eyes twinkling. "It's nonsense. It's music. It's a puzzle. It's so him."

She added it to the cart, along with a packet of dark chocolates, a pair of brown forest boots, and new clothes for him. "He won't expect it. That's why it'll matter."

By evening, their bags held more than luggage — they held thought, care, memory. A gesture for the family they were about to live with. A silent thank you before the journey even began.

**Bhagavatam Parallel | 16th Avatar - Varaha**

In an age where the Earth had vanished beneath the cosmic ocean, chaos reigned. The demon king Hiranyaksha, mad with power and pride, had seized Bhumi Devi — Earth herself — and hurled her into the deep. The demigods trembled. The balance of creation was breaking.

In their despair, they prayed to the Supreme Lord.

From the nostrils of Brahma emerged a small boar — no bigger than a thumb. Before anyone could understand, it leapt into the sky and began to grow. It grew until it touched the clouds. It grew until thunder rode its breath. Its eyes blazed like suns. Its tusks shone like crescent moons.

This was Varaha, the sixteenth avatar of Vishnu.

With a roar that shook the stars, Varaha plunged into the ocean.

Below, in the shadows, Hiranyaksha waited — fangs bared, mace raised, arrogance burning. He challenged the Lord with brute force, hurling mountains and fire, tearing through waves. But Varaha was beyond force. He fought not just with might, but with meaning.

Their battle churned the waters of the cosmos. Thunder met fury. Light met rage.

At last, Varaha struck — his tusks shining like dharma itself. Hiranyaksha fell.

And then, from the silence, the Lord found her.

Bhumi Devi.
Curled. Quiet. Waiting.

With unmatched grace, Varaha lifted her gently upon his tusks. Not as a trophy, but as a mother lifts her child. He rose through the ocean, carrying Earth back to the light — to balance, to harmony, to home.

And like Varaha, Meera and Ayan, too, were diving — not into oceans, but into forgotten forests. Not to fight demons, but to retrieve the sacred. To lift memory. To awaken the Earth once more.

---

दन्तायुधो भगवान् सुरासुरैः प्रतीयमानः पृथिवीं चिकीर्षया।
यज्ञेश्वरोऽग्न्यर्कसुदर्शनाच्युतो मेघस्वनोऽभीद्यदुरन्तविक्रमः॥

*Meaning*

***The Lord, bearing tusks as weapons, appeared among demigods and asuras, desiring to rescue the Earth. Glowing like fire and the sun, thunder-voiced and unstoppable — he plunged into the depths with boundless might.***

*(Bhagwatam: Canto 3, Chapter 13, Shloka 29)*

---

## Chapter 14

# THE ROAD TO SIMLIPAL

### Flight of Mixed Thoughts

The Chhatrapati Shivaji Maharaj International Airport shimmered like a glass hive, busy with morning echoes and rolling trolleys. Inside, it was a strange orchestra of airport announcements, coffee slurps, and unsaid emotions. Navya and Manas walked alongside their parents towards the departure gate, their bags light but their excitement heavy.

On the plane, Navya took the window seat. Below her, Mumbai stretched like a glittering web. Next to her, Manas was playing with his smartwatch. Across the aisle, Meera was flipping through printed heat maps of satellite data while Ayan sipped green tea from a flask labeled *"Soil Never Lies."*

No one spoke much.
But inside each of them, something had already begun shifting—like the ocean before a churning.

### The Long Drive

They landed in Bhubaneswar just past noon. The air was humid, earthy, full of mangoes and dust. Parag and Priya were waiting near the exit with folded hands and beaming smiles. Beside them stood a robust white Fortuner, shining despite its muddy wheels.

"Climb in, jungle rajas and ranis!" Parag called out.

The car was packed, but they managed. Manas sat in the middle, squished between Navya and Raghav, who had already begun drumming a GDP rhythm on the back of the driver's seat.

"Stop with the tabla," Priya teased. "This isn't your concert."

"It's *Great Dholak Power*, not tabla," Raghav corrected solemnly.

As the car cut through winding highways and green fields, memories tumbled like clouds.

"We came here every summer," Prisha whispered, her voice carried by the breeze.

Navya looked out and smiled. "It smells ancient. Like the soil has secrets."

In the front seat, Ayan laughed. "You four have made this drive feel like a road trip from a Hindi sitcom."

Parag, at the wheel, added cheerfully, "We're about fifteen minutes away. Once we pass the old mango orchard, the forest lodge should be on your left. You'll smell the mahua flowers before you see the gates."

Prisha looked out, eyes half-lost in the movement of trees. A butterfly flew alongside them for a few seconds. She watched it in silence. Something in her heart settled.

Before more teasing could follow, the car slowed. Ahead, a wrought-iron gate creaked open with the help of a tribal staff member wearing a handwoven cotton kurta. The nameboard above, carved in wood and painted in faded ochre, read:

**"Vanvasa Heritage Retreat – Est. 1902"**

Bougainvillea spilled over mossy stone walls, and the fragrance of mahua flowers really did linger in the air. As they drove in, a narrow gravel path curved past lotus ponds, tall sal trunks, and silent statues of forest animals sculpted in stone.

"This used to be a British forest rest house," Parag explained, "but the tribal council preserved and converted it into a heritage lodge. Our family's been visiting it since your grandfather's time."

**Arrival at Vanvasa**

By twilight, they reached their lodge nestled on the outer edge of Simlipal's dense zone. The building was a quiet blend of polished wood and stone, shaped like a crescent around a central lotus pond. Solar lanterns flickered along stone paths. Bamboo walls breathed with forest air. Wind chimes made from clay and conch whispered lullabies.

Navya stepped out first. "Is this... a jungle or a dream?"

Meera smiled. "It's where both meet."

Inside, each room was a small sanctuary—linen sheets, wide windows, desks made of reclaimed sal wood. In the dining area, copper plates gleamed beside leaf-fold napkins. Books on tribal lore and satellite ecology sat on the reception shelf.

Outside, the stars spilled across the sky like an unspoken invitation.

**Bhagavatam Parallel | 15th Avatar: Kurma**

In an age when the Earth itself seemed to tremble, the devas and asuras agreed to churn the *Ocean of Milk* in search of amrita, the nectar of immortality. They chose Mount Mandara as the churning rod. But as they began, the mountain began to sink.

Panic rose. The promise of nectar was slipping into darkness.

And then — from the divine blue sky — emerged Kurma, the turtle avatar of Vishnu. He slipped beneath the ocean, silent and vast, and supported the mountain on his back. He didn't roar or preach. He just held it steady.

The churning continued. The ocean revealed gifts and poisons. And Kurma stayed beneath it all, bearing the weight of change.

In Simlipal too, something was about to churn. And though no one noticed yet, Meera and Ayan were already becoming the turtles beneath this quiet, cosmic stir.

**Modern Parallel — The Silent Supporters**

In every great mission — in science, in families, in revolutions — some do not shout, do not shine, but simply hold steady.

The quiet researchers working behind the scenes. The parents who carry dreams on their backs. The friends who don't lead, but keep the circle from falling apart.

Meera and Ayan, like Kurma beneath the mountain, were such souls. Holding firm beneath the churn of curiosity, ambition, and ancient calls. Letting others rise while they bear the weight of what must remain grounded.

---

*कूर्मोऽवतरदम्भोधौ देवादीनां चिकीर्षया ।*
*मन्दरं धरणे कृत्वा प्रगृह्य वासुकीं रसे ॥*

*Meaning:*

***Kurma, the turtle incarnation, appeared in the cosmic ocean to help the devas. He supported Mount Mandara on his back while the serpent Vasuki was used to churn the ocean.***

*(Bhagavatam: Canto 8, Chapter 7, Shloka 8)*

---

# Chapter 15

# THE CIRCLE OF FIRE AND FLOWERS

**Morning at Vanvasa Retreat**

The soft golden breath of morning seeped through the bamboo blinds. A chorus of forest sounds greeted the children as they stirred from slumber — cuckoos, rustling leaves, the distant splash of a langur leaping into a pond.

Raghav stretched and yawned, asking Manas, "First night without snoring elephants. Victory!"

Navya was already by the window, notebook in hand. "I think that was Manas. He talks in binary when he's dreaming."

"Zero-zero-one… Simlipal," Manas muttered from under a blanket.

The breakfast hall was fragrant with steamed millets, toasted bread, jamun juice, and spiced chutneys. Meera and Ayan, already dressed in forest khakis, laid out a simple plan.

"Today is not about research," Meera smiled. "Just observe. Listen. Feel."

A tall man in his early forties entered, dressed in tribal weave — brown skin, sun-warmed, eyes like river pebbles.

"This is Dhanraj," Ayan said. "Our guide, our friend."

Dhanraj nodded, not speaking much, but his presence was rooted — like a tree.

**The Sacred Fire Circle**

After a short trek through towering sal trees and hushed bamboo paths, the group arrived at a moss-covered clearing.

It was a circle — wide, ancient, ringed with stone seats and wildflowers.

Dhanraj gestured. "Our elders called this *Agni Chakra.* Sacred ground. Where questions were asked to the forest. Not answers — only questions."

The children sat quietly.

Dhanraj built a small, contained fire using dry bark and flint stones. No matchsticks. Just patience and rhythm.

Raghav tapped his fingers on a stone. "GDP rhythm. This place has it too."

Prisha sketched the stone circle in her journal. Manas logged tree types into a notes app — secretly.

Navya collected fallen leaves and arranged them into a mandala.

There were no school bells here. No exams. Just the forest, whispering.

**Bhagwatam Parallel | Hansa: A Dream from the Ashes**

That night, after a simple dinner of rice and lentils, they returned to their rooms. Prisha couldn't sleep.

As the night deepened and forest insects sang their lullaby, she drifted into a dream so vivid, it felt carved into moonlight.

She saw four childlike sages — Sanaka, Sanandana, Sanatana, and Sanatkumara — sitting beneath a giant fig tree. The wind carried no sound. Their eyes were closed, but their hearts overflowed with questions:

*What is real? What is illusion? What is the soul? Is the world temporary or eternal?*

From the sky descended a magnificent white swan — radiant, calm, and still. It did not flutter. It did not speak in haste. It simply *was.*

The sages opened their eyes and asked. One by one, their doubts flowed like rivers. And the Hamsa answered — not always in words, but in truth.

"The body is the shell, the soul is the pearl."
"Truth cannot be described. It can only be lived."
"Time is not the enemy. Ignorance is."

And at last, when the final question was asked — *"Who am I, truly?"* — the Hamsa vanished into golden light.

Prisha woke up gasping. A feather — small, white, and soft — lay on her bedsheet. She looked around. No bird. No open window.

Just silence.

## Modern Day Parallel – The Listeners

Some truths aren't found through searching.
They arrive when we become still.

In today's world of noise — of tweets, alerts, opinions — we've forgotten how to listen.

The Hamsa reminds us that wisdom doesn't always roar. Sometimes, it glides silently.

And those who seek must also learn to ask with silence in their voice.

The children didn't know it yet, but this was the first of many circles they would sit in. Many questions they'd carry. And not all would have answers.

But that was okay.

The feather had already fallen.

---

हंसे रूपं समुद्धिश्य ब्रह्मणः प्रश्निनां मुदा।
व्याजहारात्मतत्त्वार्थं यं गृणन्ति हि सूतयः॥

*Meaning*

***Taking the form of a swan (Hamsa), the Supreme Lord appeared joyfully before the questioning sages and revealed to them the truth of the soul — the essence even the Vedas honor.***

*(Bhagwatam: Skandh 11, Chapter 13, Shloka 5)*

---

# Chapter 16

# VANVAAS KI RAAT

## The Art of Stillness

Morning spilled like golden paint across the Vanvasa Heritage Retreat. The resort — an elegant crescent carved from reclaimed *sal* wood and black granite — stood quietly at the forest's edge, its verandahs wrapped in handwoven cane, its corridors cooled by earthen tiles that whispered stories beneath every footstep.

The entire structure had taken over five years to complete, handcrafted by artisans from across the country. Priya, who adored textiles, had collected tribal wall hangings from Gujarat, *Pattachitra* panels from Odisha, and bells from Kutch. Parag had overseen the carpentry himself, sourcing antique doorknobs from Rajasthan and wooden columns salvaged from dismantled *havelis*.

Windchimes of conch and copper tinkled in the breeze. The central courtyard — lined with tall neem trees and flowering frangipani — hosted sunrise yoga and morning tea. Nearby, a curving stone path led to the café called "*The Courtyard Zest*," known for roasted jackfruit tacos and jungle berry smoothies.

Raghav was humming a *raag* by the lotus pond, where frogs had declared a musical rebellion. Navya sat in the lodge's breezy library nook with a book in her lap. Meera and Ayan were on the nearby forest trail with their equipment, decoding soil samples. Prisha walked barefoot on the pebbled meditation trail, her eyes half-closed, half-seeking something unseen.

Even the air here moved differently—like it had memory.

## Leisure in the Retreat

That afternoon, the *courtyard Zest* was filled with the laughter of antakshari. Raghav turned every Bollywood song into a *raag*-fusion remix, while Navya danced her answers with playful *Kathak* spins.

Manas, meanwhile, had assembled a mini drone from his kit and proudly presented it to curious guests.

Under the bamboo canopy, Parag and Priya sipped forest tea, sharing how they'd acquired the retreat from an old British caretaker.

"It wasn't just about building a resort," Priya said to a young couple. "It was about preserving a lifestyle that honored the forest."

From the shade of a neem tree, Meera and Ayan watched with quiet pride—occasionally pointing out how drifting clouds cast shifting shadows across the forest floor, sketching patterns that only trained eyes would notice.

**Courtyard Zest**

Dinner was quiet — the kind of meal where even silence had flavor. Overhead, the moon hung full, casting silver over the lotus pond. Lanterns flickered across the courtyard where both families sat together.

Parag and Priya leaned into their wicker chairs. Ayan sipped a hot forest brew from a bamboo cup. Meera spun a silver bracelet around her wrist. Raghav had a *dholak* across his lap. Navya played with a mango leaf. Manas had just locked the settings screen on his drone app.

"Enough technology for one day," Meera said, smiling. "Let's time-travel instead."

Parag turned to Prisha with a wink.

"Beta, we're in Simlipal and haven't heard even one story. *Tumhara Bhagavatam kahaan hai?"*

Prisha grinned, brushing imaginary dust off an invisible mic.

"Which one do you want?"

"Something... big," Navya said lazily. "Like *really* big."

"Then," Prisha said softly, "let's go to the one who came *for* dharma itself. Rama."

A hush fell. Even the *mahua* trees leaned in.

**Bhagwatam Parallel | 20th Avatar – Rama**

Long ago, the three worlds trembled under a single name — Ravana. Having pleased Brahma through severe penance, he'd earned near invincibility. No god or demon could kill him.

Drunk on power, he humiliated good beings, imprisoned sages, and claimed dominion over the heavens.

The devatas, weary and desperate, turned their gaze upward.

"O Narayana," they prayed, "descend not as thunder or trident — but as a man. Save the world not with a storm, but with silence."

And in Vaikuntha, Lord Vishnu smiled.

In Ayodhya, King Dasharatha had everything — queens, wealth, glory — but no heir. He performed the sacred *Putrakameshti yagna*, and from its flames rose a golden bowl of divine kheer.

Four sons were born:

> ***Rama****, calm as the moon*
> ***Lakshmana****, fierce and loyal*
> ***Bharata****, noble and wise*
> ***Shatrughna****, sharp and silent*

Rama was raised with kindness stitched into his soul. His teachers were the mighty sages Vashishtha and Vishvamitra.

One day, Vishvamitra came to court.

"Let Rama and Lakshmana come with me. I need not just warriors — I need purity."

Reluctantly, the king agreed.

In the forest, Rama confronted the demoness Tataka, once a woman cursed by fate. Rama hesitated. But dharma asked for protection. He lifted his bow. And silence returned to the forest.

Demon after demon fell to his arrows.

Soon, they reached Mithila, where King Janaka had announced a swayamvar. The task: lift and string the mighty bow of Shiva — the Pinaka.

Princes came from across the world. None succeeded.

When Rama stepped forward, the court paused. He didn't look proud — only reverent. He lifted the bow as one lifts a fallen tree branch. And when he strung it, it broke in two with a thunder that split the sky.

Sita placed the garland around his neck. Her eyes lowered. Her heart soared.

"Their wedding," Prisha said gently, "was not just a union — it was a promise. Of strength with softness. Dharma with love."

Navya whispered, "So… was that the end?"

"No," Prisha smiled. "That was the beginning."

**Modern Day Parallel – The Silent Strength**

As the tale ended, Meera's voice broke the stillness.

"To break the bow of ego with grace... that's the real lesson, isn't it?"

Parag nodded.

"And to choose love — without pride."

Navya looked sideways at Raghav.

"Maybe *you* should stop breaking chairs with your GDP beats and start breaking ego."

Raghav chuckled.

"Why not both?"

Laughter danced under the neem tree canopy.

---

श्रीरामं सत्यपराक्रमं हरिमिहोत्तंसं सदा
रामं रजःसत्त्वविभूतिमण्डितं रम्यं गुणैः साक्षिकम् ॥

*Meaning*

***I bow to Shri Rama, the truly valiant one, the most exalted among the manifestations of Hari (Vishnu), forever radiant with sattvic and rajasic glory, and adorned with virtues witnessed by all.***

*(Bhagavatam: Canto 9, Chapter 10, Shloka 2)*

---

# Chapter 17

# VANVAAS KI GOONJ

**Morning Whispers & Botanical Bonds**

The mist was still lifting from the valley when Navya slipped into her sandals and walked towards the herbal trail behind Vanvasa Retreat. The scent of lemongrass and wet earth mingled in the air as dewdrops shimmered on leaves like glass beads. Manas caught up with her near the bamboo grove, rubbing sleep from his eyes.

"Why do plants look shinier in the morning? Is it just the dew or some kind of photosynthetic flex?"

Navya laughed. "Partly dew. But some species, like *Calathea,* actually open up at dawn. It's called *nyctinasty*. Light sensitivity." She pointed to a crimson-veined leaf. "That's *Mimosa pudica*. Touch it."

He did. The leaf folded instantly.

"Sensitive plant," she said. "Used in Ayurvedic calming tonics. But it's shy. Like someone I know."

He raised an eyebrow. "Not me, obviously."

Behind them, a quiet pair of eyes watched — Meera and Ayan, hands entwined, leaning against a neem tree.

"She's growing," Ayan whispered.

"She's blooming," Meera replied, softly proud.

Later, as the trail opened to a clearing, Navya rattled off names like a spellbook: *Saraca indica* (Ashoka), *Celastrus paniculatus* (Jyotishmati), *Nyctanthes arbor-tristis* (Parijat).

"Parijat?" Manas asked.

"My favourite. It only blooms at night. By morning, it carpets the earth. That's why it's also called the sorrowless tree."

Meera joined them just then. "Its oil treats neurological disorders too. Very rare. Mostly grows wild now."

Navya smiled. "I want to study more of these in real forests. Maybe… even discover new ones."

Ayan nodded. "And the forest will speak to you. It always has."

**Return of the GDP**

Late afternoon, in the *Courtyard Zest*, Parag arranged a guided meditation session.
Everyone sat cross-legged on yoga mats, eyes closed, breathing deep.
And then it came.
Dum-da-da-dum… DUM!
A sudden dholak beat.
A wind chime clinked.
A frog croaked melodically.
A bamboo stick struck rhythm.
Eyes snapped open.

There stood Raghav — half in zen, half in mischief — creating an impromptu *Sound Bath of the Jungle*. He bowed dramatically.
Navya threw a cushion at him. Prisha muttered, "Great Dholak Power strikes again."
Parag clapped. "You've turned meditation into stand-up percussion."
Manas added, "GDP: *Guaranteed Disruption Protocol*."
Everyone laughed.

**Bhagwatam Parallel | Ramayana Continues**

That evening, under a velvet sky sprinkled with stars, both families sat once again on floor cushions around the open courtyard. A mild breeze carried the scent of mahua and mango blossom.
Priya passed mugs of warm ragi malt, and Raghav gently tapped his dholak.
"Shall we continue where we left?" Parag asked.
Prisha nodded, eyes glinting. "From wedding to wandering."

Long ago, in Ayodhya, joy had bloomed with Rama and Sita's wedding. But joy is a guest — it never overstays.

Kaikeyi, the queen, once kind, was poisoned by envy. Bound by promises, Dasharatha exiled his beloved Rama for fourteen years. Lakshmana and Sita chose to walk beside him, their feet kissing the dust of *dharma*.
As the trio walked into the forests, the city wept. Dasharatha died of heartbreak. Bharata refused the crown and placed Rama's sandals on the throne.

In the forests of Chitrakoot, Dandakaranya, and Panchavati, they lived with simplicity. Rama built huts, Sita cooked on stone hearths, and Lakshmana guarded with a bow drawn.

One day, a golden deer pranced by. Sita, enchanted, asked Rama to catch it. Rama left. Lakshmana stayed. But when Sita heard a cry — Rama's voice echoing in pain — she panicked.
Against Lakshmana's pleading, she drew a line — *Lakshman Rekha* — and he crossed it.

Ravana arrived, disguised as a sage, and when Sita stepped out to offer alms, he revealed his true form and abducted her in his sky-chariot.
The birds screamed. The trees trembled. The Earth held her breath.

But one soul dared to fight — the old vulture, Jatayu. He attacked Ravana mid-air. His wings were torn, his body broken, but his spirit burned bright.
Rama found the dying Jatayu. The bird whispered Sita's name before passing. Rama held him like a father and lit his funeral pyre with the respect given to kings.

Thus began the search.
Rama walked, wept, roared, and resolved. Mountains echoed his pain. Rivers mourned with him.
He met Sugreeva, the exiled monkey king, and forged an alliance. The world began to move once more.

**The Modern Day Parallel**

As Prisha finished, the courtyard stayed quiet. Only the wind moved.
Navya whispered, "That golden deer — was it illusion or destiny?"
Meera replied, "Sometimes the things we desire most are distractions… tests."
Ayan added, "And those who dare to fight even when they're broken — like Jatayu — they're the real heroes."
Raghav said softly, "I won't let anyone touch my family. GDP promise."
Manas nudged him. "Just don't fight Ravana with your dholak."
They all smiled — a small circle of light in the forest night.

---

*स वासुदेवः शुचिर्भृदुत्पत्तिप्रतिपत्तिस्थितः।*
*रामः सत्यवान् सत्यसङ्गट्टकृत्स्ने हिन्दरागसा॥*

*Meaning*

***He is Vasudeva—pure at every stage of creation, preservation, and dissolution. He is Rama—a true man of integrity, whose being carries the resonance of truth and devotion.***

*(Bhagwatam: Canto 9, Chapter 10, Shloka 50)*

---

# Chapter 18

# THE THRONE AND THE THORNS

**Nature's Classroom**

A soft morning mist settled over the courtyard of Vanvasa Heritage Retreat. The grass shimmered with dew, and the neem trees filtered sunlight like emerald lace. A gentle breeze rustled the leaves, carrying the earthy scent of blooming champa and wet stone.

Navya sat barefoot near a stone planter, sketchbook on her lap, toes nestled into the cool soil. She pointed at a plant with spiked leaves. "This is *Acanthus ilicifolius* — a mangrove associate. Usually found near tidal waters. Strange that it's thriving here."

Manas blinked. "Didn't know mangroves came with thorns."

"They usually don't. This one's special. Locals call it *Chhota Vajradanti* — little thunder-tooth. Its roots clean salt from water. Like a natural filter."

Meera had joined them silently, sipping lemongrass tea. Pride lingered in her quiet smile. "Keep going," she encouraged.

Navya flipped to another page. "This is *Clerodendrum infortunatum*, but kids call it *Bhoot Paata* — Ghost Leaf. Its paired flowers look like teeth."

"Ghost Leaf?" Manas muttered. "Sounds like Raghav's fan club."

Everyone laughed.

Navya traced a soft line along the ghost-leaf sketch. "Some plants just want to be seen," she said thoughtfully. "Like people."

## Firewalls and Footnotes

While others drifted towards breakfast, Manas lingered in the resort's shared workspace. Something had taken hold of him again — the cyberattack.

He powered up one of Parag's emergency laptops and navigated through the school's copied server logs. Pulkit Roy's notes sat open beside him, and a spectrum-filter tool ran quietly in the background.

"No brute-force. No brute code... it's a relay," he muttered.

He scribbled furiously on a notepad:

Layer 1 breached via old SSH port...
But how did they get past MAC filters?

Pulkit had once joked about *signature cloaking*. "Was it really a joke?" Manas whispered.

And then he saw it.

Four characters repeated in the logs.

क, य, म, य.

He leaned back. "Not again…"

## Bhagwatam Parallel | The Story Continues – Lord Rama's Return

That evening, fireflies danced over the courtyard as the scent of grilled pineapples wafted from the kitchen. The families sat beneath the open canopy, Raghav drumming softly on his dholak.

Prisha began. "Last night, we left just after Rama met the monkey king Sugreeva."

After Jatayu's sacrifice, Rama and Lakshmana wandered through forests and mountains, never losing hope. In Kishkindha, they found Sugreeva, the exiled monkey king. Rama helped Sugreeva win back his throne, and in return, Sugreeva's monkey army joined the search for Sita.

High atop a mountain, Hanuman leapt across the ocean, landing in distant Lanka. He found Sita, brave and unbroken, imprisoned in a garden. Hanuman delivered Rama's ring to her—a promise that help would come. He set fire to Lanka as a warning and returned with news of her safety.

The army built a bridge—*Setubandha*—across the roaring sea. With monkeys, bears, and courage as their allies, they marched to war.

On the battlefield of Lanka, brothers fought: Rama against Ravana. The earth shook with the clash of dharma and ego. In the end, Rama's arrow—blessed by all the gods—struck true. Ravana fell, and peace returned.

Rama freed Sita, who walked through fire to prove her purity. Together, they returned to Ayodhya. Lamps lit every doorway, and the city glowed for Deepavali—the festival of light and return.

Rama was crowned not just king, but as a living symbol of maryada, the dignity of dharma. His reign, Rama Rajya, became the dream of justice, kindness, and harmony for all time.

"And so," Prisha finished softly, "Lord Rama taught the world: True strength lies in keeping one's word, forgiving even enemies, and ruling with love as well as law."

Ayodhya's joy was echoed in every heart that night, as the children listened—knowing that every exile, every search, and every homecoming lives on in the world, and in them.

**GDP Strikes Again**

That afternoon, just after lunch, a staff member came running across the courtyard. "Ma'am! Someone rearranged the salad bowls to spell GHOST… and taped a sign over the chutney tray!"

Priya turned from her conversation with Retd. Major General Bakshi. "Excuse me, General. The agency strikes again."

She found Raghav hiding behind a pillar, giggling.

"What now, young man?" she asked, hands on her hips.

Raghav shrugged. "*Garam Dimag ki Pralaya, Maa.*"

"Why's your dimag so *garam* today?" Meera asked, appearing with a raised brow.

He huffed. "Nobody's paying attention to me! Everyone's sketching leaves or decoding logs or quoting shlokas. A boy needs his limelight!"

Priya smiled. "Our little Krishna is sulking because the gopis won't chase him."

Meera laughed. "Come here, you melodramatic mango." She pinched his cheek. "We'll build a GDP statue in your honour."

Raghav beamed. "Full form today: *Ghar ki roti, Daal ka tadka, Papad ke saath achaar!*"

The courtyard exploded with laughter.

रामं गुणानुचरितं रमणीयमीनं, संकीर्त्य तीर्थपदपादयुगं वियोगात्।
स्मृतिं पुनः सुखयति श्वसनेन रज्ज्वा, निर्गत्य देहमिह याति परं हि भूम्नि॥

*Meaning*

***One who remembers the beautiful deeds and divine qualities of Lord Rama, whose feet are as sacred as pilgrimages, and chants His name even in sorrow — such a person departs this life with joy and attains the supreme state.***

*(Bhagwatam: Canto 9, Chapter 11, Shloka 23)*

# Chapter 19

# THE YAJNA WITHIN

**Into the Green Unknown**

The sun rose slowly over Simlipal, painting the forest canopy in strokes of amber and jade. As the kids gathered around their breakfast table, a quiet announcement was made.

"We're going deeper into the forest today," Ayan said, adjusting his trekking bag.

"Two days," Meera added, checking her field notes. "We'll be hiking towards Khairi, near the ancient streambeds. Something's off in the fungal sequences and mineral spreads — it's not matching previous surveys."

Prisha blinked. "You mean… the soil changed?"

Ayan nodded. "In ways we can't explain yet. Even plant memory seems disoriented. Something altered the underground communication of roots. That's why we need to study this in person."

Navya leaned forward, instantly alert. "You mean the mycorrhizal networks?"

"Exactly," Meera smiled. "Did I ever tell you your name literally means 'newness'? Your brain matches it."

Raghav groaned. "Two days without you means Manas has to cook his own tea!"

"GDP special kadak chai is banned," Priya called from the kitchen. "Last time your 'tea' melted the kettle base."

**When Trees Speak**

That afternoon, as Meera and Ayan moved through the inner zones of Simlipal, Navya walked with them for part of the trail, whispering the names of trees as if greeting old friends.

"That's *Haldina cordifolia* — also called *Haldu*," she said, touching its golden bark. "And this one here is *Madhuca longifolia*. Locals survive entire summers on its fruit."

Parag and Priya trailed behind, quietly observing.

Ayan paused by a rock outcrop. "Notice this? The quartz is discolored. Possible signs of trace radiation exposure… or maybe just climate-driven mineral shift."

Priya looked confused.

Meera gently translated. "It means the ground might be reacting to something unnatural — not just weather. Could be ancient residue, or even modern contamination."

Parag frowned. "Does that worry you?"

"Not yet," Ayan said. "But it raises a question — how many secrets does this land still hide?"

**Sparks of Doubt**

That evening, a courier envelope arrived at the resort's reception. No address. No sender name. Just three words:

"To the Four."

Manas read the contents aloud. A single sentence:

"Those who fix firewalls must also learn what burns them."

Below it, a smudged symbol. A flame inside a square. Nothing else.

Navya frowned. "Is this… a threat?"

Prisha's voice was low, sharp. "Or a warning."

They gathered in the treehouse library that night — a small circular wooden room elevated between two mango trees. The breeze whispered through the lattice windows.

"This has to be connected to the cyberattack," Manas said.

Prisha read it twice, lips moving silently. "Someone knows we were the ones who helped decode it."

Navya narrowed her eyes. "But how? Only Pulkit sir knew. And Anusuya ma'am helped in the last phase."

Manas shook his head. "It could be anyone watching us. Maybe someone from the tech team? Or just someone from school who figured it out."

Raghav looked amused. "Are we famous now? The Four Hackateers?"

Navya stood near the bookshelf. "What if... we're being watched? What if this isn't over?"

Raghav tried to joke, "Maybe it's from the Great Dhamaal Patrol. Our fan club?"

But the mood was serious.

They discussed every possibility. Who knew about the firewall breach? Who knew about their late-night research sessions?

Then Prisha brought up the disc.

"It's... quiet now. But what if we were wrong about it?"

Navya's tone snapped. "We are wrong. We've been obsessing over it for weeks. What's changed? Nothing. No light, no code, no purpose."

"But maybe it's waiting," Prisha whispered.

"Or maybe we're giving it more power than it deserves," Navya replied.

That line hung in the air. Manas looked from one to the other. "So what now?"

Navya folded her arms. "We bury it. Get rid of it. The forest has taken secrets before — let it take this one."

Prisha's eyes widened. "Without even trying to understand it?"

Navya raised an eyebrow. "We've tried. We failed. Isn't that enough?"

The argument flared — quietly but deeply.
The boys remained silent.

But the fire had been lit.
The yajna of conflict had begun.

## Raag Bhookha – Symphony of the Stomach

It was nearly 7:00 p.m. The sun had dipped, casting long shadows on the wooden deck of the courtyard café. The staff was setting up a cozy dinner buffet under hanging lanterns. The scent of curry leaves and fresh rotis wafted through the air like sacred incense.

And then... came Raghav, barefoot on a low stage set for open-mic night, a napkin tied around his head like a bandana.

He tapped the microphone with flair.

"Ladies and Gentleboys, presenting the musical masterpiece that echoes in every hungry soul — *Raag Bhookha!*"

Manas groaned. "Not again."

Raghav bowed dramatically, struck an invisible tanpura, and began:

***"Ghar ki roti,***
***Daal ka tadka,***
***Papad ke saath…***
***Achaar ka jhatka!"***

He paused for effect, eyes closed in reverence. "This raag is not just sung… it is felt in the belly."

He broke into exaggerated aalaps:

"Bhoo-o-o-o-o-kh…aaaah…
Kha-naaaaaa chaaahiy-eeeeee!"

Navya burst out laughing, nearly dropping her soup bowl. "Stop it! You'll scare the guests!"

Just then, a bemused tourist couple from Delhi clapped politely. "Is this… part of the cultural programme?" the man whispered.

Raghav, not missing a beat, turned to them. "Yes, sir! Special composition from the GDP Gurukul."

Manas buried his face in his hoodie. "Oh no. What's the full form now?"

Raghav grinned. "*Garam Dholak Pratishthan.*"

"And yesterday it was '*Ghar ke Dabbe ke Popat*'," Prisha added.

"Today it's *Gustakh Dil ki Pukaarein,*" Raghav said, hand over heart. "Tomorrow? Who knows?"

Even the staff had gathered behind the buffet, giggling. Chef Sandeep raised a ladle like a microphone.

*"Beta Raghav, dinner bell baj gaya hai — ab asli raag bajao, khaane ka!"*

With a theatrical bow, Raghav whispered to Prisha, "One day this will be a Grammy-winning raag. Mark my chutneys."

**Bhagwatam Parallel | 7th Avatar – Yajana: The Yajna Within**

Later that evening, Prisha sat alone by the lotus pond behind the resort, watching moonlight shimmer on the water.

She thought about the fight.
About Navya's sharp words.
About her own stubbornness.

Then she opened the Bhagavatam — not to escape, but to understand.

She began reading the story of *Yajña*, the seventh avatar of Lord Vishnu.

"During the *Svayambhuva Manu* era, the balance between good and evil was delicate.
Demons had begun to interrupt the very yajnas that sustained the universe.
So Lord Vishnu appeared as *Yajña* — not a warrior, but a living embodiment of sacrifice.
He upheld the Vedic rites and protected the sages by leading through wisdom and example."

He did not wield a bow.
He did not slay asuras in battle.

Instead, he burned ignorance with selflessness.
His fire did not consume — it purified.

Even the demigods performed yajnas under his guidance to stay aligned with dharma.

Prisha's eyes moistened.

*Maybe this conflict with Navya is also a yajna…*
*One where ego burns, and only truth remains.*

She whispered:

"yajno vai vishnuh"
*Sacrifice itself is Vishnu — through surrender, we see the divine.*

A warm breeze stirred the lotus petals.
Somewhere deep in the woods, two scientists camped under the stars, unaware that their children were already preparing for yajnas of their own.

---

यज्ञैः साङ्गोपाङ्गपार्षदं, यज्ञैः कल्पितमक्षयम्।
धर्मस्य तत्त्वं राजर्षे, नारायणमयं जगत्॥

*Meaning*

***Through yajnas, with all their rituals and assistants, the eternal is preserved.***
***The essence of dharma, O royal sage, lies in this truth —***
***The universe is filled with Narayana.***

*(Bhagwatam: Canto 4, Chapter 6, Shloka 42)*

---

# Chapter 20

# THE VANISHING CLUES

**Something Beneath**

Meera tightened the strap of her field scanner while Ayan unfolded a compact drone with thermal sensors. They stood deep in the Khairi stretch of Simlipal — far beyond the usual research zones.

"The moisture here has risen by eighteen percent," Meera said, flipping her logbook open. "No rain in weeks. And yet, the roots are bloated."

Ayan crouched beside a sal tree. "Even algal creep on the north-facing bark. That's not normal for this temperature."

He launched the drone. A soft buzz rose into the air, and a blue thermal scan shimmered across the holographic grid in their palms.

Meera knelt beside a coiled vine. "Remember what Navya said about root silence? That the network wasn't responding to her?"

Ayan nodded slowly. "And she didn't even have our equipment. Just… instincts."

Meera straightened, brows drawn. "What child senses what machines barely register?"

A soft beep sounded. On the screen, a pulse flickered below the soil — faint veins reacting to light.

"It's changing," Ayan murmured. "This forest isn't just reacting to climate. It's… trying to reveal something."

Meera didn't speak. She had already pulled out a satellite device and begun typing — coordinates, pulse readings, timestamps.

"Sending it to the Bangalore lab. And the Haifa team," she said.

Ayan glanced sideways. "And the old contact?"

She hesitated. Then nodded. "Yes. We need his eyes, too."

**Silent Frequencies**

By afternoon, they were tucked under a rocky outcrop, their gear scattered around them. A rugged laptop blinked with jagged graphs.

"Electromagnetic activity is rising below the basalt layer," Ayan noted. "Every few days. Like… a system rebooting."

Meera wrapped her scarf tighter. "You think it's connected to that fossil pattern we found last month?"

Ayan didn't look away from the screen. "I think the fossil was a warning."

She tapped her communicator. A bearded man appeared on the screen — his room a blend of ancient manuscripts and modern instruments.

"We've confirmed the second pulse," Meera said.

"Frequency match?"

"Ninety-two percent."

The man's face grew grim. "Then it's the same source. You're standing over one of the gates."

A moment of silence passed between Ayan and Meera.

"What now?" Ayan asked.

"Observe. Record. But tread carefully. If this stirs beyond your zone, the awakening won't stay gentle."

The screen blinked off.

**The Debate Deepens**

By a murmuring forest stream, the kids sat in a circle. The letter lay between them like a fifth presence.

Prisha picked it up. "*Those who fix firewalls must also learn what burns them.*"

Navya leaned back against a mossy boulder. "I'm tired. Tired of secrets, codes, theories… of always waiting for the next twist."

Raghav tossed a pebble into the stream. "I kinda liked being GDP. *Garam Dimaag ke Pichhle Janam.*"

Manas grinned. "*Great Dahi Pakode.*"

Prisha's smile didn't reach her eyes. "We're not the same anymore. This… whatever it is, it's changed us."

Navya's voice rose. "Then let's go back to who we were. Bury the disc. Seal the letter. Be kids again."

Manas nodded. "Maybe we were never meant to carry this. Maybe it belongs to the school."

Prisha hesitated. "But what if it comes back?"

Silence.

Only the wind rustled the leaves, as if the trees themselves whispered an ancient answer.

**Raag Bhookha — The Sequel**

That evening, the courtyard café glowed with hanging lanterns. Laughter floated in the air as tourists relaxed under the stars.

And then Raghav took the makeshift stage — towel-cape billowing, ladles in hand.

"Presenting: *Raag Bhookha — Bhojan ke Bina Bharat Bandh!*"

*"Roti ki yaadon mein,*
*Bhookh ke geet likhe,*
*Khaane ke raag chhedo,*
*Tandoor ke beat sikhe!"*

Manas clapped. "GDP of the day?"

Raghav struck a pose. "*Ghaas Phoos ke Dushman!*"

"*Gussa Dimaag ka Parikshan!*" Prisha offered.

"*Galtiyon ka Data Processor,*" Navya muttered — but her smile betrayed her mood shift.

A tourist kid chimed in, "*Garam Dhokla Party!*"

Chef Sandeep emerged from the kitchen, holding a ladle like a scepter. "Beta Raghav! Come taste this new kheer before your audience riots!"

Raghav bowed. "My art is complete."

**Bhagwatam Parallel | 12th Avatar – Hayagreeva: The Horse-Headed One**

Later that night, Prisha sat alone in the treehouse library. The letter still rested in her palm like a puzzle unsolved.

She opened the Bhagavatam and turned to a story Anusuya ma'am had once mentioned — the tale of Hayagriva, the horse-headed form of Vishnu.

"When the demons Madhu and Kaitabha stole the Vedas and hid them in the cosmic ocean, Lord Vishnu appeared as Hayagriva. With the face of a radiant white horse and a thunderous cry, he dove into the depths and reclaimed divine wisdom."

She read on — of Hayagriva's burning eyes, the deep underwater battle, and the truth that can never be destroyed.

*"Even the darkest depths cannot drown knowledge."*

Prisha closed the book. She thought of the disc. Of the warning. Of the weight of mystery.

She whispered aloud, "Some things must be protected. But some must be let go."

She looked up. The moon shimmered through the trees — a distant, watchful eye.

And somewhere in the forest, Meera and Ayan worked by their lanterns, unaware that the land beneath their feet was slowly awakening.

---

वेदं च धर्मं च सदाशयं च अदत्तमासन् हरिरग्रहीषीत् ।
हयग्रीवरूपेण यथावत्समाप्तम् नमो नमः ते हयग्रीवदेव ॥

*Meaning*

***To the divine Hayagriva, who descended to retrieve the Vedas, Dharma, and eternal truth from the abyss — we bow again and again. He restores what was lost, with wisdom that cannot drown.***

*(Bhagavatam: Canto 2, Chapter 7, Shloka 11)*

---

# Chapter 21

# THE BURIAL

### The Forest Calls Again

The sun had barely crested above Simlipal's canopy when the four children began their silent journey.
Each carried a small satchel, but only one bag felt heavier than it should. Inside, wrapped in layers of muslin and dried leaves, lay the disc — silent, unblinking, as if in slumber.

Manas walked ahead, his head bowed low.
Raghav hummed a soft tune, hoping to slice through the tension.
Navya and Prisha stayed quiet — no teasing, no chatter. Just thoughts, tangled and unspoken.
No one needed to speak of the path. Their feet remembered.

### Final Goodbye

They reached the banyan grove near the old stream — the same place they had once tried to decode the disc's carvings.
Navya looked around and whispered, "This feels right."

Prisha knelt by the roots, brushing away moss and memories. "It began here... and it ends here."

They dug a shallow pit with their hands. None of them cried — but their fingers moved slowly, reverently.
The earth seemed to resist at first, reluctant to reclaim what had never belonged.

Raghav held the disc one last time. "It gave us more questions than answers."

Prisha rested her palm gently over his. "And still... it brought us together."

He folded his hands, then cleared his throat and began dramatically:

*"Here lies the GDP of mystery,*

*Global Destructor of Peace and history,*
*Gave us stress, thrill, fear, and glee,*
*Now rest, O disc, beneath this tree."*

Manas smirked. Navya rolled her eyes — but smiled.

Prisha placed the bundle into the pit with care. They covered it in silence.

For now, it was over.

**Letters with No Names**

That afternoon, four envelopes arrived at the resort reception through a local courier.
No name, no return address—just five words:
"To the One Who Knows."

Inside, each letter bore the same line:
"Those who remember must also forget."

Manas stared at his. "Who keeps sending these?"

Navya frowned. "And how do they even know we're involved?"

Prisha hugged her knees, voice low. "Should we tell our parents? Or maybe call Vice Principal Asha?"

Raghav shook his head. "If this is meant for us, maybe it's because we're the only ones who can solve it. Telling anyone else might make things worse."

After a long, uneasy pause, the four decided—just for now—to keep the letters secret.
Outside, the breeze shifted. The mystery grew, but so did their sense of unity.

**The Return**

Late afternoon. A jeep rattled up the forest trail, kicking up dust and dusk.

Meera and Ayan stepped out — exhausted, dusty, but glowing with some invisible discovery and hands full of soil samples.

Navya was the first to spot them. "You're back!"

"We are, sweetheart," Meera said, hugging her tightly. "And starving."

Raghav grinned. "Raag Bhookha strikes again?"

Ayan ruffled Manas's hair. "You two survived without us?"

Manas whispered, "Barely."

They didn't speak of what they found.

Not yet.

But in their eyes — a glimmer of urgency, wrapped in affection.

**Under One Roof, Under One Bond**

Lamps flickered along the wooden dining patio, casting dancing shadows on the floor. Simlipal's silence settled like a shawl — not heavy, but hushed, like the jungle itself had paused to listen.

On the special request of Meera, dinner was simple: khichdi, kadhi, and roasted papad. But it felt like a feast.

The long day of mystery and goodbye had drained them, yet strangely, none of them wanted to leave the table. Conversations lingered like old friends reluctant to part.

Meera looked at her son.

Manas was leaning against Parag, laughing at something Raghav said, his eyes brighter than they had been in weeks. Across the table, Navya was poking Prisha's arm with a fork, mimicking her strict tone from earlier that day.

Suddenly, Meera's throat tightened.

"They've changed," she whispered.

Ayan, sitting beside her, followed her gaze. "Yes," he said. "And maybe... so have we."

He reached for her hand beneath the table.

Parag smiled gently. "They're stronger than we ever knew. But even the strongest kids need people who believe in them."

Meera blinked back tears. "I don't know how to thank you both."

"You already did," Priya said, smiling. "You raised children who still care… in a world that teaches them to shut down."

A pause.

Ayan looked away. "Sometimes I feel... we missed so many moments. Always researching. Always away."

"And yet," Parag said, "they turned out brilliant. Maybe it's because you gave them curiosity, Meera and Ayan gave them grounding."

Later, as the kids went inside — giggling, sleepy, tangled in tales of ghost-letters and GDP obituaries — Meera and Priya stayed back on the balcony.

Cicadas had begun their midnight chorus.

"I worry, Priya," Meera said. "What if life scatters them? Different paths. Different places. They're so close now, but..."

Priya's voice was firm. "Then let's make a promise."

Meera turned towards her.

"Let's promise," Priya continued, "to keep showing up for each other's kids. Even if they drift. Even if they forget. We remind them. We bring them back."

Meera smiled, tears shimmering. "Like a second set of parents."

"Exactly," Priya nodded. "When the world pushes them apart, we become the gravity."

Inside, laughter exploded again — Raghav had apparently declared that tonight's GDP stood for "Grateful Dinners & Parents."

And in that moment — with full stomachs, quiet tears, and hopeful hearts — two mothers stood like sentinels.

Guardians not of mystery or magic, but of the bonds that make such magic possible.

**Bhagavatam Parallel | 4th Avatar - Nar Narayan**

That night, Raghav lay quietly on his bed, reading.

He had reached the story of Nar Narayan, the twin sages born to Dharma and Murti.
Together, they performed penance to uphold dharma across the ages.

"When the world trembled — not from war, but from confusion — Lord Vishnu manifested as Nar and Narayan.

Nar acted. Narayan meditated.

Together, they maintained balance —
One in karma, one in dhyana."

He paused, whispering to himself,

"Prisha didi did the right thing, agreeing with Navya di to bury the disc.
Sometimes… letting go is also dharma."

This was not a story of weapons or war —
It was a story of patience.

Of silence.
Of inner restraint.
Of standing guard even when no one watches.

Maybe this, too, was a kind of tapasya —

Burying, not running.
Pausing, not fleeing.
Waiting, not quitting.

---

नारायणं नरं चैव ऋषी नरा-नारायणौ यदा ।
धर्मं स्थापयितुं भूमौ तपश्चक्रतुः सदा ॥

*Meaning*

***Nara and Narayana, the twin incarnations, performed eternal penance to uphold dharma on earth. They are the silent protectors through tapasya.***

*(Bhagwatam: Canto 11, Chapter 4, Shloka 5)*

---

## Chapter 22

# FAREWELLS AND FOOTSTEPS

**Departures and Divides**

The morning mist still clung to the grass as Navya zipped up her backpack. Her parents were already loading equipment into their jeep.

"You sure you want to come?" Meera asked, adjusting her field vest. "It won't be easy. We'll be deep inside for a week."

Navya didn't flinch. "Exactly why I'm coming. You said I could assist this time."

Ayan chuckled. "She knows half our species names better than we do."

Manas gave her a mock salute. "Try not to name any trees after me."

Navya grinned. "Only the twisted ones."

Meanwhile, Prisha rolled her small duffel onto the gravel. Parag was helping her fasten the buckle.

"Five days at the Bakshi Foundation is a big deal," he said. "Wild Life conservation isn't a weekend project."

"I know," Prisha nodded, serious. "Major General Bakshi runs a tight camp. But it's worth it."

Raghav frowned. "Why don't I get invited to any of these cool missions?"

Priya teased, "Because your last expedition was to the mess kitchen to rescue leftover jalebis."

He placed a hand on his heart. "I was preventing food wastage. A noble cause."

Laughter softened the goodbyes.

### Backup Plans

As the jeeps stood ready, Meera pulled Priya aside. In her hand was a thin, worn field diary.

"Just some backup notes," Meera said, slipping the file into Priya's hand. "In case we lose connection or… the forest eats our Wi-Fi again."

Priya smirked. "That, I can believe."

Ayan added quietly, "Some of the newer findings… they're hard to explain. If anything feels off, just read the last two pages."

Then, with a final wave and a trail of dust, both jeeps disappeared into the forest, leaving behind a strange stillness.

### Sanctuary of the Wild

Far from the resort, Prisha crouched beside an injured leopard cub, gently applying herbal balm under the guidance of a young wildlife vet. The sounds of the sanctuary — distant hoots, rustling grass, and monkeys calling from the treetops — filled the air.

Major General Bakshi, tall and composed, stood beside her with folded hands.

"You're a fast learner," he said. "Most freeze around wild animals."

Prisha smiled, eyes still focused on the cub. "Maybe they don't feel wild to me."

He studied her for a moment. "Do you talk to them?"

She hesitated. "Not in words. But… there's something. A feeling."

Bakshi placed a hand on her shoulder. "Sometimes, the forest doesn't speak in language. It speaks in silence. You're one of the few who can hear it."

In her pocket, her fingers brushed the edge of her diary. She'd already filled six pages with animal behaviour notes — and strange, vivid dreams of conversations with birds and tigers.

She hadn't written those dreams down yet. Not yet.

### Ripples and Rhymes

Back at the resort, Raghav stretched out in a hammock, sunglasses on, strumming his ukulele.

"I declare this zone a no-disc, no-cryptic-letters, no-GDP area," he said.

Manas laughed. "Back to being the prince of puns and pranks?"

"I'm telling you, bro," Raghav grinned. "For once, I'm not the confused, philosophical musician. I'm just me. A free bird. And all eyes are on me now."

Priya served lemonade while Parag read aloud from a wildlife magazine. The mood was easy, sun-drenched, light-hearted. It felt… normal.

Until the letter arrived. A staff member handed Parag a cream envelope with no sender. Again:
"To the One Who Knows."
Inside, just one line:
"Some silences are not empty. They are pregnant with a return."

Parag passed it to Priya, who read it twice and frowned. Before she could say anything, Manas snatched the envelope and shrugged, forcing a laugh. "Oh, it's nothing—just our friends being silly. They always send weird riddles during the holidays. Summer vacation pranks, you know?"

Raghav piped up, "Yeah, probably Aryan and Simran. They get bored easily."

Priya smiled, still puzzled but not worried. Parag just shook his head, amused.

The grown-ups went back to their magazine and chores, but the boys exchanged glances—knowing the truth was theirs alone.

**Bhagwatam Parallel | 6th Avatar - The Story of Dattatreya**

That evening, as the sky dimmed into a golden hush, Raghav sat with Manas in the courtyard. A thick silence rested between them — not heavy, just reflective.

"I remembered something," Raghav said.

Manas looked up. "A few days ago, Prisha didi told me and you one story. I think this moment needs that story."

"Go on."

Raghav opened the *Bhagavatam*. "It's about Dattatreya — a form of Lord Vishnu, born with the wisdom of Brahma, Vishnu, and Shiva. A yogi unlike any other. He didn't teach by talking. He taught by observing."

Raghav flipped a page.

"He had 24 gurus. But none were human. He learned from a tree, a pigeon, a snake, fire, water — even a prostitute. Every element in nature became his teacher. The wind taught detachment. The earth taught patience. A python showed acceptance. A bee warned against hoarding. And from the courtesan, he learned about the illusion of desire."

Manas sat up, fully listening. "And the point?" he asked.

"That the world is always teaching us, bro," Raghav said, closing the book. "Even now, while we rest. Even without discs or codes."

Manas smiled. "So… this break is a teacher too."

Raghav laughed. "Only if it lets me sleep past 6 a.m."

They clinked their buttermilk cups.

**Modern Day Parallel | Learning from All Around**

Later, the sun melted behind the sal trees. Manas polished his camera lens on the porch. The resort felt quieter now — Prisha was away at the sanctuary, Navya deep in the forest.

"I was thinking about what you said," Manas said. "That Dattatreya learned from a dog, a fish, even fire. That's wild."

Raghav nodded. "And cool, right? It means your teacher doesn't have to be perfect. Just pay attention."

Manas leaned back. "Like how Navya notices stuff others miss. Or how Prisha connects with animals."

"Exactly. Or how you spot patterns the rest of us can't."

Manas looked thoughtful. "Even the disc… maybe it wasn't a puzzle. Maybe it was a mirror."

"Or a reminder," Raghav said. "To learn from everything. Even from silence. Even from letting go."

The wind brushed the railing. Then Raghav smirked. "Also, Guru Salad Maharaj taught me stealth and surprise."

Manas laughed. "Don't tell me you still believe that ghost salad was a spiritual guide."

"I believe in learning," Raghav said, winking. "Even from papad bowls."

And behind the jokes, a quiet truth pulsed —
Not all teachers stand on podiums.
Some arrive in silence.
In friendship.
In change.

दत्तात्रेयमहं वन्दे ज्ञानानन्दमयं गुरुं ।
यो जगत्गुरुणा साक्षात् आत्मतत्त्वं प्रकाशयेत् ॥

*Meaning*

***"I bow to Lord Dattatreya, the joyful and wise teacher, the true Guru of the world, who lights the path of self-knowledge for all."***

*(Bhagwatam: Canto 11, Chapter 7, Shloka 33)*

SECTION THREE

# ECHOES BEGIN

## *Chapter 23*

# THE FORGOTTEN FOOTSTEPS

*(Lore Chapter – Pre-Independence Era, Year 1892)*

**May 1892 – A Commission from the Crown**

The sky over Calcutta was a blazing blue, heavy with heat. In a tall chamber of the Calcutta Presidency, the sun filtered through Venetian blinds onto polished teakwood desks. Harold Statham, a 28-year-old officer of the British Civil Services, stood before a table of dignitaries. Behind them, the Queen's insignia gleamed. The words on the scroll handed to him were crisp and cold:

"You are to travel the provinces of India and implement a gradual replacement of native educational structures with the more advanced British system, using subtlety and regional adaptation where resistance may arise."

But behind the language of policy lay a deeper motive—one that had been whispered through halls in London:

*"Destroy the spine of their unity—their ancient learning. Without it, India is just a body without breath."*

Thus began his mission.

## Across Provinces – The Quiet Replacement

He began studying hundreds of ancient books and brittle manuscripts, palm-leaf texts, copper plate etchings, and reports from various Indian presidencies. A peculiar pattern repeated across many documents — a triangle nestled within a circle, sometimes accompanied by a flame, a conch, or a lotus.

For months, Statham travelled. From the bustling town of Madurai to the spiritual lanes of Varanasi, and the tribal hamlets of Chhattisgarh to the Bengali pathshalas, he took meticulous notes. He established schools along Western lines—teaching English, geography, arithmetic—and in each city, tactfully dissolved native curricula. He charmed local elites and promised temple priests cultural respect.

His real triumph was merging— Vedic verses were recited before English grammar lessons, and European etiquette was masked behind Sanskrit quotations. The plan was working.

But then he heard of something… different.

In his journey logs, he scribbled notes about one mysterious institution mentioned repeatedly by old scholars and monks:

"An academy in the hills of Dehradun… older than memory. Knowledge not just taught, but guarded."

## Whispers from the North – Saraswati Vidyapeeth

In Agra, an aging librarian handed him a folio bound in jute, eyes lowered in reverence. "You are researching ancient Gurukuls, are you not? Then this might interest you."

It was a handwritten memoir of a 17th-century scholar who spoke of a school hidden near Dehradun, referred to only as "Saraswati Vidyapeeth."

"Established by a disciple of Vallabhacharya, though the master himself never visited. The gurukul lies nestled in a valley where the Saraswati once whispered. Not just a centre of learning, but of something else—a deeper force of preservation."

Statham dismissed the spiritual overtones, but the sheer frequency of mentions across unrelated records piqued his curiosity.

He headed to Dehradun.

## The Arrival – A School Unlike Others

Dehradun greeted him with crisp mountain air and measured hospitality. The officer walked through winding paths and sal forests until he stood before a sprawling structure — ancient stone walls blended with newer repairs.

Locals spoke in low tones when asked about the Gurukul. "It is not a school," one said. "It is a living mantra." Another whispered, "They don't just teach there. They remember."

Finally, the carriage halted before an expansive stone gate flanked by ancient peepal trees. A name etched in Sanskrit:

"Saraswati Vidyapeeth."

Inside, marble floors bore no dust. Boys and girls of varying ages recited scriptures, solved mathematical riddles using vedic sutras, and debated astronomy using both Indian and Greek terms. Statham felt like he had stepped into a world that hadn't bowed to time.

Within, he found something unsettling — not resistance, but calm mastery. The principal, Acharya Divyavarna, greeted him with poise. His eyes shimmered like someone who had seen centuries pass. The man spoke fluent Sanskrit, Hindi, and — to the officer's surprise — polished English.

The school grounds radiated something beyond knowledge — it was presence.

**Something Deeper – A Question of Roots**

The officer stayed for weeks. He pored over the ancient library, discovering journals that traced the school's lineage back over 400 years.

Over these weeks, Statham observed everything. The curriculum was rigorous. Students studied six *darshanas* of Indian philosophy alongside languages like Persian and Pali. But something felt… hidden. There were locked rooms in the eastern wing. Some maps revealed not current geographies but mythical lands.

He found journals in the library detailing rare spells and shlokas, with footnotes describing events that felt... unreal. But repeated. Documented. Preserved.

One such journal had a symbol drawn at the end, a phrase:

"Truth will echo, long after kings are gone."

Statham asked the Acharya about it.

The Acharya replied, "This school does not teach only to inform, Mr. Statham. It teaches to awaken."

And in that moment, the officer knew—he could not simply dismantle this place. Not without arousing revolt. He had to be... smarter.

### Closing Note & Foreshadowing

One evening, as he sat by the main shrine reading a worn manuscript, he felt the prickle of being watched.

A young boy, no older than ten, crouched behind the shrine steps, silently listening.

The boy was always nearby — alert, not mischievous. Eyes wide, always observing. The officer ignored him at first. But the boy watched and learned — not just from the books, but from the officer's expressions, his changing moods, and his muttered English notes. That boy would grow up to protect what Statham tried to veil.

### Seeds of Legacy — And a Forgotten Melody

The officer eventually submitted a rebranding proposal with a respectful tone. With gentle diplomacy and disguised intentions, he proposed blending Eastern thought with Western structure.

The name Saraswati Vidyapeeth was quietly modified to Saraswati Valley Academy — a name the locals could still accept, while the British could control its curriculum.

What he didn't know was that the boy behind the shrine had understood more than expected. He had seen through the officer's polished respect and noted the unease in the elders' eyes.

When the officer left, the boy followed a different path — not towards the academy, but away from it. Deep into the forests of Simlipal, where he would plant the true seed of knowledge — a sect devoted to guarding what the world forgot.

### Bhagwatam Parallel | 3rd Avatar – Narada

In the forests of Naimisharanya, long before empires rose and fell, lived a divine sage known across realms — Narada. He was not born of a man and woman, but from devotion.

Once a humble son of a servant woman, young Narada absorbed spiritual wisdom by simply listening to the sages who stayed at their home. After his mother's death, he wandered into the forest, meditated deeply, and was graced with a vision of Vishnu. That single glimpse burned away his worldly ties.

He became the divine messenger, moving across worlds with his veena in hand, singing praises of Narayana. He would appear where chaos brewed, not to stop it, but to plant seeds of divine curiosity. Through stories, questions, and songs, he awakened dharma in the hearts of seekers.

Narada's role was never to resolve — only to stir. He sowed unrest that led to higher truth.

And perhaps, like him… the boy behind the shrine became a modern Narada — not with a veena, but with silence and foresight, bearing the torch of ancient memory through a forest path the world had long forgotten.

---

एतावान्साङ्ख्ययोगाभ्यां स्वधर्मपरिनिष्ठया।
जन्मलाभः परः पुंसाम् अन्ते नारायणस्मृतिः॥

*Meaning:*

***The true success of human life, whether through knowledge or action, lies in remembering Narayana at the time of death.***

*(Bhagwatam: Canto 1, Chapter 6, Shloka 34)*

---

# Chapter 24

# SEEDS OF SOLITUDE

**Prisha – Boundaries**

Her boots were caked in forest mud. The kind that clings and won't let go. Prisha sat cross-legged on a bamboo mat inside the small rescue enclosure, gently pressing antiseptic cream onto the side of a trembling rescue rabbit.

It had been brought in that morning — a deep cut on its flank, probably from a thorn fence or stray dog. She was focused, hands steady, heart calm.

This, she was allowed to do.

But her eyes kept drifting towards the fence line. Just beyond it, barely visible through the branches, was a young muntjac — a small forest deer — limping, its hind leg bloodied. It had emerged from the trees about twenty minutes ago and had stood there since. Watching. Waiting.

Her hands froze.

She looked up at the ranger on duty — Shubh, again. Shubh's tired eyes missed little.

"No," Shubh said quietly, not even looking up from her notes. "Not our perimeter. Not our animal."

"But—"

"Protocol, Prisha."

Prisha turned back to the rabbit and resumed dabbing ointment, but her grip had stiffened.

A minute passed. Then another.

A voice came from behind the enclosure.

"That look on your face?" said Arjun, half-smiling. "That's called passive-aggressive protest."

She didn't answer.

He leaned on the pillar. "You're not breaking the rule. But you're judging the heck out of it. With your eyes, your frown, your elbows."

Prisha gave him a flat look. "You're annoying."

"And you're noble. Dangerous combination."

She looked at the deer again. Still standing there. Still bleeding.

Still out of reach.

"Don't get emotionally attached to what you can't help," Arjun said more softly now.

"That's a cruel thing to say," she whispered.

"It's not cruel. It's just... surviving this work."

Prisha wiped her hands and set the medicine aside. Her breath came a little harder now, like exhaling hurt.

"I didn't ask for this job to become numb," she said.

Arjun didn't reply. He just sat down next to her, knees brushing.

The rabbit's breathing slowed. The deer limped into the trees. The silence grew thicker.

But somewhere in the center of that silence, Prisha felt the earth breathe beneath her.

And inside her — something old stirred awake.

**Navya – The Weight of Knowing**

The humidity clung to her skin like a second shirt. Navya's backpack felt like it weighed half her body, packed with sample containers, pH strips, humidity meters, and four boxes of labelled petri dishes. The straps dug into her shoulders, but she didn't complain.

She never complained.

Her parents were twenty steps ahead, locked in one of their high-speed scientific debates.

"The anthocyanin concentrations don't explain the mutation," Ayan was saying.

"Because we're not measuring the right cycle. It's not stress. It's response," Meera replied.

Navya crouched under a leafy branch and collected three fallen petals — deep purple, unlike anything in their regional guidebook. She placed them in the slide box, avoiding contamination.

Sweat trickled down her neck. Her hands were streaked with dirt and chlorophyll.

She noticed something under the roots of a wild guava tree — a moss patch shaped strangely, not in a cluster but in deliberate arcs.

She leaned closer. Under the moss, on the tree bark, was a clean triangle. Barely visible. But precise.

She looked up.

Say something?

Her mother had just launched into a monologue about stomatal behavior in fungal adaptation. Her father was correcting Latin nomenclature.

No point.

She made a quick sketch in her pocket notebook, wiped her brow, and resumed walking.

She knew what she saw. And somehow, the forest knew she saw it too.

**Manas & Raghav – Mangoes, Mishaps, and Mission Control**

The drone wasn't flying.

Again.

Manas stood stiffly on the balcony slab behind their room, shoulders locked, eyebrows furrowed. He was silent for five minutes. The small quadcopter sat on the ground in front of him, motionless — like it, too, was scared of disappointing him again.

He ran another diagnostic on his tablet. "Wing angle algorithm mismatch," he muttered.

From the steps, Raghav was lounging with his usual snack combo — peeled mango slices, a bowl of green chutney, and a spoon he refused to use. He licked his fingers like a king on vacation.

"GDP update," Raghav declared loudly. "Gadget Destruction Program."

Then laughed at his own joke.

Manas didn't respond.

"C'mon, bro. Even NASA fails on launch day," Raghav offered, munching.

"This isn't launch day. This is every day," Manas snapped, not angrily, just weary.

Raghav waved a mango slice like a wand. "Okay, fine. Not a failed mission. Just a delayed mission."

Manas finally turned. "You've been saying that since I flopped the last code run."

"Delayed is my new spiritual state."

He tossed a mango piece his way. Manas caught it without thinking.

"You think that I should consult some ISRO engineers on how to make it fly?" he asked quietly.

Raghav frowned. "What, you think the forest is jamming your drone?"

Manas didn't answer. He just stared at the triangle diagram scribbled next to his code.

He didn't know why it mattered. He just knew it did.

**Four Dreams, One Call**

That night, across three different corners of the country, four children lay in separate beds — under different skies, among different trees — but stirred by the same hush.

Prisha turned in her bunk, breath shallow.

Navya clutched her sweat-damp pillow.

Manas opened his eyes once, then shut them tighter.

Raghav hummed a tune in his sleep and didn't know why.

And then, they saw it.

A dark mountain with no path.

A doorway carved not with tools, but time.

And standing before it — four childlike figures, glowing faintly in white, neither boys nor gods.

They said nothing. Just looked.

A gust of wind blew from behind, carrying only a phrase — not in voice, but in thought.

त्रैवर्णिकं द्वारं प्रतीक्षते।

"The triad doorway awaits."

Then, silence.

And each of them woke — at nearly the same moment — with a whisper on their lips they didn't recognize.

Raghav sat up, heart beating fast.

Prisha opened her diary and wrote: "I saw them again."

Navya checked her phone clock: 3:33 AM.

Manas stared at the triangle symbol he had drawn the night before.

None of them spoke to anyone about it.

Not yet.

**Bhagwatam Parallel | 2nd Avatar Sanat Kumaras**

The next afternoon, while walking back from her field shift, Prisha sat under a shady banyan and pulled out her worn copy of the Shrimad Bhagavatam. She let it fall open where it wanted.

The page fluttered to Canto 3, Chapter 15.

"From the mind of Brahma, the creator, were born four sons — Sanaka, Sanatana, Sanandana, and Sanat Kumara. Though blessed with the power to rule, they chose renunciation from the moment of their birth. Eternal children in form, eternal sages in spirit."

They had no interest in kingdoms.

No need for rituals.

Only a thirst for truth.

They once walked into Vaikuntha, Lord Vishnu's realm — without invitation, without fear — their hearts so pure that even the gatekeepers trembled.

But the gatekeepers blocked them.

Sanaka spoke first. Calmly.

"We do not seek power. We seek the Source."

When the gatekeepers mocked them as mere children, the Kumaras placed a gentle curse — not from ego, but from the pain of being misunderstood.

The Lord Himself appeared, not angry but smiling.

"You are always welcome here," Vishnu said.

"Because those who seek Me without seeking reward — they are Me."

Prisha read that line three times.

They are Me.

She looked up at the wide, ancient banyan branches.

She didn't know why, but her throat tightened.

Somewhere deep in the forest, someone had once walked barefoot, like those sages.

Maybe still did.

She closed the book and scribbled in her journal:

Eternal children.

Seekers of only truth.

Not all wisdom grows old."

---

नैषां मतिस् तवदुरुक्रमाङ्घ्रिम्..

*Meaning:*

***"The mind that clings to sense-bound logic cannot grasp You, O Infinite One.***

***But even a moment of surrender can break the cycle of birth."***

*(Bhagavatam; Canto 3, Chapter 15, Shloka 45)*

---

# Chapter 25

# WHISPER ROOTS

**The Leaf That Whispered**

"Did you just smell that?" Navya asked, still crouched beside a thick patch of ferns.

Meera looked up from her soil sampler. "Smell what?"

"That… minty… no, like tulsi but sharper. It came out of nowhere."

Meera shrugged. "Could be spores. Or decaying bark. Focus, sweetheart. Did you note the chlorophyll density?"

Navya nodded but didn't answer. Her eyes were still fixed on a creeper tangled across the fern bed. A second ago, when she reached towards it, a sharp scent had hit her nose — familiar but strange. Almost like it had replied to her touch.

She stretched her hand again. Nothing. Just the scent of mud and morning.

"Navya!" Ayan called from farther ahead, "Don't fall behind."

She grabbed her bag and jogged to catch up, but looked back once. The creeper hadn't moved. But she felt something.

**Like the creeper had said, a word only she could hear.**

**The Dream Under the Banyan**

Prisha had just finished cleaning out the injured rabbit's enclosure. It had begun nibbling again — a good sign. A small langur baby in the cage next to it watched her movements with its head tilted sideways, fingers curled around the metal mesh. She offered it a sliced banana through the opening, and it took it gently, more curious than greedy.

The air felt heavier today. Quiet, but not in a peaceful way. Like the forest was watching.

She stepped outside the enclosure just as a low grunt sounded from beyond the wire fence.

A wild boar.

It stood maybe fifteen feet away, half-hidden in the bushes, eyes fixed on her. Not charging. Not startled. Just… looking. Its body stiff, ears twitching, snout lifted slightly.

Prisha froze.

But something stopped her from stepping back.

The boar grunted again. This time softer. Almost like a word that wasn't a word.

She didn't *hear* anything in her head. But she *felt* something. Confusion? No — worry. A sense of waiting. Of something unfinished.

She blinked.

The boar didn't move. It just stared a moment longer… then turned and vanished into the woods.

Prisha stood still, breath held. Her chest felt warm, her skin buzzing.

She didn't understand what it wanted. Not exactly.

But she knew it had said something. Not with sound. With… presence.

She returned to her bunk and opened her diary. She wanted to write, but her eyes kept closing.

She didn't remember falling asleep.

One moment, she was staring at her own sentence half-written, the next — a huge tree. A banyan, older than anything she had seen. Roots hanging like ropes. The ground is soft and smoky. No sounds. No birds.

And four children standing still.

They weren't facing her. They stood near the roots, hands pressed together like in prayer — silent, glowing faintly in the mist. Not magical. Just... unreal in a very real way.

She tried calling out, but no voice came. One of them turned slightly. He looked younger than Raghav, but his eyes were ancient — not tired, but full. Like someone who had already heard everything in the world and was just waiting for you to catch up.

Then she saw it. Carved into the bark behind them — a triangle, small and perfect.

Before she could move closer, the mist rose.

And a sentence floated through it. Not loud. Not whispered. Just… **there.**

**"त्रैवर्णिकं द्वारं प्रतीक्षते।"**
*The triad doorway awaits.*

She woke up with her palm pressed against her chest and her forehead damp.

Arjun was still asleep in the bunk below. Outside, a peacock called.

She didn't feel scared.

Just… watched. In a kind way.

**The Map That Drew Itself**

Manas didn't remember deciding to draw it.

He had just finished fixing the last drone wire for the day and was lying on the cool stone floor of their room at the resort, a notebook open beside him. Raghav was on the bed, humming a raag under his breath, flipping between two songs like they were flavours of ice cream.

Manas turned to the next page of his notebook and let his pen drift.

Triangle. Triangle inside triangle. A second triangle upside-down. Then, lines connecting corners.

By the time he noticed, the shape had grown into a full pattern — like a forest map made of geometry. A central triangle ringed by three outer ones. It wasn't neat. It wasn't pretty. But it felt… correct.

"Nice alien doodle," Raghav said, glancing over. "Planning to contact Mars next?"

Manas didn't answer.

He tilted the page. Held it up. Then down. Then added a circle connecting the corners.

He didn't know what it was. He just knew it wasn't random.

For a second, he thought of the disc again — the one now buried in Simlipal. It had made him dream of triangles too. But this time, there was no dream. No disc. Just instinct.

He labeled nothing. Said nothing.

But inside his chest, a strange calm had settled.

Like part of him had remembered something his brain still didn't know.

## The Raag That Reached

Raghav had no plan when he walked down to the resort's small amphitheatre.

The place was nearly empty — just a few tourists loitering, some staff arranging chairs for a folk-dance event later that night. He wasn't performing or rehearsing. He just wanted some air… and maybe a quiet place to test a tune he'd heard in his sleep two nights ago.

He sat on the back steps, far from the spotlight zone, and pulled out his little keyboard. It was battery-powered, barely louder than a loud whisper. He switched it on, adjusted the volume, and played the first three notes of the melody.

*Ka… Ya… Ma… Ya.*

He still didn't know what it meant. But it came naturally now — fingers moving like they'd done it a hundred times.

Down below, near the refreshment stall, two middle-aged guests were arguing. Loud enough to turn heads. Something about room allocations, children playing near restricted zones, and someone cutting ahead in the meal line. The tone was sharp.

Raghav kept playing.

His tune wasn't loud. It wasn't even meant for them. He was barely audible over the crickets and murmurs.

But slowly, the voices faded.

Not completely. Just… softened. One of the men turned to leave mid-sentence. The other exhaled, mumbled something about not ruining the trip, and walked away in the opposite direction.

Raghav didn't notice.

He was still playing. A soft loop now. Ka–Ya–Ma–Ya.

Then he laughed softly to himself and muttered, "GDP full form: Great Divine Peace."

No one heard it but a passing waiter, who blinked and kept walking.

Raghav shut off the keyboard and leaned back.

He didn't know he had just calmed two strangers with sound.

He just knew the tune felt right. Like a fingerprint he hadn't known was his.

## The Unnamed Shift

That night, four homes in four corners of India shared the same kind of silence.

**At the resort**, Raghav sat on the stone boundary wall outside their room, licking the last of the mango chutney off his fingers. His keyboard sat beside him, switched off. The stars were brighter tonight, clearer.

Inside, **Parag** was reading aloud from a travel blog while **Priya** tried to fix the loose handle on her suitcase. "This writer says Simlipal is older than any written forest record," Parag said. "Maybe even prehistoric…"

Raghav half-listened. His mind was somewhere between the tune he'd just played and the triangle Manas had once shown him in a scribble.

He wasn't worried. Just curious.

He tapped out the raag's rhythm softly against his leg.

*Ka… Ya… Ma… Ya.*

**In Satpura**, Prisha sat on her cot, arms wrapped around her knees. The rescue center was quiet — only a soft rustle outside and the occasional sound of animals shifting in their cages. Arjun was snoring gently two bunks down.

She opened her diary and drew what she remembered.

Not the whole banyan this time. Just the part where the roots touched the ground — and four faint outlines near it. Then, without fully realizing it, she added a symbol next to the tree: a small triangle.

She stared at it for a long time.

She didn't know what it meant. But it didn't feel like something new.

It felt remembered.

**In Simlipal**, Navya lay curled in her sleeping bag beside a half-zipped tent flap, listening to the soft clicks of insects in the trees.

Her parents were still awake in their own camp tent nearby, murmuring in hushed tones — something about mutation cycles and leaf growth. She didn't interrupt.

She pulled out her sketchpad, meant to record plant samples, and instead drew the vine she'd seen that morning — the one that had responded to her. Just before closing the pad, she added a small triangle near its base.

She didn't know why.

It just felt… true.

**Back in the resort**, Manas was lying in bed, phone on airplane mode, staring at the ceiling. He reached under his pillow and pulled out the torn triangle-map page he'd drawn earlier.

He traced the lines again.

Somewhere, something was aligning. He could feel it in his fingers.

But he didn't know what it was yet.

They were still miles apart.

Still thinking in silence.

But inside each of them, a single thought began to settle like mist:

**Something is calling us.**
And we're already answering.

**Bhagwatam Parallel| 8th Avatar Rishabhdev**

*"Not every teacher speaks. Some simply walk away."*

In a time long past, there was a king named **Rishabhdev**, born to King Nabhi and Queen Merudevi. He was no ordinary ruler — for he was **an incarnation of Vishnu**, sent to demonstrate how the highest wisdom could be lived, not just spoken.

As a king, he ruled wisely and with justice. His people prospered. His palace was filled with wealth, but his heart was never attached. He taught his children not just with words, but through **how he ate, how he walked, how he stayed silent.**

To his hundred sons, he gave only one real teaching:

"The body is not for chasing pleasure. It is a boat, meant to cross the ocean of suffering. Use it wisely. Use it with restraint."

After fulfilling his duties, Rishabhdev did something no emperor had ever done.

He **gave up everything.**
His crown.
His speech.
Even the clothes on his back.

He walked away into the forests, naked and silent.

Not out of shame — but out of **freedom**.

People mocked him. Threw stones. Called him mad.

He didn't flinch. He didn't explain.

Because Rishabhdev had realized a truth beyond words:
The world doesn't need more sound.
It needs stillness strong enough to **change the air around it**.

He spent the rest of his life **wandering as a silent yogi**, untouched by praise or insult, fear or comfort. The Bhagavatam says he became **so powerful in his silence** that even wild animals grew calm around him.

His silence was his message.
His walk — a sermon.
His restraint — the loudest roar of all.

**How It Echoes Today:**

Like Rishabhdev, the four children don't know their strength yet.
They don't seek power.
They are not trying to impress.
But still — vines respond, animals hesitate, melodies calm strangers.

They haven't been taught.
They are remembering.

And in that quiet remembering, the world is already listening.

---

*ऋषभ उवाच —*
*नायं देहो देहभाजां नृलोके कष्टान् कामानर्हते विड्भुजां ये।*
*तपो दिव्यं पुत्रका येन सत्त्वं शुद्ध्येद्यस्माद् ब्रह्मसौख्यं त्वनन्तम्॥*

*Meaning:*

***This human body is not meant for indulgence like that of pigs, who eat filth. It is meant for divine austerity, by which the soul becomes purified and attains unending spiritual happiness.***

*(Bhagwatam: Canto 5, Chapter 5, Shloka 1)*

---

# Chapter 26

# RINGS OF MEMORY

**Beneath the Microscope**

The lab tent was warmer than outside. Not because of the sun, but because no one had opened the flaps since morning. The smell of damp cloth, crushed leaves, and ethanol made Navya's eyes sting.

Meera stood hunched over the microscope, not blinking.

Ayan sat nearby, scribbling calculations onto a page he'd already crumpled twice. "I re-checked the fungal count. No contamination. It's not the soil."

Meera didn't answer. She adjusted the focus again. "Three rings in the root cross-section."

Navya looked up. "That's... normal?"

"No," Meera said quietly. "Four is normal for this species. Sometimes five."

Ayan flipped the sample chart. "And this one has **three**. But the center is hollow. Completely blank. Like the innermost memory was erased."

"Could it be lightning damage?" Navya offered.

"No scorch. No heat trauma," Meera said.

She finally looked up.

Her eyes weren't angry. Just... tired. And deeper than usual. Like something else was playing in her mind.

Navya had never seen her like this. Her mother was the kind who faced collapsing cliffs with field notes in hand. But right now, she looked almost small — not because of fear, but because of **the size of the question she didn't yet know how to ask**.

Ayan spoke again, voice lower this time. "Second sample from the moss bed shows the same — triple rings and hollow core."

**They exchanged a heavy glance.**

Navya shifted in her seat, pretending to reorganize the plant boxes.

She didn't want to intrude.

But **she couldn't ignore the weight in the forest either.**

**Tracks in the Stillness**

"Migration pattern," Shubh said, pointing to the red marks on the laminated map. "Last spotted herd is here. Near the northern ridge of the sanctuary."

Prisha squinted at the circles. "Isn't that trail too narrow for tagging?"

"That's why we're not tagging. Just tracking," Shubh replied, adjusting the strap on her field bag. "Walk the perimeter. Note hoof prints, grazing signs, fur patches. Don't enter the gorges alone."

She handed Prisha a GPS marker, half-faded from sun exposure. "You're on your own this time. Last assignment. Make it count."

Satpura wasn't like the lush forests of Simlipal. This central Indian range was rougher — its landscape dotted with sharp ridges, deep sandstone gorges, and dense teak trees that could swallow light before it hit the ground. Leopards had been spotted here, though rarely.

But Prisha wasn't thinking of leopards.

She was thinking of silence — the kind that sits on her shoulders.

Near the fork, under a moss-covered log, Prisha spotted a hoofprint—sharp, fresh, pressed into the damp earth. She knelt, tracing its edge with her finger. It was just a print… but no deer was there. The stillness seemed to thicken.

She walked slowly, notebook in hand, thumb ready to jot markings. But none appeared. No scat. No broken branches. No fresh prints.

She stood up and turned slowly, every sense on alert.

She knelt beside it. Her fingers brushed the edge — and froze.

The wind wasn't moving.

The air felt… aware.

There—a few yards away, in the dappled shade, a tiger stood watching her. Its stripes melted into the bamboo shadows, eyes calm and focused. For a heartbeat, Prisha's body wanted to run, but her feet stayed rooted. Her heart thumped so loud she could almost hear it in her ears.

Her breath caught.

She gripped her notebook harder than needed. Every instinct said turn back.

But her feet held. Just one step forward.

Her heart was thumping now. Her throat dry.

The tiger's gaze met hers—steady, measuring, not cruel. It flicked its tail once, then, with the silent authority of the wild, turned and slipped away, vanishing between the trees.

The silence returned, heavier and alive. Prisha let her breath out, slow, her legs weak, but her mind lit with awe.

Sometimes, **courage wasn't about feeling brave.**
Sometimes, it was just about **not stepping back.**

### The Cave and the Silence

That night, at different hours but with the same moon above them, four children across four places fell into a sleep deeper than usual.

**Navya's dream came first.**

She was walking through a mist-covered valley. Not dark, not scary—just quiet. The air shimmered with the scent of damp leaves and hidden roots. Every breath felt green, alive.

Before her rose a cave mouth, wide but shallow, carved into a hill of obsidian rock. No torches. No glow. Just the presence of something old.

She noticed saplings growing at the cave's entrance—tiny, trembling, but thriving. The moss on the stones glimmered as if whispering.

Four childlike figures stepped out of the cave.

Not floating. Not glowing. Just walking—barefoot, calm, quiet. Their skin was pale gold. Their robes are the color of uncut stone. Their expressions were unreadable.

As they passed, the grass around their feet seemed to lean in, as if listening. A vine curled softly around Navya's ankle—friendly, not frightening.

Navya wanted to speak, but something inside her said: **Don't. Just see.**

She watched as one of the figures reached out and touched a sapling. Instantly, a tiny bud bloomed.

They didn't look at her. But she felt seen—and, for a moment, deeply rooted, as if the silent language of trees had finally let her in.

**Raghav dreamt next.**

In his version, the cave was smaller, cloaked in soft moss. The wind curled around the entrance, humming a melody just beyond memory—a tune only he could almost catch.

He recognized the children, though he couldn't say from where. One of them turned towards him. The child's eyes sparkled as if catching a private joke only Raghav could hear.

No words were spoken. Instead, the child raised two fingers to his lips—not as a warning, but as if sharing a secret chord, or granting a gentle blessing. The air shimmered, and for a moment, Raghav felt the familiar spark—the strange, joyful charm that made people laugh, listen, and linger near him.

**The message was clear:**

**Some truths are not sung.** They're remembered. And sometimes, what is remembered has its own silent music—one that can open hearts, or shift the air itself.

**Prisha's dream came while the forest creaked faintly around her bunk.**

She didn't see the cave from the outside. She was **inside** it. Earthy. Cool. The walls were covered in tiny handprints—hundreds of them—as if children and creatures had passed through for generations. She noticed, between some of the prints, the faint imprints of paws, claws, and feathers, all mingling together in harmony.

Somewhere in the distance, she heard a low growl—a leopard cub, maybe, or a wolf—but it didn't frighten her. She sensed eyes watching from the shadows: soft, trusting, wild.

The four sages stood by a doorway. Not stone. Not wood. Just a gap in reality, outlined in shifting light. As she watched, a gentle breeze rustled through, carrying the scent of wet fur and fresh earth.

The sages stepped through the opening, one by one, without hesitation. When the last one turned to glance back, he looked almost… familiar. Like Raghav. But not.

Prisha reached out her hand instinctively, as if calling a lost animal. For a heartbeat, she felt the brush of a warm nose against her palm.

She woke up sweating—her heart thumping with a strange comfort, as if she had just been welcomed by every wild thing in the world.

**Manas's dream came last.**

He found himself high above the cave, not entering but observing, as if mapping it from a new dimension. He wasn't drawn by instinct—he was analyzing, drawing it out: lines, angles, spirals, dimensions—shapes within shapes, codes within codes. It shouldn't have made sense, but somehow, to his logical mind, every symbol clicked together.

As he sketched, he noticed patterns: a triangle enclosing a spiral, a circle floating just outside the center. His hands moved almost on their own, breaking the cave's mystery down into parts and sequences.

The four sages emerged from the cave and glanced up at him. Instead of approaching, they simply nodded in acknowledgment—recognizing his search for order and meaning—then continued on their path, leaving him alone with his puzzle.

Manas tried to keep drawing, flipping the page in his dream, but suddenly his pen wouldn't work. He tapped it, frustrated. At that moment, the triangle he'd doodled on his hand earlier shimmered faintly, as if reminding him: Sometimes, logic must meet mystery.

He woke with the image of the triangle glowing in his mind—a riddle unsolved, but alive with possibility.

None of them spoke about it the next day.

But all four wrote down the same phrase — in different notebooks, at different hours:

**"The ones who walked out of the cave… were waiting for us."**

### The Inscription and the Stranger

It was almost dusk when the forest official reached the ridge.

The slope near the third waterfall in Simlipal had always been unstable — but this week, two large boulders had shifted after a minor tremor. The clearing behind them was unexpected.

He stepped through carefully. What he saw wasn't a cave, exactly — more like a **shallow stone face**, carved with **symbols that weren't tribal, weren't modern, and definitely weren't decorative**.

They looked old. **Mathematical. Aligned. Intentional.**

He lifted his radio to report — but paused.

There was **someone already standing there**.

A man, back to him, facing the wall, crouched low and tracing one of the shapes lightly with a gloved finger.

No backpack. No tent. Just a satchel and a quiet presence.

The official cleared his throat.

The man stood slowly and turned. His eyes were steady. Calm.

"Department clearance?" the official asked, trying not to sound rude.

The man nodded and flashed a worn badge. **"Dr. Roy. Linguistics & pattern analysis. Here on behalf of ECHO. You're welcome to notify Meera or Ayan Agrawal."**

The official hesitated. "You're with them?"

Pulkit smiled faintly. "Not with. Just… near."

He turned back to the wall. His fingers paused over a symbol that looked like a triangle enclosing a curled leaf.

"Do you know what it says?" the official asked.

Pulkit didn't answer right away. He stepped back, took a photo, and then finally replied.

**"It's not saying something. It's asking something."**

### Notes No One Reads

The forest hut was quiet, except for the soft clinking of glass vials being packed.

Navya watched her mother seal another sample case, hands moving with clinical precision. Meera hadn't spoken much during dinner. Ayan had tried to lighten the mood with a joke about humidity being the real enemy of science, but even he had drifted into his own thoughts soon after.

Navya stood near the open flap of the tent, staring at the dense outlines of sal trees under moonlight.

"Mom?" she asked quietly.

Meera looked up but didn't answer right away.

"Do you think… forests can forget?" Navya said.

Meera blinked. "Why do you ask that?"

Navya hesitated. "Some of the plants today… felt like they were missing something. Like they wanted to say it, but didn't remember how."

Her mother didn't dismiss it. Didn't laugh.

She just said, "Some memories don't vanish. They go… quieter."

Then Meera zipped the bag and stepped out to join Ayan at the edge of the field tent, leaving Navya alone inside.

She sat down, pulled out her notebook, and scribbled softly:

"Three rings. Hollow center.
Plants that don't speak, but feel heavy.
Something is wrong. Not with the forest. With what it used to be."

She paused.

Then added one more line, right at the bottom of the page:

**"Mom is worried. This time, she's not pretending she's not."**

She didn't tear the page out.

She just folded the notebook closed and went to bed.

**Bhagavatam Parallel | 23rd Avatar Buddha**

He was born not with thunder, but with a silence that would shake empires.
In Kapilavastu, between the Himalayan foothills, a prince was born to King Suddhodana and Queen Maya of the Shakya dynasty. Sages foretold two destinies: *"He will be either the greatest king or the greatest teacher."*

Named Siddhartha — "one whose every wish is fulfilled" — he grew up within palace walls, never seeing sickness, pain, or death. Surrounded by gardens, music, art, and study, he mastered languages, logic, and martial arts. Yet his gaze lingered on a dying leaf, a bird's silence, a servant's hidden sigh.

At sixteen, he married Princess Yashodhara, and they had a son, Rahula. But the palace began to feel small. One night, he ventured out with his charioteer Channa and saw, for the first time: an old man, a sick man, a corpse… and a serene ascetic. *"All this awaits me too?"* he asked. *"Yes, my Prince,"* came the reply.

The seed had been planted. One night, out of compassion, he kissed his sleeping wife and child goodbye, left his jewels and title, and walked into the forest. For years, he studied under renowned teachers, endured extreme penance, and debated truth — yet peace eluded him.

Then, in Bodh Gaya, beneath a fig tree, he vowed: *"I will not rise until I know."* Through the night, he faced not demons but doubt. At dawn, the illusion broke — he saw the wheel of life, cause and effect, suffering and its end. He became the Buddha, the Awakened One.

He claimed no divinity, sought no worship. He taught the Middle Path between indulgence and renunciation, the Four Noble Truths, and the Eightfold Path — a way of mindful, compassionate living. His stillness transformed more than any army could.

### Why Vishnu Took This Form

In Sanatan thought, this Buddha was Vishnu incarnate — not to convert, but to correct. He came to silence the corruption of rituals, expose the misuse of dharma, and awaken self-reflection in an age of arrogance.

---

*ततो बुद्धः कलौ सम्भवितान्नञ्जनसुतः।*
*सञ्ज्ञयन् बलिनां मोहेन सुरद्विषां॥*

*Meaning:*

*Then, in the age of Kali, the Lord shall appear as **Buddha**, son of Anjana, to **delude those who are enemies of dharma**, misusing Vedic knowledge for selfish gain.*

*(Bhagawatam: Canto 1, Chapter 3, Shloka 24)*

---

# Chapter 27

# THE RISING SIGNS

**Return to Base**

The jeep rolled back into the Simlipal research resort. Navya jumped down first, her braid bouncing, backpack stained with leaf marks. Ayan and Meera followed, their bags packed with notes and samples.

Raghav was the first to spot them.

"Well, well! Look who's back from Forest Hogwarts!" he called, holding up a mango slice.

Navya rolled her eyes. "At least I didn't spend my week peeling fruit like a royal monkey."

Before he could reply, Manas came jogging up, waving his tablet. "Guys! I finally got the drone to lift a little!"

"Lifted and dropped, you mean?" said Prisha, arriving from the side trail, scarf dusty and arms scratched.

"Yes," Manas replied. "It flew, paused, then gave up."

Raghav nodded. "GDP: Gadget Disaster Program."

Everyone laughed.

They sat under the mess tent, sipping juice. It wasn't a big celebration. Just comfort. Familiar. Like the group was complete again.

**Leaves and Lies**

Later, they lounged in the library. Navya on a beanbag, Manas tapping on his tablet, Raghav lying across two chairs, and Prisha fixing a scraped elbow.

Near the corner window, Meera stood facing outward, speaking softly into a satellite phone. Her voice was low but sharp.

"Yes, the root samples from Sector 7 showed the same arc pattern. It's not chemical — it's something else, like memory or more like asma...."

A long pause.

"No, I don't think it's random. Ayan believes it's signaling. EcHO needs to take this seriously before it spreads across zones."

Another pause. Her tone grew colder.

"I said no. We're not involving them until we confirm the correlation. The kids stay out of this."

She ended the call and quietly slipped the phone into her notebook pouch, walking towards the exit.

At the same time, Navya opened her own sketchpad. "I saw this in the forest," she said, almost to herself. "Under a guava tree. The moss wasn't random. It formed... this."

She held up the drawing — a neat triangle nestled in arcs of shaded green.

Manas leaned in. "That looks like what I—never mind." He flipped open his drone logbook, eyes wide.

"Like what?" Prisha asked.

Before he could answer, Raghav snatched the notebook and raised it dramatically. "Behold! The triangle that unlocks... extra dessert!"

He darted to the front desk. "Madam, we discovered a talking plant. We demand paneer tikka in exchange!"

Everyone burst out laughing.

Manas passed him a paper napkin. "For your next trick: GDP — Goofy Distraction Protocol."

Even Navya chuckled.

### Broken Wings and Echo Raag

That evening, Manas stood on the side deck. The drone's wings flapped, hovered, then flopped over like a tired bird.

"Ugh," he said.

Raghav tossed him a mango slice. "GDP. Glorious Dive Parade."

Manas shook his head.

"Just joking," Raghav added more gently. "It's getting better."

Navya walked over. "We should give it a medal for trying."

Prisha added, "Let's name it Sir Fall-a-lot."

Manas smiled.

Later, in the music room, Raghav sat at the keyboard, playing random notes. Then he hummed a tune — soft and slow.

The moment he played the seventh note, a breeze came in through the window.

In the reception area, two guests who had been arguing suddenly went quiet.

Raghav didn't notice. He kept humming.

"This tune's got its own mind," he said.

**Games and Glimpses**

After dinner, they played carrom. Navya kept winning. Raghav kept cheating. Prisha scolded him like a strict schoolteacher.

During the game, Prisha's scarf slipped, revealing a small drawing on her wrist — a wild boar's eye.

Raghav noticed. "That from the forest?"

"He looked at me," Prisha said quietly. "Not like an animal. Like… he was trying to say something."

Everyone paused.

Navya shrugged. "I'd still take boars over bugs."

They laughed again.

Prisha, while packing the board, said softly, "What if animals remember things we've forgotten?"

Manas replied, "But what it would be, it doesn't seem logical, you think too much".

**Scribbles and Silences**

That night, after lights out, Prisha sat by the window with her diary open. The others were still whispering jokes and teasing Raghav for his mango obsession.

She drew the boar's eyes, a rabbit's ear, and a muddy footprint.

"They don't talk. But they remember.<br>
I care more than I expected.<br>
And I feel something changing."

She closed the book and climbed into bed.

Raghav, still humming softly, drifted into sleep.

**Bhagavatam Parallel – 5th Avatar: Kapila**

Long ago, the sage Kardama and his wife Devahuti had a child named **Kapila**, an avatar of Vishnu.

He never wielded a weapon, never sat on a throne — but with words, he shattered illusions. He didn't rule kingdoms. He taught truth.

He explained how the world is made of matter and spirit — and how we must learn to tell the difference.

He taught his mother and the world that true sight came not from the eyes, but from clarity of mind. He birthed the **Sankhya philosophy**, the separation of prakriti (matter) and purusha (spirit). His truths didn't demand temples. Real freedom comes not from escape, but understanding. Only introspection.

"You don't need to run from the world. You just need to see it clearly."

Kapila walked quietly, but his words still echo.

Kapila didn't battle demons. He dismantled ignorance.

He taught that to know the self is to know God, and left behind no ashes, only awakening.

**"Liberation isn't escape. It is understanding."**

---

*आहमेव्यममेवाग्रे नान्यद् यत्सदसत्परम् ।*
*पश्यतां मायया स्पष्टं रुद्धं नभ इवोदितम् ॥*

*Meaning:*
***"I alone existed before creation. Neither truth nor illusion — only Me.***
***What you see now is covered by illusion."***

*(Bhagwatam: Canto 3, Chapter 25, Shloka 15)*

---

# Chapter 28

# THE PATTERN BENEATH

### The Trailside Reunion

That morning, the kids had wandered down a short forest trail behind the resort — just a walk, nothing intense. A break from schedules and syllabuses. Navya carried a sketchpad, Manas had a screwdriver behind one ear, and Prisha walked barefoot for exactly eleven minutes before regretting it.

Raghav, as always, brought snacks.

They sprawled out on a sun-dappled boulder and shared everything — forest mischief, leaf-shaped bruises, trail jokes, and how GDP now apparently stood for "Great Drone Panic."

Manas tried defending his drone again. "It's not failure, it's delayed optimization."

Navya raised an eyebrow. "Even the squirrel that dodged your drone disagrees."

Raghav smirked. "GDP: Genius Defies Physics."

They all laughed — and for a moment, the weight of recent dreams and strange instincts loosened. Just kids in a forest. But beneath the humour, something else pulsed quietly between them. Like they were part of something... forming.

### The Monkey and the Moment

Later, near the kitchen garden behind the resort, Prisha stepped away from the others to wash her hands at the outdoor tap.

That's when she noticed the monkey.

It sat on the edge of the spice shed roof — a young one — nibbling at something it had clearly stolen from the porch basket. When it noticed her, it froze.

So did she.

There was no panic. No threat. Just eye contact.

And suddenly, in her chest, Prisha felt a flicker — a wave of frustration and pride. As if the monkey wasn't just watching her, but judging her for interrupting his little victory.

She blinked.

The monkey tilted its head… then tossed a half-chewed fruit onto the ground and scurried away into the trees.

She stood still for a long time, hand dripping under the tap.

"What was that?" she whispered.

Not fear. Not imagination. Just… a connection. Brief and strange.

**Leaves and Listening**

Later that afternoon, Meera and Ayan had stepped away towards the old pond trail — a quiet clearing just past the bamboo grove. Navya followed sometime after, wanting to collect the pressed leaf samples she had left tucked between flat rocks to dry.

As she neared, she heard Meera's voice.

She was speaking into her satellite phone, barely audible.

"No, the root patterns from Sector 7 show deliberate spirals. Not a fungal spread."
"We can't ignore the behavioral sync in Zone Delta. The boar, the monkey troop, even the birds."
"Yes, I know. But we are not accelerating the program. Not until the markers repeat."
"The kids are responding. Especially Navya. But she doesn't know yet."

Navya stood frozen in the curve of the trail. She backed away slowly, the pressed leaves forgotten.

**The Parents' Quiet Tension**

Back at the resort, Meera and Ayan sat on the cottage porch, poring over field notes and leaf-pressed samples. The air was thicker than usual — not from humidity, but from silence.

Ayan ran his thumb along a sample record. "This one's showing spiral responses again. Under stress, the roots restructured — deliberately."

Meera nodded slowly. "And this moss formation… it's not random."

They both looked at each other.

"This is spreading faster than we calculated," she said.

Ayan lowered his voice. "And aligning."

There was no need to say more. They'd both been feeling it — an echo between the forest's response and the children's subtle shifts. Things were no longer data points. They were signs.

"We'll need help," Meera said eventually.

"Let's wait another day," Ayan replied. "See if it stabilizes. Then we reach out."

They sat in silence a while longer, their tea growing cold.

### The Sound of Noticing

Manas was hunched over his latest drone build. The stabilizer system had come to him in a flash — a half-dream at dawn. He hadn't even drawn it before assembling it.

Raghav arrived, licking bhel puri off his fingers. "Chef Sandeep made it on special request."

Manas gave a distracted smile. "Let's see if version 6.1 survives air."

Navya joined them with a basket of fallen flowers and leaves. "It's weird. The plants... they're trying to show us something."

Prisha arrived, still thoughtful. "I think the animals are too."

Manas asked, "How do you know that?"

They all fell silent for a moment.

Then Raghav said, casually, "We're special, remember?"

Manas grinned. "Speak for yourself. I'm three circuits away from world domination."

They laughed again — but not too loudly.

### Bhagavatam Parallel: 10th Avatar Dhanvantari

That night, under the soft flicker of lanterns, Prisha opened her Bhagavatam journal and flipped to the next marked section. Navya read aloud:

"Long ago, in an age when even the devas were vulnerable, a crisis stirred across the three worlds. The asuras had grown too strong. Their power tilted the balance of existence, and even the gods suffered defeats. Weak and uncertain, the devas turned to Lord Vishnu."

"Help us," they said. "We are losing dharma itself."

Vishnu gave them a strategy: Samudra Manthan — the churning of the cosmic ocean. It was not just a test of might, but of patience, cooperation, and cosmic alignment. Both devas and asuras were to churn the ocean of milk together, using the serpent Vasuki as a rope and Mount Mandara as the churning rod.

From churning, emerged wonders — the moon, the goddess Lakshmi, the divine horse *Uchhaishravas*, the wish-fulfilling cow Kamadhenu, the deadly poison *Halahala*... and then...

Rising on a platform of radiant lotus light, appeared a tall, serene figure, blue-skinned like the deep sea, eyes with wisdom, bearing a golden pot — the *amrit*, nectar of immortality.

He was none other than Dhanvantari, the tenth avatar of Vishnu — the celestial healer, father of Ayurveda, divine physician to the gods.

He was not invoked —born from cosmic churn to heal a world spiraling into imbalance.

Dhanvantari was more than just a bearer of *amrit*. He carried within him the secret codes of health, herbs, balance, and inner vitality. His teachings were not just about medicine, but about dharma through wellness, the strength to hold truth by holding one's own health, internally and externally.

**Modern Day Parallel**

Raghav stretched out on a mat. "A god of medicine?"

"Yes," Prisha said. "But also of restoration. Of balance. Of remembering nature's logic."

Manas tilted his head. "The forest is reacting because it's wounded."

Navya added, "And maybe... it trusts us enough to help."

They didn't say anything more after that.

But somewhere nearby, the banyan leaves rustled — not with wind, but with listening.

---

*त्वं वै नराणां ऋषभः सुसूनुः संसारतप्तान् तरयेथा विद्वान्।*

*भिषक्तमं त्वां भुवनत्रयस्य कथं वयं नानु नमामि भक्त्या॥*

*Meaning:*

***"You are the supreme physician, O Lord Dhanvantari — born to heal the pain of the world. To you, the greatest among beings, we offer our deepest devotion."***

*(Bhagwatam: Canto 10, Chapter 14, Shloka 14)*

---

# Chapter 29

# THE RETURN OF THE LISTENER

**Breakfast Briefing**

The dining veranda at the Simlipal resort was unusually quiet that morning. No forest chatter, no teasing. Just the rhythmic clinks of cutlery and the occasional rustle of leaves.

Priya looked up from her bowl of poha and smiled. "By the way," she said casually, pouring herself some chai, "Pulkit Roy is visiting the resort today. He's been assigned to help with some forest-related research. He's meeting Meera and Ayan."

Raghav nearly dropped his spoon. "Pulkit *sir*? From school?!"

"Yes, the same," Priya smiled. "The cybersecurity guy during your mid-term tech fiasco."

Navya leaned in. "Wasn't he also into Sanskrit stuff?"

"He wears many hats," Priya chuckled. "Brilliant mind. He's working on something bigger now, but he keeps helping old colleagues."

Manas muttered, "That explains his firewall-fu."

"Don't bother him with questions," Priya warned playfully. "Let him finish his meetings first."

But curiosity was already thick in the air like jungle mist.

**A Quiet Arrival**

Pulkit's arrival wasn't dramatic. Just a jeep pulling in, its tires dusted with dried forest mud. He stepped out in his usual practical outfit — part professor, part field agent — with a canvas bag and a half-smile.

Meera and Ayan met him by the cottage steps. No greetings, no hugging — just nods.

Inside the shaded porch, away from ears, the conversation began.

Pulkit placed a few folded documents on the table. "Data from Borneo and the Andes. Same response curve. Root memory, cell transference, and electromagnetic feedback."

Ayan raised an eyebrow. "But the acceleration here is different."

Meera added, "It's evolving with interaction. And the forest... it's behaving like it's aware."

Pulkit's tone shifted. "Then we've moved past anomaly. This is alignment."

They all fell silent for a moment, hearing the wind stir the sal leaves.

"We'll share a partial report," Meera said. "Enough to stay ahead. But not enough to trigger... outside interest."

Pulkit nodded. "That's wise. But eventually, you'll need to let someone in."

"Maybe," Ayan replied. "But not today."

**Chatter, Pranks, and Patterns**

Meanwhile, the kids sprawled out under the shade of a jamun tree near the kitchen trail.

Navya was sketching curled leaves. Raghav was licking bhel puri off his fingers. Manas tinkered with a bent propeller. Prisha had taken off her shoes and was humming something old.

"Guess what GDP stands for now?" Raghav asked with a grin.

"Godly Drone Problems?" Navya offered.

"Great Data Prank," said Manas.

"Grumpy Dancers of Prisha," Raghav declared and ducked as she threw a spoon at him.

They laughed loud and long — real laughter, not distracted or suspicious.

But now and then, Navya glanced at the faint triangle she'd drawn on her wrist the night before. Prisha absently traced a flame shape on the earth with a stick.

They didn't talk about those symbols.

Not today.

## The Informal Meeting

Pulkit found them later in the evening, by the edge of the resort lawn. He approached quietly.

"Still building things that don't fly?" he asked Manas with a wink.

Manas straightened. "It flies. Just... temporarily lands."

Pulkit chuckled. "I believe in temporary genius."

The others gathered around. There were questions waiting in their eyes — about dreams, symbols, maybe even letters — but none of them spoke them aloud.

"You're here for forest stuff?" Navya asked carefully.

"Partly," Pulkit said, smiling. "Mostly I'm here for good tea and older friends."

"And secret maps and encrypted leaves," Raghav added.

Pulkit didn't deny it. He just looked at each of them, one by one — as if scanning something deeper than expressions.

"Take care of yourselves," he said. "And listen to the silence between the trees. Sometimes, it says more than books do."

Then he walked back towards the cottages, boots crunching softly on gravel.

## Bhagavatam Parallel | 13th Avatar - Ved Vyasa

That night, Prisha sat with her Bhagavatam journal under the porch lamp. The others joined her quietly, the day still lingering in their bones.

She opened to a bookmarked page and began:

*"Born to Sage Parashara and the fisherwoman Satyavati, Ved Vyasa was no ordinary child. He was born on an island, thus named Krishna Dvaipayana.*

*His mind absorbed the Vedas, his heart craved clarity."*

"He compiled the Vedas into four," Navya added, "so that people could actually understand them."

Prisha nodded. "And then he wrote the Mahabharata, the longest epic in human history."

Raghav tilted his head. "Wait—he also wrote this? The Bhagavatam?"

"Yes," said Prisha. "But even after all that, he felt... incomplete. Something was missing. That's when Narada appeared and told him — you've written about dharma, but not enough about devotion."

Manas murmured, "So this book... was his way of remembering what matters most."

*"He wasn't a warrior," Prisha added softly. "But he was a warrior of memory. He passed on the light through words, so the next world wouldn't forget."*

They all sat quietly then.

And in that moment, a breeze lifted Navya's pages, revealing — unintentionally — a triangle drawn beside a leaf.

---

सूत उवाच

नारायणं नरं व्यासं देवीं सरस्वतीं तथा। वन्दे गुरूं नमस्यामि सम्स्मरणात् पापनाशनम्॥

*Meaning:*

***Suta said:***

***I offer my respectful obeisances unto Narayana, unto Nara, the greatest human being, unto Mother Saraswati, the goddess of learning, and unto Vedavyasa, the author. By remembering them, all obstacles to progress are destroyed.***

*(Bhagwatam: Canto 1, Chapter 4, Shloka 14)*

---

# Chapter 30

# THE SECOND DEPARTURE

**The Parents' Quiet Pact**

Later that afternoon, Meera and Ayan stood at the edge of the resort, backpacks fastened, boots mud-ready. The forest ahead seemed thicker than ever.

Pulkit joined them for a brief moment under the guise of handing over field maps.

"No transmission beyond Zone 8," he said.

"We know," Meera replied.

"If it responds again," Ayan added, "we mark, don't touch. Observation only."

They exchanged one final look. Quiet. Old friends. War veterans of a different kind.

Pulkit hesitated a moment, then said, "This isn't what we thought it was, is it?"

Ayan's voice dropped. "Not even close. It's deeper. The patterns are older than we assumed. The reaction across multiple species… it's not a coincidence."

Meera added softly, "But there are clues—trails forming. Something is guiding this. Maybe even waiting."

Pulkit nodded. "And we're close. The signals are aligning faster. Whatever's unfolding—we're on the edge of cracking it."

Ayan added, with rare conviction, "Give us a few more weeks. We'll come back with answers."

Meera smiled faintly. "And clarity." "Keep the kids steady," she said.

Pulkit nodded again.

Then the two scientists turned and vanished into the trees.

## Farewells on the Bridge

By the wooden footbridge near the creek, the four kids watched Meera and Ayan disappear. The moment felt longer than it was.

Navya hugged herself.

"They said two weeks," Prisha offered. "Maybe three."

"Yeah," Manas said. "And I said I'd clean my inbox last Diwali."

Raghav gave a half-smile. "Relax. You still have Priya Aunty and Parag Uncle."

"And Pulkit Sir," Navya added, though her tone didn't hide her mixed feelings.

## New Rhythms Begin

That evening, the mood of the camp shifted. Not drastically. But subtly—like someone had turned down the forest's brightness by a few notches.

Parag brought extra blankets to the porch.

Priya walked Navya to her tent, just like old times.

Pulkit moved around quietly, setting up his small workstation near the satellite router.

The kids kept glancing at him.

Manas whispered to Raghav, "If he pulls out another Sanskrit-coded hard disk, I'm out."

Raghav grinned. "We're special, remember?"

"You keep saying that," Prisha said, "but I don't see any magical weapons yet."

"Maybe we're the weapons," Raghav said, mock-dramatic.

No one laughed.

## Bhagavatam Parallel | 24th Avatar - Kalki

That night, while lightning flickered faintly beyond the hills and a restless breeze swept through the sal trees, Prisha opened her Bhagavatam notebook and turned to the final page.

Raghav lay nearby, humming something soft. Manas tapped his stylus rhythmically against a notebook. Navya just stared at the dark clouds, listening.

"There will come a time," she read aloud, "when adharma—untruth, greed, confusion—will rule not just kings, but common minds. People will forget the rhythm of nature, the meaning of stillness. Words will lose value. Knowledge will be commercial. Violence will wear new clothes."

She paused, then continued.

"In that time, when the world has forgotten itself, **Kalki** will rise. Riding a white horse, carrying a sword as radiant as the sun, He will bring the last cycle to a close — Not with destruction, but with truth sharp enough to tear illusions."

"Where will he be born?" Manas asked, genuinely curious now.

"In the village of Shambhala," Prisha said, "to a wise and humble Brahmin named Vishnuyasha."

Navya murmured, "Will he end everything?"

"No," Prisha replied. "He will begin again."

---

*कल्किर्नाम भविष्यामि जगत्पातः सनातनः।*
*धर्मसंस्थापनार्थाय सम्भविष्यति विष्णुयशसः कुले॥*

*Meaning:*

***"In the future, I will appear as Kalki, the eternal Lord and protector of the universe, born in the family of Vishnuyasha, to restore dharma in a time of darkness."***

*(Bhagavatam: Canto 12, Chapter 2, Shloka 19)*

---

# SECTION FOUR

# THE THREADS BEGIN TO PULL

## Chapter 31

## THE ASHES OF SILENCE

*Year: 1893 | Location: Saraswati Vidyapeeth, Dehradun*

"What you burn in words, I will remember in silence."

**The Scholar's Visit**

Harold Statham dismounted the horse cart in Haridwar with the stiffness of a man who had traveled too far with too many questions. The sacred city buzzed with pilgrims, but he wasn't here for salvation. He was looking for a man who once translated the Atharvaveda into Latin.

He found him in a chai shop behind a crumbling arch, sitting cross-legged, eyes milk-white with age but voice as sharp as a winter river.

"You are the one from the Vidyapeeth," the old linguist said before Harold could speak. "Your boots carry the dust of that place."

Harold blinked. "You've been there?"

The man didn't answer directly. He sipped slowly. "Some doors open with keys. Others... with silence. Saraswati's guardians use the latter."

Harold leaned in. "I've seen symbols there. Triangles, spirals... on ceilings, on manuscripts. Are they rituals? Coordinates?"

The man shook his head. "They are memories. Mnemonics to remember that which cannot be written. What is passed by vibration, not ink. Born of silence."

"Then why paint them?" Harold asked.

"To warn those who ask the wrong questions," the old man replied.

**Shadows in the Courtyard**

It was raining when Harold returned to the Vidyapeeth. The droplets fell in straight lines, like invisible needles trying to stitch the sky back together.

He stayed in the guest chamber that night, pretending to review textbooks and curriculum charts. But at midnight, he lit his lantern and stepped into the open courtyard.

He moved like a man certain of both purpose and guilt.

The eastern wing — sealed for decades — had no guard. Just a sandstone door with no handle, a rusted padlock, and beneath it, a stone tile that rattled underfoot. He pried it loose.

Inside the gap was a faded copper key.

But just behind a peepal pillar, silent and wide-eyed, stood a small boy — barefoot, barely ten, watching through the rain.

**The Room Without Time**

The door creaked like a whisper breaking after years of holding back.

The eastern wing smelled of dry turmeric, camphor, and dust layered like tree rings. Harold stepped in slowly, his lantern flickering against arched ceilings carved with ancient geometry.

He looked up.

On the ceiling, just above the central alcove, was a painted triangle — **three flames at its vertices**, and a spiral emerging from the center. Around it were shlokas, but not from any Veda he recognized.

He opened his notebook and began sketching.

One wall bore a map — but not of India. The landmasses were abstract, fluid, marked by **sacred syllables instead of names**. Near the center:

"त्रैवर्णिकं द्वारं प्रतीक्षते।"
*"The triad doorway awaits."*

In a wooden box, he found a journal titled:

"Echoes of Soundless Teachers."

Inside, the entries were fragmented — each one a mantra paired with a memory. Not explanations. Experiences.

His breath slowed. His hands stopped writing.

It felt… like the room knew it was being watched.

### The Confrontation

A soft cough broke the silence.

Harold spun, nearly dropping the lantern.

Acharya Divyavarna stood at the threshold, robes unruffled, eyes deep as a still lake.

"I wondered when you would come," the Acharya said gently.

Harold straightened. "You locked this room."

"I preserved it," he replied.

"From whom?"

"From those who measure meaning by conquest."

There was no anger in his voice. Only a terrible, patient sadness.

"You cannot erase a forest by burning its trees, Mr. Statham. You must silence its roots. That's what your mission asks of you."

Harold said nothing.

The Acharya walked slowly to the mural. "You see a triangle. I see the breath between sound. You see patterns. I see memory."

"Then what are you hiding?" Harold asked, almost whispering.

Divyavarna looked at him. "Not hiding. Holding. For those who listen."

And then he stepped aside. "You may report what you like. But truth… does not fear paperwork."

### Fire at Dawn

The fire came just before sunrise.

The eastern wing blazed like an offering — orange flames licking up against the rain-stained sky.

The children were ushered to safety. No injuries. No panic. Only silence.

Harold stood beside the guards, watching the smoke curl like a serpent. His hand tightened around his report scroll — already half-written.

He said nothing. Just watched the mural crumble in red heat, the inked ceiling collapse like a dying breath.

No one could prove how it started.

Later that day, he submitted his summary to the Calcutta Presidency:

"The Saraswati Vidyapeeth remains… an institution of local myth and moral discipline. Records lost to accidental fire. Curriculum adaptable. No further anomalies."

But he knew better. And he knew… **someone else had known too.**

### The Boy's Departure

That night, when the rains had washed the ash clean, the boy stood barefoot in the courtyard.

He had not spoken to Harold. He had never entered the room. But he had seen enough.

He knelt and dipped his fingers into the soft mud, drawing **a single triangle** with a small flame at its center.

Then, with a cloth bag slung across his shoulder, he turned away from the charred wall.

No ceremony. No farewell.

Just a child walking into the forest.

He didn't walk in anger. He walked in purpose.

He would carry the memory — not of the fire, but of **what came before it.**

### Bhagavatam Parallel | The Tale of Gokarna

**"There was once a devout Brahmin named Atma Deva, wise in the Vedas and revered in his village — yet torn within by sorrow."**

He had no children. And to a man bound by worldly attachments, this felt like the absence of immortality itself.
One day, a wandering sadhu visited his hut and warned:

***"O Brahmin, you are not destined to bear a child. Seek liberation, not lineage."***

But Atma Deva would not listen. In despair, he begged for a blessing. And so — by divine arrangement or fate — a child was conceived, not by dharma but by **deception**.

His wife, **Dhunduli**, fearing pregnancy, **secretly adopted her sister's newborn** and passed him off as their own. This boy was named **Dhundhakari**.

He grew not in wisdom, but in **greed, anger, and indulgence**. As a youth, he consumed wine, consorted with thieves, and brought ruin upon their home.

Distraught, Atma Deva finally renounced all, **leaving his house, his wife, and his name**, to wander into the forest and seek moksha.

But what Dhunduli had not revealed was that **she later bore another son** — born from divine intervention — a child of strange stillness and bright gaze.
They named him **Gokarna**, for his ears were shaped like the holy cow's.

Unlike his brother, Gokarna was **silent and observant**. From his earliest days, he studied scriptures by lamplight, questioned nothing aloud, but **saw everything**.

When the house grew too heavy with sin,
when his brother brought courtesans and shame,
when his mother turned bitter from guilt —
**Gokarna left**.

No words. No letters. Just silence — like the last star before dawn.

He wandered into hermitages, sat with saints, and let **dharma** rise like the sun within him.

Years passed.

Dhundhakari, swallowed by lust and rage, was **killed by his own companions**. But death was not escape — for his sins chained his soul to the house he had defiled. He became a **preta** — a ghost, neither living nor dead.

It was Gokarna, now a scholar and pilgrim, who returned upon hearing whispers of this unrest.

He did not curse. He did not judge.
He gathered villagers. Lit a lamp. Began to **recite the Śrīmad Bhagavatam for seven days**.

Each word was a cleansing flame.
Each shloka a ladder between worlds.

At the end of the 7$^{th}$ day, a divine light descended — and **Dhundhakari's spirit was freed**.

Even the most fallen, said the sages,
may find grace in the river of devotion.

**Modern World Parallel: The Boy Who Chose Silence**

He had read the Gokarna story not once, but many times —
once in a torn scroll, again in whispered prayers, and lately… in the reflection of his own life.

He had lived it, unknowingly.

The **Saraswati Vidyapeeth**, once a haven of sacred learning, had become a place of suspicion, agendas, and betrayal. He had watched **Harold** — the very man entrusted with reviving truth — **twist questions into traps**, and knowledge into possession.

He had watched letters burn.
He had watched silence punished.

He had seen enough.

Like Gokarna, he **chose not to rebel with fire**, but with **absence**.

He left quietly.
Not because he was afraid —
But because he understood:
**Some sanctuaries are not saved from within. They must be rebuilt from afar.**

He would carry the stories. He would carry the symbols.
He would find others who still believed in the ancient rhythm.
And one day, like Gokarna did for Dhundhakari,
**he too would return — not to accuse, but to liberate.**

Until then, his path was the forest.
And his voice… the wind.

---

*शृण्वतां कथा कृष्णस्य नित्यं भागवतं यः पठेत्*
*तस्य पापानि नश्यन्ति मोक्षं लभते ध्रुवम्॥*

*Meaning:*

***Those who listen to the divine stories of Krishna,***
***and read the Bhagavatam every day with love —***
***their sins melt away, and liberation comes… steady and sure.***

*(Bhagwatam: Canto 12, Chapter 13, Shloka 23)*

---

## Chapter 32

# WHISPERS BENEATH THE CANOPY

**Triangle of Sugar**

The sun was still lazy, stretching behind the veil of Simlipal's morning mist, as a faint chirp of barbets rose from the sal trees. Inside the *Courtyard Zest,* Raghav sat with his plate, grumbling quietly about the idli being "less fluffy than Abdul chacha's clouds."

Parag folded his glasses and sat opposite him. "You know," he said, pointing at the random scattering of spilled sugar grains on Raghav's plate, "sometimes patterns show up when we're not even looking."

Raghav frowned, still chewing.

Parag leaned forward and tapped gently on the plate. "See this?" The sugar had formed, by pure coincidence — or maybe not — a crude triangle. Three points, one grain sitting boldly in the center.

"You think it's just messy sugar," Parag said, "but what if someone was trying to show you how to begin a map?"

Raghav raised an eyebrow. "That's… oddly specific."

Parag smiled. "That's parenting, beta. Oddly specific without explanation."

There was a pause. Raghav picked up one grain of sugar and placed it at the center. "There. Now it's a pyramid."

"Or a mountain," Parag added. "And what's hidden in a mountain?"

Raghav thought. "A cave? Or... silence?"

"Exactly." Parag tapped his own forehead. "The quiet ones know the way."

Raghav looked up, curious now.

Parag stood, brushing imaginary dust from his kurta. "Come to me when you're ready for the next riddle," he said. "Till then, finish that tragic idli."

**Leaves? Nope. This Time It Walked**

The forest was supposed to feel calmer today — warmer sun, friendlier air, and no surprises in the shadows.

And yet.

"I swear this place gets a new vibe every six hours," Navya muttered, flipping her sketchbook shut. "If it had Instagram, we'd be tagging moods by the minute."

Prisha laughed, then paused. Her gaze shifted sideways — not towards trees or leaves, but something low, silent, and breathing.

A **lean Indian pariah dog**, short-haired, sun-browned, with one crooked ear and sharp, thoughtful eyes, stood quietly behind a sal tree. It wasn't growling. Just watching — head tilted, tail low.

It took three slow steps forward. Then turned. And walked away — deliberately. Like it was waiting.

Prisha whispered, "We're following it."

Navya sighed, "Of course we are."

They followed through the undergrowth and lichen-draped roots, the dog trotting just ahead — leading them through a narrow space between two mossy boulders.

Then it stopped. Sat. And looked up at them with a quiet breath.

Navya raised her eyebrows. "That's new."

Before either could say more, a calm voice called from the left. "You met Ghostie?"

A woman stepped out, wiping her hands with a sal leaf. Dusty jacket. WRC patch on her shoulder. Crescent-shaped scar over one brow. She knelt and gave the dog a fond pat.

"He only shows up when he senses kindness," she said. "You must be good people."

Prisha crouched beside the dog — Ghostie, apparently — and the animal leaned gently against her leg. "He led us here."

The woman nodded. "Yeah. He does that."

"Who are you?" Navya asked, not unkindly.

"Shiwani," she said. "Wildlife field rescue. I've been around these trees for three years now."

She rose, brushing her hands. "You'll find the forest doesn't always send dangers. Sometimes it just sends a friend."

And with that, she clicked her tongue at Ghostie and disappeared behind the mahua grove.

Navya pulled out her sketchbook again. "Okay… that was actually poetic."

**Mango Lassi, Room Keys, and a Familiar Face**

It was nearly lunch, and the resort had started humming like a well-fed beehive.

The four kids had taken over the swing-corner near the garden café — Prisha's feet dangling, Raghav sipping from a copper tumbler, Navya sketching something leafy, and Manas flipping through his field notes with a frown like he'd lost a bet with himself.

"Why does this resort serve *three* kinds of mango lassi?" Raghav asked, holding up a tiny menu card.
Navya snorted. "Because we're in Simlipal. This is mango land, GDP boy."

"Great Dessert Paradise," Manas mumbled without looking up.
"Gross Daily Pranks," Prisha offered innocently, just before smirking.
"Gigantic Dosa Planet," added Raghav with a proud nod. "I'm versatile."

Before Navya could one-up him, they heard the resort bell chime — and the soft rumble of an SUV parking at the gravel porch.

A man stepped out first — mid-forties, sturdy build, a tan that spoke of long expeditions. He adjusted his bag, looked around once, and started towards the reception.

"Who's that?" Raghav murmured.

Just then, the man greeted one of the forest officials with a loud, familiar baritone. "Alok Sinha, Central Symbolic Research Authority. Reporting after two years, boss!"

Manas blinked. "That name sounds familiar."

They watched from behind the hedge as the man chatted cheerfully with the receptionist. Then something unexpected happened.

The receptionist leaned in and said something. Mr. Sinha's eyebrows rose. He looked towards the garden.

And then — he dialed a number.

A minute later, **a teenage boy** stepped out of a second car parked near the gate. Tall, quiet, dark curls. His eyes scanned the open café lazily — and then stopped.

"Wait…" Navya squinted. "That's—"

"**Gaurav?!**" the four of them said at once.

The boy turned, a little startled, then smiled. "Well. This wasn't in the brochure."

He walked over slowly, looking as awkward as ever — but somehow sharper around the edges.

"Wh—what are *you* doing here?" Prisha asked, rising halfway.

"My dad's doing a forest symbology review project with the conservation team," he said. "He didn't mention *you guys* were here. I thought it was just going to be... vacation, with birdcalls and spotty Wi-Fi."

"You followed your dad into a jungle for vacation?" Raghav raised a brow.
"I thought there would be hammocks," Gaurav said honestly.

They laughed. And just like that, the air shifted — something new, someone familiar, another dot on the map of their strange summer.

Manas was already pulling out a second chair. "Come. You're late. We've already decoded half the jungle."

"I brought snacks," Gaurav added.

Raghav perked up. "You can stay."

**ECHO, Delhi: Quiet Minds, Loud Maps**

In the heart of Delhi, nestled within the aged sandstone walls of the **National Centre for Forestry & Environmental Conservation**, a discreet wing existed — one not marked on public directories.

This was **ECHO** — the **Earth and Culture Heritage Observatory** — a cross-disciplinary think tank working under the Ministry of Environment and the Ministry of Culture. Few beyond government circles even knew it existed. Even fewer understood what it actually did.

On the **fifth floor**, past a coded elevator and a quiet hallway, a **frost-glass room** sat in one corner. Curtains were drawn to keep out the sun. Inside, plush beige **sofa sets** lined one wall, and a large **interactive display table** flickered softly. A single mug of black coffee sat untouched.

At the center of this silence stood **Dr. Anusuya Pant**.

She was dressed in a **tailored charcoal-grey blazer**, pale cream blouse, and well-cut trousers. Her hair was neatly tied back. In her hand, a stylus hovered over a projected scan.

On the screen: a **notebook page**. The kind children use.
But the sketches weren't childish — they were ceiling symbols. Curved triangles, dotted circles, sundials. Some darkened more than others.

A voice echoed softly from the wall speaker.

**"This one's from the Simlipal logbook,"** Pulkit Roy said.
**"Page 19. Ayan's handwriting. These same shapes are etched into the ceiling of Rock Chamber 3C — eastern ridge, near the old waterfall basin."**

Anusuya didn't reply immediately. She zoomed into one of the drawings, layered it with a translucent geometry file, and tilted her head.

**"I don't think," she said. "I observe first."**

Pulkit paused. "Understood. Forwarding the alignment overlays now."

Anusuya continued studying the image. She didn't blink much when she was focused — her team had learned to recognize that. A stillness before insight.

Then quietly, to herself more than anyone else:
**"This is not recent. This is memory resurfacing."**

She turned slightly, speaking towards the intercom again.

**"Also send this to Dr. Khan,"** she added.
**"He's tracked these symbols since the Bhujpetra site collapse. He'll spot what we can't."**

Outside, a junior assistant passed the glass wall and slowed — wondering, again, what exactly went on inside this part of the ministry.

The curtain shifted slightly.
The room fell still again.

### The Stone That Dreamed

The next afternoon, Gaurav sat under the flame tree, quiet as always.

He was holding something.

Navya noticed it first. "Gaurav? What's that?"

He didn't answer right away. Just stared at the **smooth, flat stone** in his hand — the color of burnt almond, with lines across it like river maps drawn by the wind.

"I found it yesterday near the forest trail while coming to the resort," he said finally. "Didn't pack it."

Prisha tilted her head. "Where was your bag kept?"

"In the room. Next to yours, I think."

Navya stepped closer. "Can I see it?"

Gaurav nodded and handed it over. The stone was warm — not hot, not cold, just... present. Like something recently alive.

"It feels like it's thinking," Prisha whispered.

Raghav leaned over from where he was pretending not to be interested. "Everything feels like that around here. Even the salad."

Navya smirked but didn't laugh. She was flipping through her sketchbook now, brows furrowed.

"I've drawn something like this before," she murmured. "Not exactly. But close."

Manas looked up from his tablet. "A copy?"

"No," she said. "A... memory, maybe."

Gaurav didn't say much. He just sat down cross-legged and looked into the treetops, voice low.
"I had a dream last night. A dome. People chanting. And someone — not me, but someone I was — drawing circles in the air. Like instructions."

"You remember details?" Prisha asked.

He nodded. "Sort of. A spiral staircase. Fireflies. A whisper I didn't understand."

Raghav, who had been casually munching a biscuit, paused mid-chew. "Just asking—did anyone else's vacation come with this much cryptic poetry?"

Navya rolled her eyes. "Nope. Just yours. Must be that elite GDP package."

Everyone chuckled, and the heaviness lifted for a moment.

But deep in her chest, Prisha felt something tighten.
The stone.
The dream.
The fact that none of this — none of it — was random.

## Circles, Crows, and Something Odd

Later that afternoon, the Simlipal sun mellowed into its golden mood. The kids had returned to their rooms — a lazy post-lunch haze had settled over the resort like a warm shawl.

But Gaurav couldn't sleep.

He wandered to the shaded bench outside the main lodge, a wooden notebook in hand — not the kind you buy in stores. Handmade paper, rough twine binding. His father's habit.

Prisha spotted him while fetching hot water for tea. "Still drawing weird shapes?"

Gaurav smiled. "They're not weird. They're just... not meant to be forgotten."

She sat beside him. A jungle crow hopped along the path, watching them like it knew something they didn't.

He flipped the notebook towards her. The page showed a **circle inside a square**, with a leaf pattern repeated in sets of eight. Along the edges were odd symbols — something between script and geometry.

"Where did you see this?" Prisha asked.

"In my dad's lab folder, long back. He had labelled it **'Ceiling – Eastern Chamber, SCP 3C'**. I thought it was just one of his failed projects. But yesterday, he said something strange."

He paused, tapping his pencil against the paper.

"He said: *'Some knowledge lies flat until time lifts it into pattern.'* I didn't get it."

Prisha tilted her head. "Rock Chamber 3C... that's the same one your dad mentioned earlier, right?"

"Exactly. And now he's suddenly here. Called me out of nowhere."
Gaurav exhaled. "Something's up. I can feel it. And it's not just the resort food."

Prisha looked at the sketch again — those eight leaves along the rim. Almost like a time wheel. A spiral of memory.

Behind them, the crow cawed once and flew off.

She returned the notebook slowly. "You'll show the others?"

"In a bit," Gaurav said. "But not all of it. Some things... are better whispered first."

Prisha nodded, then grinned. "That's fine. We've gotten good at whispers lately."

## Bhagwatam Parallel | Story of King Muchukunda

Long ago, in an age when the lines between devas and humans blurred, there lived a noble king named **Muchukunda**, a fierce protector of dharma and beloved by the people of Earth. When the gods were embroiled in cosmic battles against the asuras, it was Muchukunda who came to their aid.

For **years beyond counting**, he fought on behalf of the devas, never asking for rest, never seeking reward. But time moved differently in the celestial realms. When peace was restored, and Muchukunda asked to return home, the devas looked away.

His kingdom... his family... his people...
All long gone. Hundreds of years had passed on Earth while he had only blinked.

The devas, grateful but helpless, offered him a boon.
Tired, heart-heavy, and without a place to belong, Muchukunda asked for **undisturbed sleep** in a cave, hidden from time, where no one would trouble him.

They granted his wish — but added a mysterious twist:

"Whosoever awakens you shall be reduced to ashes by the fire of your gaze."

And so, King Muchukunda slept. Beneath the mountains. In a cave dark as forgotten memory.

Centuries later, Lord Krishna was pursued by a barbaric warrior named **Kalayavana**, who had no respect for dharma or divinity. Krishna, knowing Muchukunda's cave lay nearby, **lured Kalayavana inside**.

The demon king stumbled in, found the sleeping figure, and mistook him for Krishna.
He **kicked the king**, shouting in arrogance.

Muchukunda awoke.

With eyes that had once protected the innocent... now blazing with celestial fire...
He looked once, and Kalayavana turned to ash.

Silence returned.

Then Krishna stepped forth from the shadows, radiant and serene.
Muchukunda, finally awake in more ways than one, recognized the Divine.

Humbled, he bowed low. Krishna smiled.

"You have burnt away your past. Now walk the Earth as a sage," he said.

And so the warrior became a wanderer. A king became a seeker.

And deep within a cave... a fire that had slept for ages... had found its purpose.

## Modern Day Parallel – The Cave Within

As the wind danced across the Similipal skies and a boy quietly sketched eight leaves on a napkin, a different cave stirred in memory — the **cave of King Muchukunda.**

He had fought for the devas. Loved fiercely. Lost everything.
And then, he slept — beneath the mountains, hidden from the noise of the world.
But even in sleep, he held **fire in his eyes**. A power that could awaken or destroy.

Just as **Muchukunda's cave** waited for a careless footstep to open its secret, perhaps this world too is lined with **dormant flames** — wisdom that sleeps in caves of stone and hearts of silence.

Gaurav's drawings weren't just doodles.
They were **doorways.**
And something, or someone, had just stepped closer.

---

*शान्तिं लब्ध्वा न पुनरावर्तते न स विषण्णः।*
*स्वात्मारामो निरुपधिः सुखमश्नोति शाश्वतम्॥*

*Meaning:*

***He who has found true peace never returns to sorrow.***
***Detached and content in his own Self,***
***He tastes a joy that never ends.***

*(Bhagavatam: Canto 12, Chapter 12, Shloka 50)*

---

## Chapter 33

# ECHOES IN THE FOREST, WHISPERS IN THE HALLS

**The Long Path Inward**

It had been more than a week since Meera and Ayan stepped into the forest's deeper veins.
What began as an eager expedition had now blurred into muddy tracks, damp notebooks, and quiet glances exchanged without words.

The trees here were not the ones that welcomed them at the forest's edge — tall and familiar, with obedient canopies and well-behaved roots. No, these trees seemed older… shyer… or maybe just more stubborn.

Some had **leaves shaped like long spoons**, others with **rounded, waxy fans** that shimmered despite the humidity. There were thick-fronded sal trees standing like sentries, **ghost-white dhak trees** whose leaves looked like hands cupped in silence, and one particular banyan whose aerial roots had formed **a tangled cage around nothing**.

"They're all different," Meera said softly, brushing her thumb along the jagged leaf of a Karanj. "But none of them are leading anywhere."

Ayan grunted, more mud than man by now. "Every pattern breaks before it becomes something."

He flipped his notebook open — pages dotted with quick sketches: leaf sizes, vein structures, tree bark impressions, a crude attempt to trace their looping routes. His pen hesitated as he looked up at the trees again.

They weren't repeating.
But neither were they random.

That's what was getting to him.

Some trunks were marked — **tiny notches**, unnatural but faint. Too precise to be weather. Too inconsistent to be tribal.

Behind them, the young local assistant — **Dhanraj** — trailed silently. Even he had stopped offering suggestions. When Meera turned to ask him something, he only muttered, "This part... no one really comes here. Animals avoid it too."

That was new.

A bird flapped once overhead. The forest fell back into hush.

They hadn't found anything decisive — no carved rocks, no symbols, no answers. Only these trees... these stubborn, whispering trees... with leaves too quiet and paths too circular.

Meera rubbed her forehead. "I thought we'd be closer by now."

Ayan didn't respond.
He was staring at a **tree whose branches had bent into the shape of an arch**, like a doorway that had long since forgotten its purpose.

He tore a page from his notebook and began sketching.

**The Resort: Gaurav's Sketchbook**

"Guys, don't laugh," Gaurav warned, holding his sketchpad like a shield.

Raghav had already smirked. "Whenever someone says that, it means it's going to be hilarious."

They were all gathered on the grass slope behind the resort — a lazy afternoon stretched between two hills, cicadas humming in the background like a low drumroll.

Navya leaned over. "Is this... a frog riding a tiger?"

"It's *symbolic,* okay?" Gaurav huffed. "Dream I had last night. And also, I was bored."

Prisha took the sketchpad gently. "This is good, Gaurav. Really. See these curves?" She traced the tail. "You've done it with rhythm. That's hard."

Manas peered in, lips pursed. "Wait—what's this weird line behind the tiger?"

Gaurav shrugged. "Dunno. It just came. Like some kind of net or... pattern."

Navya's eyebrows lifted. "Pattern?"

He flipped to another page. "This one I made this morning. It started with that leaf we were talking about yesterday — the one with eight veins. Then I kept adding lines. Then it looked like... this."

They all stared.

It looked vaguely like a **wheel**, with thin jagged rays and something like **eyes** between the spokes.

Raghav looked up at the trees. "Okay, that's freaky."

"Not freaky," Prisha murmured. "Familiar."

They all fell silent.

A breeze rustled past them — light but oddly warm. For a moment, no one said anything.

Then Gaurav laughed, shaking the awkwardness off. "It's just a sketch. I'm not channeling aliens."

Raghav rolled his eyes. "You sure? Because I'm starting to think *everyone* who hangs out with us ends up in a conspiracy."

"Welcome to GDP," Manas quipped. "Great Drawing Project."

"Great Doomsday Prophecy," Navya added.

They all laughed, the tension defused for now.

But somewhere beneath the laughter, in the sketchbook held casually in Gaurav's lap, the **wheel with the jagged rays** waited.
Like it had something more to say.

**The Decision**

The curtains were drawn slightly tighter today in the south glass room of ECHO. Morning light seeped through faintly, glinting off the digital panel that hovered in mid-air. On it, a field-sketched page blinked open — a scan from Meera's notebook.

Pulkit had just entered.

He didn't announce himself. He didn't need to. Anusuya was already turning towards him.

"That page," she said, without looking at the screen, "is from their eighth day. Note the pattern shift. The carvings aren't just getting complex — they're aligning in reverse symmetry now."

Pulkit crossed his arms.

"And you think it's intentional?"

She paused.

"I don't know yet. But there's a logic forming... something that wants to be noticed."

There was a flicker of warmth in her eyes — not at the data, but at his presence. Pulkit smiled softly.

"You haven't changed. Still whispering to geometry as if it might talk back."

"It always talks. You just haven't learned how to listen."

The moment sat quietly between them, full of years they hadn't spoken of. It didn't need defining. It only needed space.

Anusuya turned back to the hovering symbols — two concentric curves, with a dot in the middle, not unlike what Ayan had reported near **Chamber 3C**, the real one in Simlipal.

She zoomed in, then spoke with a sudden crispness.

"I'm going," she said.

Pulkit blinked. "You mean—"

"Yes. To the site. Simlipal. If I wait for Delhi's paper clearances, the monsoon will seal half those paths. Tell Khan I'll file a field mission request, but I'm not waiting for approval."

He looked at her carefully. "You'll go alone?"

"No. Dhanraj is already there. And I'll need someone who knows the terrain. Maybe even..." she hesitated, then shrugged, "maybe even Meera's old GPS team."

Pulkit nodded slowly.

Anusuya walked towards the console and pulled out a compact field log tablet, tucking it under her arm.

"Meanwhile," she added, voice softer now, "keep the kids ready."

Pulkit raised an eyebrow. "For what?"

She didn't answer directly. She turned to face the hovering scan one last time.

"Whatever is calling out from those leaves, those rocks... it's not done yet. And they're part of it now — whether they know it or not."

Then she turned.
Straight-backed. Quiet-footed. Gone.

### The Pause Before the Puzzle

The forest was quiet today — not silent, but softer. As if the trees were breathing slower, watching from above.

By the shallow stream near the resort's eastern edge, the kids had gathered without much planning. Raghav was tossing flat stones over water. Navya sat with her feet dipped in, eyes closed, letting the stream speak. Gaurav leaned back against a rock, sketching something absent-mindedly. Prisha was unusually quiet, her gaze following a group of spotted deer grazing beyond the tree line.

"You're too quiet," Manas said to Prisha, flicking water at her with a leaf. "Did a leaf offend you again?"

She half-smiled. "No. Just… look at them," she nodded towards the deer. "They haven't moved from that spot in ten minutes. That's not normal."

"They're grazing," Raghav said, skipping another stone. "That's literally what they do."

"No. See the youngest one? Ears up. Muscles tight. Like it's listening for something," Prisha said softly.

Navya opened her eyes. "She's right. That's alert behaviour."

Manas squinted. "Maybe they're picking up something we can't."

"Like a predator?" Gaurav asked, suddenly interested. "Or a vibration?"

Raghav shrugged. "Or maybe they just don't like our playlist."

Everyone laughed. The tension melted for a moment.

Gaurav leaned forward, flipping open his sketchbook. "By the way… my dad showed me something weird last night. Some carvings from inside a jungle cave near here. He thinks they match the ceiling patterns Meera Ma'am had sent him long ago — leaves, yes, but also animal shapes."

Navya sat up straighter. "Animal shapes?"

"Yeah. One looked like a langur… but with eight tails."

Prisha's eyes narrowed. "That's not a mistake. That's a message."

There was a long silence.

Raghav cleared his throat. "So… operation GDP just got an upgrade?"

"Grossly Disturbing Patterns?" Manas offered.

"Or," Navya said, grinning, "Gaurav's Dad's Puzzles."

They all broke into laughter again — but it lingered only a moment.

Because in the distance, the deer had suddenly vanished.

## The Grove That Wasn't on the Map

It was late afternoon now. The forest light had grown golden, but the deeper they walked, the less sunlight seemed to follow.

Meera was adjusting the strap of her satchel again. Her boots were caked in layers of dark mud, and even her ponytail had gathered leaves.

Ayan trailed behind, scribbling in their weather-beaten field notebook. The previous pages were already filled — leaf sketches, bark textures, patterns of moss, fungal growths. And yet, none of it led anywhere conclusive.

Dhanraj was a few paces ahead, machete in hand, swatting vines gently aside. "This patch," he called out, "wasn't marked on any forest trail."

"That's the fourth unmarked area today," Meera muttered.

Ayan paused near a gnarled old tree with roots like frozen serpents. "No — this one's different. Look." He bent low. "These aren't natural twists. It's as if… something carved the path to grow this way."

Meera crouched beside him. A cluster of long leaves, shaped like fans, stood perfectly upright around the base. Their edges had fine dotted marks, almost too neat to be from insects.

"Eight again," she whispered, counting.

And then — a rustle. Low, heavy.

Not the flutter of birds. Not the scamper of squirrels. But a gait. Grounded. Measured.

Ayan held up his hand, stilling Dhanraj and Meera. From the grove ahead, a large shadow moved — not human, not familiar. The leaves trembled, and for a moment, the shape of a massive **wild gaur** could be seen in silhouette. Its curved horns gleamed briefly in the dying light before it vanished behind a curtain of green.

Dhanraj's voice was low. "That… was no ordinary bull."

Ayan nodded. "No. And it didn't run. It watched."

Meera touched the notebook. "This place isn't resisting us. But it isn't welcoming us either."

As they began to retreat for the day, Meera stopped one last time — staring at the old tree. Someone had scratched something into the bark.

It was faint. But readable.

**'Chamber 3C… is never empty.'**

She looked at Ayan. His expression had turned grim. The same chamber where symbols were seen. The same chamber Anusuya was now heading towards.

Meera shut the notebook slowly. "We need to send this tonight."

**Bhagavatam Parallel | The Story of King Nriga: The Unseen Mistake**

Long ago, there lived a benevolent and dharmic king named **Nriga**, from the lineage of the solar dynasty. He was known for his generosity — every year, he donated thousands of cows to Brahmins, ensuring each had proper lineage, gold-plated horns, silver hooves, and garlands around their necks.

But fate played a strange trick.

Unknowingly, one cow from his donations wandered into another Brahmin's herd — and the same cow got donated twice. Years passed. And when the two Brahmins realized the mix-up, they came to the king, both claiming the cow was theirs.

King Nriga, though innocent in intent, was now caught in a moral tangle. He begged both sages for forgiveness and offered them thousands more in return. But they refused. **"We want only what was given to us,"** they said.

In his next life, King Nriga was cursed to be born as a **giant chameleon**, trapped under the earth in a dry well, until Lord Krishna himself would liberate him.

That day came during Krishna's youth. When the boys were playing, they peered into the well and saw a strange creature glowing below. Krishna pulled him out — and the curse broke.

King Nriga appeared, humbled, radiant, and freed. He bowed to Krishna, thanking him for grace beyond merit.

His final words before ascending to heaven?

**"Even the smallest mistakes leave marks. Offerings done in ego can become shackles. True dharma is in awareness."**

**Modern Day Parallel – The Forest That Remembers**

Meera and Ayan had done no wrong — not by law, not by intention. But something about that unmarked grove felt like a whisper from the past. Like an unresolved memory in the belly of the Earth.

The Eight leaves. The silent gaur. The phrase carved into bark — *"Chamber 3C... is never empty."*

It was as if the forest carried an old wound. One that wasn't healed by science or mapped by drones. It asked for humility, not conquest. Awareness, not answers.

Like King Nriga's tale, the message was subtle yet clear:

**Even nature remembers missteps. And sometimes, silence is her way of marking it.**

---

*श्री-नृग उवाच —*
*यं त्वं विबुद्ध्य कृतवांश्च शपंस्तथा मां*
*किं मे पुनः प्रति गृणन्स्वकृतं शुचिः स्यात्।*
*संसारचक्रमपि धावति मे शिरस्य्*
*यन्मे कृतं त्वयि तथैव ततः पुनः किम्॥*

*Meaning:*

***King Nriga said:***
***"O Lord, You have become aware of the curse upon me and have delivered me. What use would it be for me to be purified again by You accepting my actions? The cycle of birth and death continues over my head; what further purification is left, when all my deeds are already offered to You?"***

*(Bhagavatam: Canto 10, Chapter 64, Shloka 32)*

---

# Chapter 34

# THE QUIET BEFORE THE CALL

**Delhi Skies, Faint With Rain**

The sky above Delhi was the kind that whispered, not thundered — muted grey clouds gathering like silent witnesses. In the corner office of the Department of Forest Conservation, the curtains moved gently as Anusuya Pant packed her travel bag. Notebooks, a khaki folder marked "SV_OLD," a silver USB drive — and at the bottom, a small, weathered compass. A gift from a much younger Ayan, years ago, during their research in the north.

Pulkit hovered at the door. "So you really want to go alone?"

Anusuya didn't look up as she zipped the bag. "I need to see it myself. The carvings, the ceiling, the forest. And something about Meera's sketches… they don't match her usual hand. It feels… urgent."

Pulkit hesitated. "You'll check the last GPS ping?"

"Already mapped it. Near the southern stream — where the rock ridge bends east."

He stepped closer, offering a brown envelope. "Director Khan sent this. Official permissions and some older terrain maps. Also, an email from the vice principal of SVA. Apparently, they're... a little worried too."

She opened the envelope silently and read a few lines. Then she folded the letter, tucked it into her bag, and finally looked up.

"Something is shifting, Pulkit. The forest… feels like it's revealing something. Or waiting."

He didn't reply. Just handed her a thermos. "Lemon tea. No sugar. Just the way you hate it."

She smiled. "I observe first."

**Somewhere Deeper in Simlipal**

After three more days of intense exploration, Meera and Ayan had pushed further — this time venturing southeast of the basin near **Chamber 3C**, following a natural curve of the forest that twisted between moss-covered boulders and streams fed by the monsoon's early breath. Something about the overlapping root structures and clustered leaf patterns had caught Meera's trained eye.

Before leaving, they'd instructed **Dhanraj**, the young tribal aide, to remain at the base camp and maintain regular communication — both with them and with the ECHO office. He was used to their rhythm, their silences while working, and the odd hours when the relay line would buzz with field logs.

But now, more than 24 hours had passed without a word.

"Maybe they've just gone deeper… too busy marking something new," he muttered, more to the rustling bamboo than himself.

Still, something tugged at his instincts.

While restocking the camp supplies that afternoon, he noticed faint boot imprints fading eastward — the kind left behind by people walking slowly, scanning the ground.

Near the edge of the trail, something flapped. A single sheet of Meera's waterproof notebook, caught under a root.

He picked it up carefully.

On the page: a banyan leaf, its veins mapped like river systems… but one vein was circled twice. And beside it, a word: **"Hollow?"**

**Saraswati Valley Academy – Vice Principal's Office**

Back at SVA, Vice Principal Asha clicked her tongue as she reread the forwarded mail. She had written to Anusuya, mentioning that the Agrawals hadn't checked in for more than 24 hours. Not unusual for researchers — but still, her instinct had stirred.

She looked at the message from Director Khan. **"We're initiating quiet contact. No public panic."**

Asha muttered to herself, "These forests… they hold too many silences."

**Bhagwatam Parallel |The Heart That Gives- King Ranti Deva's Story**

That evening, children sat around a small campfire. Raghav face dimly lit by the flames. "You know… some days feel heavy even when nothing bad happens," he murmured.

Just then, a soft cry echoed from the trail — it was **a wounded baby deer**, limping and lost, barely visible through the shrubs.

Before anyone could react, **Prisha was already moving.** She knelt beside the deer, murmuring something. The others followed — Navya checked for bruises, Manas quickly pulled out water, and Raghav offered his scarf as a makeshift bandage.

Later, Prisha sat beside Raghav and whispered, "This reminded me of a story…"

**King Parikshit** asked **Shukadeva Rishi**, during the fateful seven days before the king's death, the very crux of the Shrimad Bhagavatam's setting.

**"What is the highest dharma? What kind of life truly pleases the Divine?"**

And so, Shukadeva said with serene eyes:

**"O King, let me tell you of a ruler who conquered not lands, but his own desires — King Ranti Deva."**

He was born in the Ikshvaku dynasty, lineage of Lord Rama. But unlike kings who sought fame or heaven, He only desired **to serve.** He chose the path of **austere renunciation.**

Once, he and his family fasted for **forty-eight days**. Not for penance, not for siddhis, but to feel the hunger of the poor — to live their pain.

At the end, a modest meal was prepared. Just as he sat to eat — emaciated, trembling — a **hungry Brahmin** appeared. Without hesitation, Ranti Deva offered him the first portion.

As he took the next bite, a **shudra**, thirsty and pale, arrived. Ranti Deva handed him water.

Then, a third visitor — a weary **chandala** (outcaste) appeared, with **four hungry dogs** by his side. Without even blinking, Ranti Deva gave away the remaining food.

Now he had **nothing.** No food, no water. Yet his eyes glowed with joy. He folded his hands and whispered:

"I do not desire mukti, nor swarga.
Let me remain where pain exists,
So I may serve and ease the burden of others."

Suddenly, the three visitors transformed — they were none other than **Brahma**, **Vishnu**, and **Shiva**, testing his heart.

And Vishnu blessed him, saying:
**"He who sees God in all beings… becomes God-like himself."**

**Modern-Day Reflection**

Navya leaned back, eyes glowing from the story.

"So… he gave away everything," she said slowly. "Even when he had nothing left."

Manas added, "He didn't need magic or weapons. He had… compassion."

Raghav grinned, "GDP — Great Deer Patrol, huh?"

They all laughed, but in the middle of it, something sacred lingered. No one said it out loud, but it was understood:
Sometimes the **greatest quest** is not about solving ancient puzzles — it's about noticing someone in need, and answering. Quietly.

---

*न कामं कामये राजन् स्वर्गं नापुनर्भवम्।*
*कामं कामामि दुःखानां प्राणिनामार्तिनाशनम्॥*

***Meaning:***
*"I seek not heaven, nor freedom from rebirth.*
*What I desire is to remove the suffering of living beings."*

*(Bhagavatam: Canto 9, Chapter 21, Shloka 12)*

---

# Chapter 35

# MANGOES AND MISCHIEF

**Morning Laughter, Mango Madness**

It had been **many weeks** since they'd reached Simlipal. The mornings had grown into a rhythm — light filtering through sal leaves, birdcalls layered with chatter, and Parag humming tunelessly as he hunted for the best mangoes with Raghav in tow.

"Papa!" Raghav giggled, balancing a sack of fruit over his head, "You're picking the raw ones again!"

Parag blinked innocently. "They're not raw. They're... pre-ripe. Very trendy."

Prisha rolled her eyes from a distance. "It's not a start-up pitch, Papa."

Nearby, Priya was brushing Navya's hair gently. The younger girl had been a little quiet the past couple of days — that kind of silence only parents noticed.

"You okay, Navya?" Priya asked softly.

Navya nodded. "Just... missing them a little more today."

"I know," Priya said. "And they'd be so proud of you. Especially of how you're handling everything."

Navya glanced at Parag and Raghav, pretending to swordfight with mango branches. A smile crept back. "He's weirdly good at this parenting thing."

"He practiced on two wild cubs in the jungle for years," Priya said. "Now it's just a bigger den."

**Gaurav's Family and the Spilled Secrets**

Later in the day, as the sun mellowed into an amber hue, **Gaurav's parents** arrived at the base lodge from a morning trek. Alok, his father, carried an old map scrawled with etchings.

"Looks like tribal geometry," he murmured, eyes focused, "The kind that speaks of movement, not just shape."

Gaurav peeked over his shoulder. "That means... like migration patterns?"

His mother, Sunita, laughed, "More like the way ants decide where to march or the way rivers bend when no one's watching."

As they sat together for a break, Priya joined them, offering tea and banana chips.

Sunita turned to her, eyes kind. "Your daughter... she's got something unusual. The way she speaks of animals — it's like she listens first. That's rare."

Priya smiled. "She was born among them. Her first lullabies were owl calls and monkey chatter."

Gaurav leaned into the firelight. "She said once that a deer blinked in her direction three times — like it was talking."

"She probably wasn't wrong," Priya whispered, her voice trailing like smoke.

### Mango Heists and Yashoda Jokes

That evening, a sleepy chaos had descended after dinner. Raghav was on a mission to sneak an extra mango — again. He tiptoed towards the fruit basket when Manas caught him red-handed.

"Don't eat all the mangoes," Manas whispered, "or I'll tell Yashoda Ma."

Raghav paused dramatically, stuffing the slice in his mouth. "Oops. Too late."

"You're not Krishna," Navya snorted.

"Nope. I'm better. Krishna had cows. I have you people."

They all broke into laughter, tumbling over pillows and empty bowls.

### Bhagwatam Parallel | Krishna's Butter Heist – A Bedtime Tale

Priya walked in just then with a mischievous glint in her eye. "Talking about mango thieves, are we?"

She sat cross-legged, gesturing them to come closer. "Let me tell you about the boy who stole butter with the same pride Raghav steals mangoes."

And so, under flickering lantern light, the **Krishna leela** began.

"There was once a village — Gokul. A muddy, musical hamlet where cows mooed and flutes sang. And in one small house lived a boy so sweet, so naughty, that the gopis had to hide butter in rafters."

"Krishna would gather his monkey army, stack wooden pots, and climb like a cat on sugar. He'd knock down the clay pots and share the loot."

"One day, Yashoda caught him — cheeks full of butter, fingers covered in cream."

She chased him through cow sheds and gardens, finally cornering him under a tree. "But when she raised her hand... she looked into his eyes and saw something more. Not a boy. Not a thief. The whole world."

"And in return, he just smiled... and offered her the last dollop of butter."

**Modern Time Parallel**

As the laughter faded and yawns took over, Prisha whispered, "You know... Krishna never kept the butter for himself."

Navya nodded, eyes half-shut. "He always shared it with everyone... even the monkeys."

Raghav stretched like a lazy lion. "Joy's not in hoarding... it's in the stealing— I mean— sharing."

Manas chuckled. "In today's world, we chase so much — likes, grades, stuff. Maybe all we need is to share mangoes and stories."

Priya smiled from the corner, watching them. In that moment, the message of Bhagavatam felt simple and true — happiness multiplies when passed around.

---

दृष्ट्वा तं मातुः प्रणयमयीं ईक्षां विलासात्
शङ्कास्पदं दृष्टमतिकरुणां श्रीव्रजाध्यक्षपुत्रम्

*Meaning:*

***"Seeing the playful yet loving glance of his mother, Krishna stood like a boy caught in mischief. Yet in her gaze, he found only deep affection — not fear, not anger. Just love."***

*(Shrimad Bhagavatam: Canto 10, Chapter 8, Shloka 32)*

---

# Chapter 36

# WHISTLES, WONDERS & GOVARDHAN'S GRACE

**Cricket, Cartwheels & Kohli**

Unaware that Meera and Ayan had not been seen for over twenty-four hours, the children spent the morning wrapped in sun and laughter behind the cottages. The world outside might have been quietly shifting, but in their clearing, the only thing that mattered was the game.

A makeshift pitch had been set—a fallen tree trunk for the wicket, a taped-up ball, and limitless enthusiasm. Raghav, in his full GDP avatar, stood like a sportscaster. "Ladies and Gentlemen, presenting the grand finale of the Simlipal Champions League! Will Manas hit a six, or will Gaurav's underarm wizardry get him out?"

Manas smirked and swung—a clean hit!
But just as the ball soared, Gaurav dashed, caught it mid-air, and tumbled into a bush. The crowd went wild.

"Whaaat a catch!" Raghav shouted. "That's one for the history books!"

Later, everyone crowded around the TV, cheering as Kohli faced a nail-biting over in the India match. Priya clapped the loudest, yelling, "Come on, Kohli! Show them who rules!"

Parag, half-asleep, muttered, "Every time I sit down, someone's screaming. I demand earplugs."

**Splash & Serve**

By mid-morning, the group moved to the edge of a crystal-clear forest lake. A net had been stretched across the sands.

"Volleyball time!" Navya called.

Manas dived with dramatic flair. Navya spiked. Raghav missed entirely and blamed the wind. Gaurav just laughed.

Even Parag tried once, tumbling with a comic 'thud' that had the kids rolling in laughter.

"I've officially retired from national-level gymnastics," he announced.

Later, the kids cartwheeled in the shallows. Mango peels floated on the water. The sun above was kind, and the wind whispered joy.

**Temple Bells & Twilight**

As twilight deepened, the families walked to a small Shiva temple nestled beneath twin peepal trees. A tiled path, half-lost in moss, led them in.

Manas rang the bell. Its echo cut clean through the forest hush.

They offered bilva leaves, lit diyas, and knelt together.

"ॐ नमः शिवाय," they chanted softly. The mantra wove around the trees like an invisible thread.

Parag whispered to the kids, "This is the heart of Sanatan — not just temples, but quiet moments, shared prayers, and nature's rhythm."

The priest blessed them with a warm tilak and smiled, "Bhagwan sab dekh rahe hain."

**Bedtime Story — Bhagwatam Parallel | Krishna and the Govardhan Hill**

Back in the cottage, the night deepened. Fireflies blinked through the window as Priya gathered the children.

"Today, I'll tell you one of my favourite stories," she said. "The day Krishna lifted a mountain."

The kids gasped.

In the sweet land of **Vrindavan**, nestled amidst forests and hills, the villagers of Gokul once prepared for the grand annual **Indra Yagna** — a festival to appease the rain god, **Indra**, so their fields may flourish.

Krishna, only a boy of seven, tilted his head curiously as he saw the preparations.

"Why do we worship Indra?" he asked Nanda Baba.

Nanda explained that Indra, the king of heaven, sent the rains, and without him, their cows and crops would perish.

Krishna's eyes sparkled with deeper wisdom. "Shouldn't we rather worship **Govardhan Hill**? It gives us grass for the cows, herbs for medicine, and shades us when we're tired. It is *here*, with us. Close. Nurturing."

His words, though simple, stirred truth in their hearts. And so, for the first time, the villagers of Vrindavan offered their food, music, and hearts to **Govardhan Parvat.**

But up in the heavens, Indra thundered in fury.

"How dare they forsake me?" he roared. "This Krishna! He's just a child!"

Blinded by pride, Indra sent monstrous black clouds to drown Vrindavan. Torrential rain lashed the land. Winds tore through huts. The Yamuna swelled in wrath.

The villagers panicked. Cows mooed helplessly. Children cried.

Krishna simply smiled.

He walked to Govardhan and, with his tiny hand, **lifted the massive hill like an umbrella**, holding it aloft on his **little finger**.

"Come!" he called out. "Take shelter beneath Govardhan!"

Men, women, children, cows — the whole of Vrindavan gathered under the divine canopy. For **seven days and seven nights**, Krishna stood firm, without flinching, holding the hill aloft like a blooming lotus.

The villagers sang songs. Gopis brought him butter and sweets. Balaram stood proudly beside him.

Seeing this divine feat, **Indra's pride shattered** like thunder in retreat. He descended, humbled, and bowed before Krishna.

"You are no ordinary boy," he admitted. "You are the Supreme. Forgive me."

Krishna forgave him, smiling with the grace of the eternal. "All are my children," he said. "But pride blinds even the gods."

### Modern Day Parallel

Priya smiled as the wind played gently with Navya's curls and Manas tried balancing a mango on his forehead. "Want to know something?" she said, lowering her voice like she was about to share a secret. The kids leaned in.

"There's a Govardhan in everyone's life. Not just a hill… but someone or something that quietly protects us when things go wrong."

Raghav blinked. "Like who?"

"Hmm," Priya said, pretending to think. "Like your father, Parag, who stayed calm when the power went out last week and made everyone laugh in candlelight. Like

Abdul chacha, who waters every sapling even when no one's looking. Or your teachers, who don't just teach you formulas but teach you how to be human."

She paused, letting the silence speak.

"Long ago, people thought only the gods in the sky could protect them. But Krishna showed them that the earth beneath their feet, the hill that gave them shelter, the cow that gave them milk — all deserved love and gratitude."

Navya hugged her knees. "So we should worship nature too?"

"And people," Priya added softly. "Not just the powerful ones. But the silent ones. The ones who lift the world without asking for praise."

Gaurav was quiet. "Like my mom. She doesn't say much, but… when I'm sick, she just knows."

Priya smiled. "That's your Govardhan, beta."

A little hush settled between them. Even the birds had grown quieter, as if listening.

"True joy," she said finally, "is not in hoarding gifts from the sky. It's in honouring the mountains that stand quietly behind you — every single day."

---

एकेन हस्तेन धृतः स पञ्चछैलः
कृष्णेन भक्तेन सतां गतिर्हि।

*Meaning:*

***That very Govardhan—consisting of five hills—was held aloft with one hand by Krishna, the supreme devotee and the ultimate refuge of the virtuous.***

*(Bhagavatam: Canto 10, Chapter 25, Shloka 19)*

---

# Chapter 37

# SHADOWS BENEATH THE CANOPY

**The Checklist**

"Emergency pack, terrain sensors, secondary relay modem… forest ordinance clearance," Anusuya ticked off each item with calm precision, her marker gliding over the whiteboard in her cabin.

"You're sure about this solo route?" Director Khan asked from the doorway, his voice casual, but the crease on his forehead giving him away.

"I've mapped two pockets that the earlier scans didn't cover. Southern quadrant near the old temple ruins. I'll meet Dhanraj at the base. After that, I go alone."

"At least let the Alliance team stay in the loop. In case you run into... anything strange."

"They're already looped in. Kyoto cell has the live heat-signature data. They'll route anomalies straight to us."

Khan studied her for a second, then smirked. "You still trust those fellows?"

"I trust the system. People are unpredictable."

He laughed. "You haven't changed."

She finally looked up, that slight glint in her eyes. "I hope I have. But not in the wrong places."

The tablet on her desk pinged — a new forest log file synced from the Simlipal relay tower. She silenced it without reading. Her eyes were already on the tree line in the distance.

**Alliance Call**

"Zoom's acting up again," muttered Deshmukh, fiddling with the router tucked behind the kettle.

Anusuya ignored him, fingers tapping steadily on the keyboard. The screen showed the header: **ALLIANCE FOR ECO-CULTURAL HERITAGE – INTERNAL SECURE LINK**.

"Try again," she said. "Use the alternate bridge link — the one tagged 'Singapore node.' It's faster."

Deshmukh clicked twice and stepped aside. The feed flickered, then steadied. A tired-looking woman in her late forties appeared on the screen — dark-rimmed glasses, hair in a loose bun, eyes sharp. **Dr. Helena Ortega**, head of the UN Eco-Cultural Alliance, Southeast Asia division.

"Hello, Dr. Anusuya," she greeted with a polite nod. "Your request came through flagged as 'orange-tier urgency'. I'm listening."

Anusuya took a deep breath.

"We've intercepted ancient symbols recently — eight-leaf variants — appearing in southern Simlipal. Similar to the ones we discussed last year for Kyoto. Only now… they're showing up in living formations. Rooted. Breathing."

Helena raised an eyebrow. "Rooted?"

"Yes. Organic patterns, fractal symmetry. We've documented at least two locations so far. One of our research units is in the field. I leave tomorrow."

"What are you expecting to find?"

"I don't know," Anusuya said frankly. "But whatever it is… the resonance is too old, too intentional. I thought the Alliance should know."

Helena hesitated. "Are you suggesting it's linked to the **'Amsa Codex'** theory?"

Anusuya didn't blink. "I'm not denying the possibility anymore."

Silence.

Then Helena spoke, slow and measured. "I'll notify Haifa also. We'll keep a silent watch. But you're on your own for now."

"I expected that," Anusuya replied. "I just didn't want to be *off the radar*."

Helena nodded. "Be safe. And Anusuya—if you find any signs of coded transmission or **symbolic transfer interfaces**, record them. We're still trying to decode the Cambodia alignments."

Call ended.

Anusuya sat back, exhaled. Then turned to Director Khan, who'd been silent at the corner, arms crossed.

"I'll keep the lines open," he said. "And make sure no press gets a whiff. But if something goes wrong…"

She looked him dead in the eye. "Then we follow the leaf trail anyway."

**The Gap**

Dhanraj tugged off his forest boots and sat on a log, brushing dried mud from the soles. He looked exhausted — like the forest had stolen a few hours of sleep from his eyes.

Anusuya offered him a flask of buttermilk. "Slow down. Just tell me exactly when they left."

"They left three days ago," he said, sipping gratefully. "Headed southeast, past Chamber 3C. Took basic supplies — sat-phone, GPS beacon, food. First two days, I got regular check-ins… one even late at night."

He looked up, suddenly alert. "But since last one day—nothing. No pings, no messages. I've tried their line. Static."

"Do you think they just went out of signal range? Or something else?"

Dhanraj hesitated. "I don't panic. But they've never gone quiet for this long without warning. Not even once."

Anusuya nodded. "We'll go there ourselves. And we'll go prepared."

"Now?"

"Tonight," she said. "We won't announce anything to the families yet. Not unless we're sure something's wrong."

She turned to Dhanraj. "Keep the forest team calm. Tell them they're deep in research. Nothing more."

He nodded, tension tightening around his shoulders.

**The Mango Match**

Meanwhile, back at the resort, the mood was entirely different.

"Out!" Raghav shouted, chasing after the soft tennis ball that had bounced off Manas's shin. "That's LBW! Leg before wicket!"

"It's not cricket without a proper umpire," Manas huffed, hands on his hips.

"Priya Aunty is the umpire," Navya grinned, waving from the garden bench with a bowl of sliced mangoes. "And she's already bribed."

"Only with mangoes," Priya called out playfully. "Which Raghav keeps stealing."

"I'm just checking them for sweetness, Ma!" Raghav teased, munching one and tossing a wink.

Prisha lay on a mat nearby, watching the clouds shift. "This is the first day I've seen all of you relax."

Parag arrived with his arms full of lemon soda bottles. "Everyone needs hydration after six overs of chaos," he announced, "and someone tell me who hit the ball into the neighbor's laundry line!"

Laughter burst out. Even Gaurav was smiling, helping untangle the net they'd fashioned between two tree trunks.

Gaurav's mother, Sunita, watched fondly from under the shade. "He looks happy," she said softly to Priya. "And that's rare these days."

Priya smiled. "He should be. You've raised a brilliant child. You just wait till he teaches Raghav a trick shot in chess later tonight."

The sky above held no omen — just orange streaks of late sunshine, and the sound of someone shouting "Catch!" before a soft thud and another round of cheering.

**Patterns in the Dust**

The sun had sunk low behind the forest ridge, painting the resort lawn in gold and amber. Kids had returned from their cricket match, limbs dusty and laughter echoing through the trees. Some ran straight to the mess hall for water, others flopped dramatically onto the grass as if they'd played a World Cup final.

Gaurav sat near the old pebble fountain, doodling with a stick in the soil. It wasn't unusual — he often drew patterns, spirals, or symmetrical designs. But today's sketch was different. It looked like a half-lotus. Or maybe a wheel. Even he wasn't sure.

Sunita, who had just returned from the kitchen carrying mango slices in a steel bowl, stopped beside him. "Again shapes?" she asked, amused.

He looked up sheepishly. "Just... lines. They come into my head."

Priya, who had stepped out for fresh air, noticed the design. She crouched next to Gaurav, brushing away some loose dust.

"This is familiar," she murmured. "We saw something similar in that stone carving near the waterfall trail, didn't we?"

Gaurav nodded, "Yeah. I didn't copy it, though. It just… happened."

Sunita chuckled, sitting down beside them. "Since he was little, he'd draw circles inside triangles, trees with stars as roots, suns that had eyes. His father says he has the gift of remembering what hasn't been taught."

Priya smiled gently, brushing Gaurav's hair aside. "Sometimes, the forest teaches in silence. It speaks to those who listen quietly."

Just then, Navya and Raghav came running, mango juice dripping from their chins. "Ma!" Navya shouted. "Tell Sunita Aunty what Raghav did — he ate five slices and blamed the crow!"

Priya burst into laughter. "That sounds exactly like something your papa would've done."

Sunita rolled her eyes. "Come inside before ants follow you, little monkeys."

Gaurav, meanwhile, had etched something new. A spiral connecting dots — four small circles around a central sun.

He didn't know why.
But he smiled as the last light touched the stone.

**Memory Beneath the Banyan**

The forest had gone quieter. Anusuya paused near a stream trickling through roots and fallen bark. The trees stood ancient, unmoving, as if watching her. Her phone still blinked *No Signal.* She sat down on a low stone, took a sip from her copper flask, and closed her eyes.

*"Yam yam smarati…"* she whispered.

And suddenly, her mind drifted back to a courtyard in Kashi, decades ago, where her grandmother had once woven magic through words.

**Bhagavatam Parallel | Markandeya and the Child on the Banyan Leaf**

When time itself was swallowed, when worlds had disappeared into silence, one sage remained afloat — **Rishi Markandeya**. He had been granted the boon of witnessing the **pralaya**, the end of an age. The elements had merged into chaos — fire into water, air into void.

Markandeya drifted, alone on the vast cosmic ocean, his soul battered by the force of destruction. Days passed. Or centuries. Time had no meaning.

And then… he saw it.

A child. Sleeping peacefully on a **banyan leaf**, floating on the water. **Dark as the monsoon clouds, glowing with a strange radiance, his feet curled towards his face, and a smile like moonlight dancing on waves.**

Markandeya was pulled closer without moving. He gazed into the child's eyes — and saw **galaxies swirl**, **ages pass**, **avatars rise and fall**. The child opened his mouth — and **Markandeya saw the universe** inside. Planets. Sages. Mountains. Himself. Everything.

And then — stillness.

When he opened his eyes again, the world was restored. The waters had receded. The sky had returned. And the **child was gone**.

That child, he later realized, was none other than **Narayana**, the eternal.

**Modern-Day Parallel | The Child and the Leaf**

Anusuya opened her eyes. A single **peepal leaf** fluttered down beside her.

*This world,* she thought, *is not made to be understood by logic alone.*

Sometimes, in the face of devastation — in wars, in forest fires, in scientific failure, in personal loss — it is the **innocence**, the **calm smile of a child**, that reminds us of what remains after the storm.

The **mystic leaf** is still floating. Maybe in a tribal boy sketching patterns in dust. Or a little girl chanting a shloka she doesn't fully understand. Or even in these four children, who didn't ask to be protectors of Dharma, but are being quietly prepared.

---

बालः क्रीडनकं रूपं बिभ्रद् वटपपत्रकः ।
शयानः पादसव्येन लीलायां लोकचिन्तकः ॥

*Meaning:*

***"There, as a child, resting on a banyan leaf,***
***Holding his foot in play, he lay —***
***And yet in that play, he was the silent thinker of worlds."***

*(Bhagavatam: Canto 12, Chapter 8, Shloka 32)*

---

# Chapter 38

# THE FOREST SHIFTS

**The Path Less Remembered**

*Location: Girls' dorm room, late night — the fan whirring softly, moonlight spilling like secrets on the tiled floor.*

Prisha sat cross-legged on her bed, sketchbook in lap, a pencil twirling between her fingers like it had a mind of its own.

Navya, sprawled upside down on her own bed — head near the floor, legs up on the pillow — tossed a half-eaten guava from hand to hand. "Do you think trees move?"

Prisha looked up, blinking. "Like... walk away at night?" "No," Navya grinned, "like... not legs. But I swear that weird banyan near the trail had a root twisted out like a snake yesterday. Today? Gone."

Prisha chuckled. "Maybe it didn't like you staring at it."

Navya sat up now, hair a mess, face thoughtful. "No, really. Even that bird — the one with the squeaky-swing voice — it didn't come today. Something's... different."

Prisha flipped her sketchbook around. "That's what I was trying to tell you."

She had drawn the forest path they'd taken two evenings ago. But on the same page, faint lines of another trail began to take shape — a fork, a new bend, a circle of trees that she didn't remember seeing but somehow... felt right.

"I didn't walk this path," she said, tapping the page, "but my hand just… drew it." Navya leaned in. "Maybe we're sleepwalking cartographers now."

They both laughed — but not for long.

Prisha, quieter now:
"You ever get that feeling like the forest is—watching?"

Navya nodded. "Yeah. But not in a scary way. More like... I want to dance with their rhythm."

They were silent for a beat.

Then Navya flopped back down dramatically. "Ugh. Too much nature talk. We sound like those podcast hippies."
Prisha giggled. "The kind that say things like 'the leaf chose me'?"
Navya in a faux-wise tone: "Breathe with the bark, sister."

Both burst into laughter.

But the laughter lingered with a question.

**Subtle Shifts**

Morning in Simlipal had never felt this still. Too still.

Raghav sat on the swing at the far end of the lodge's garden, his keyboard unplugged but resting on his lap like a pet owl. He wasn't playing it. Just... tapping one key.
"Sa... Re... Re... Re... Re...?"
His fingers hovered, unsure why the 'Re' felt different today.

Inside, Manas was updating a digital map on his tablet. He'd traced three old forest paths the day before, but now... one of them had vanished.

"Prisha," he called out. "This green trail, the one with the yellow moss patch near the fallen sal tree — it's not showing on today's view."

Prisha walked in barefoot, her trousers streaked with muddy prints. She had just returned from a quick walk from the forest. "No, it's there. I walked it this morning. But... there were new hoof marks. And no birds. None. Not even the mynahs."

Navya stepped in, drying her hair. "A frog came into the bathroom."

Everyone stared at her.

She shrugged. "It knocked over my shampoo. Just saying."

That made them laugh — but only for a moment.

**The Sabbatical Forms**

The resort's study room was quiet that afternoon, sun-dappled and filled with the scratch of pens. Ayaan's form had been submitted days ago. Now, it was Parag and Priya who sat at the thick wooden table, reading through the sabbatical study forms with slow, sure hands.

"I don't want them to feel left behind," Priya said, her voice barely above a whisper.

Parag looked up. "Manas and Navya?"

She nodded. "They are here with us… they've shared the soil, the rains. If our kids leave, it'll feel like something's been uprooted for them."

Parag smiled. "I've seen how Navya looks at Pri. Like a little deer following an older tigress."
"And Raghav," Priya added, "he's the only one Manas lets adjust his drone settings."

They both chuckled. And then Priya said what had been sitting in her chest for a while.

Parag just handed her the pen. "Let's write the reason as 'environmental immersion and joint family research extension.' That'll keep Bhargava sir and Asha Ma'am happy."

She signed with a quiet laugh. "And let's call it what it really is — *love*."

**The Shifting Grove**

Anusuya paused.
It wasn't hesitation. It was… memory.

This trail hadn't been here before. She was certain. The banyan roots curled differently now—like they had tiptoed sideways in the night. Even the slope of the ground had changed, gentler somehow, nudging her towards the east.

She bent down, pressed two fingers against the soil. Still damp. Still warm. Still whispering.

"Forest speaks to those who listen silently," she murmured, almost without realizing.

A sudden crack of twigs behind her made her start. Turning, she was surprised to see Bakshi—boots muddied, cap askew, breathless from the walk.

"Bakshi? What are you doing here?" she asked, genuinely surprised.

He caught his breath. "Heard a report from one of the rangers—someone spotted a wounded Bengal tiger not far from this trail. I came straight from the sanctuary to check it out. Didn't expect to find you out here."

She straightened. "No, this path was a dead end yesterday. Today it bends."

Bakshi frowned, glancing at the roots. "You think it's shifting?"

"I think," she said softly, "it's revealing."

Bakshi looked unconvinced. "Animals don't move rocks."

Anusuya smiled. "But nature moves us."

There was a silence, earthy and echoing.

Then Bakshi added, almost as an afterthought, "Signal tower's been acting strange. The ranger reported jamming. No GPS lock for the past twelve hours."

Anusuya turned to face him fully. "You didn't mention this before."

"Didn't want to worry anyone," he admitted. "Could be weather, solar interference, monkeys chewing wires… or maybe just this tiger drama."

"Or," she said, "someone who doesn't want to be found."

The words hung like dew—heavy but glinting.

Bakshi gave a short nod. "I'll get the backup frequency tested."

She nodded back, then turned and stepped further into the woods. The roots no longer curled sideways—they had formed an arch, like an ancient doorway.

She didn't need to say it aloud. The forest was watching.

**A Quiet Notebook — Clues Return**

Prisha sat curled in the study room, flipping through a thick, hardbound journal. It wasn't even labelled properly — just "Wildlife Index, 2020" scribbled in Meera Agrawal's familiar slant. It's the same journal that Meera left with Priya before going to the forest.

She wasn't searching for anything. Not consciously. But then, tucked between pages on butterfly species, a folded sheet fluttered out.

Prisha opened it. Her breath caught.
It was a **map**.

Not the regular one Meera used for their eco-trails. This had extra ink—faint **dotted lines**, **tiny circles**, and what looked like coordinates scribbled in the margin. Some paths had question marks. Others were underlined twice.

She traced one loop with her finger. "Why does this feel like something we missed?"

Just then, a thump broke her focus.

Raghav had walked in, a plate of chopped mangoes balanced on one hand, and a flute tucked under his arm. "Treasure hunting again?" he grinned, placing the plate down.

Prisha didn't respond immediately. She kept staring at the map.

Raghav sat across her. "Prish?"

She finally looked up, eyes darker than usual. "I think… maybe something was left unfinished. Something Meera Aunty didn't get time to complete."

Raghav glanced at the sheet. Then back at her. "Want to ask Dad?"

She shook her head slowly. "Not yet. Not till we understand what this even is."

Outside the window, a crow called thrice. Short. Shrill. Oddly rhythmic.

Raghav narrowed his eyes. "That's not how they usually sound."

Prisha didn't answer. Her finger was now resting on a point marked **'Kalya Tala Path – loop returns'**.

"Loop returns…" she whispered. "That sounds… like a clue."

### A Message from Pulkit

*Somewhere in Simlipal Forest, Nightfall*

Anusuya sat in her tent that night. Dhanraj was keeping a sharp watch outside, her boots still dusty from the forest, a half-empty thermos of tulsi tea beside her. She had just finished syncing the trail camera footage when the laptop screen blinked with an encrypted message.

It was from Pulkit.

**"Leaving now. Keep them unaware for now. Forest has started its own song."**

She stared at it for a long moment. The cursor blinked.

Her fingers moved slowly across the keyboard as she typed back:

**"Understood. They don't know it's a song yet."**

She leaned back. The forest outside rustled in the dark — not with fear, but with a rhythm older than words.

She whispered, almost to herself,

"It's not music. It's movement. Patterns. Breath. The wind changing course… roots shifting… creatures avoiding paths they once trusted. That's the song. Nature has its own warning system."

She turned to the old map pinned beside her — trails marked years ago, now subtly blurred by new lines.

"And only those who listen… will hear it begin."

## "Enough Waiting"

A quiet bonfire crackled in the background. The stars blinked wide as if leaning closer to listen.

Manas tossed a twig into the fire. "So... we're all pretending nothing weird is happening?"

Navya raised an eyebrow. "You mean aside from birds flying in loops, maps with secret marks, and trees that forget their positions?"

Raghav exhaled through his nose. "And me composing ragas in my sleep. Totally normal."

Prisha sat cross-legged, silent. Then softly:

"Maybe it's not about *one* big mystery. Maybe it's a hundred tiny ones — like fireflies. Alone, they flicker. But together... they light a path."

There was a pause. The fire popped.

Manas leaned forward. "So what do we do?"

Navya answered, "We follow the glow."

Raghav grinned. "Operation GDP. But this time, it's '**Great Discovery Period**.'"

They laughed — not loudly, but with that strange, thrilling stillness that only friends and forests understand.

Prisha slowly opened Meera's old journal again — the one she'd been poring over earlier that day. Her finger paused over the same faded, dotted lines.

She looked up, voice calm but certain.
**"We start here. Very soon. Kalya Tala Path.**
Maybe... an auspicious rhythm-path is waiting for us."

### Bhagavatam Parallel | The Tale of Ashwatthama's Rage and Draupadi's Forgiveness

That night, four kids and Gaurav were reading together -

The battlefield of Kurukshetra was soaked not just in blood, but in silence. The Great War had ended. The Kauravas had fallen. Dharma had won — but at a heavy price.

As the Pandavas mourned their fallen, a single act shattered even the hard-won peace — **Ashwatthama**, son of Dronacharya, enraged by his father's death, stole into the Pandava camp under the cover of night.

He did not raise his sword against warriors.

He crept into the tents where **Draupadi's five sons** slept — sons born of each of the five Pandavas — the hope of the future.
And there, like a shadow, he slew them all.

The next morning, when Draupadi beheld her lifeless children — their soft brows pierced, their dreams stolen — she wailed, not just as a queen, but as a mother.

### The Trial of Forgiveness

Arjuna, righteous and wrathful, chased Ashwatthama down. With Krishna as his charioteer, he caught him like a storm swallowing a spark.

He dragged him back to camp — to Draupadi. To justice.

Bhima thundered, "Kill him! Let the sword speak now!"

But Draupadi — eyes swollen, heart shattered — stepped forward...
And *did not demand blood.*

She folded her hands and said:

**"He is the son of our guru — Dronacharya — who once taught you all. I cannot bear the thought that my sorrow becomes his mother's sorrow."**

A gasp rippled through the camp.

Even Arjuna hesitated.

Krishna watched in silence — the test of dharma unfolding not in war, but in the wounded quiet that comes after.

Arjuna then made a choice.
He did not raise his sword.
Instead, he **cut the jewel** from Ashwatthama's forehead — the divine gem that gave him strength, pride, and immortality. He **banished** him from all kingdoms, cursed to wander with the weight of his karma.

Justice was done. But vengeance — that fire — was left unlit.

### Modern Day Parallel | A Quiet Resolve

Back in Simlipal, the children were no longer just curious minds. They were hearts shaken by fragments — the broken disc, the echoes in the forest, the strange silence from the station, the shifting trail.

A part of them wanted to rush. To storm into the woods.
To question, confront, accuse.
But they chose otherwise.

They chose to *wait few more night.*

To plan together.
To watch the rhythm of the forest like Arjuna once watched Draupadi's face before making his choice.

They weren't heroes seeking glory.
They were friends learning something deeper — **that action, without wisdom, becomes harm.**

Sometimes the right path is not paved with reaction, but with reflection.

Their whispering resolve was not unlike Draupadi's tearful restraint.
Their unity — like the Pandavas' patience.
Their silence — like Krishna's eyes.

---

शान्तस्य च प्रसन्नस्य, ज्ञानं स्यान्नात्यहिंसकः ।
वैराग्येण समायुक्तो, धर्ममेवाचरेत्सदा ॥

*Meaning:*

***One who is peaceful, joyful, and non-violent — one who is balanced and detached — walks always in the light of dharma, with true wisdom***

*(Bhagavatam: Canto 11, Chapter 19, Shloka 36)*

---

# Chapter 39

# WHAT THE FOREST WHISPERS LAST

**The Email Confirmation**

The tablet pinged with a cheerful chime.

"Please let it be good news," Raghav muttered, diving for it like a fielder saving a boundary.

He tapped it open — and the screen bloomed with the emblem of **Saraswati Valley Academy**.

*Subject: Sabbatical Approval – Final Confirmation*

*Dear Mr. and Mrs. Jain,*

*We are pleased to inform you that the sabbatical education request for your children, **Prisha Jain** and **Raghav Jain**, has been formally approved for the upcoming term. They may continue their integrated curriculum under the guidance of designated mentors, including facilitators from the affiliated Foundations.*

Raghav leapt up and high-fived the nearest soul, which happened to be Manas, still half-asleep.

"Confirmed!" he announced. "We're forest scholars now!"

Prisha grinned. "That means no return ticket for now."

Navya hugged her. "Now it feels complete."

Priya stepped in from the kitchen, drying her hands on her dupatta, overhearing the excitement. "The school finally realised what we already knew."

Raghav tilted his head. "Which is?"

"That you don't learn everything from textbooks," Priya smiled. "Sometimes the forest is the finest teacher."

Just then, **Gaurav entered with his sketchbook tucked under his arm**, a nervous look on his face.

"Hey…" he started, "I tried something. You know, the path from Meera Aunty's journal — the dotted spiral and all?"

Manas lit up. "Did you sketch it?"

"Sort of," Gaurav replied, flipping open the sketchbook. "I mean… I don't know if it's accurate. I'm not a professional or anything. But I followed the symbols, the curve sequences, and terrain hints."

Earlier that morning, the **four kids had asked him** for help.

Navya had said, "You see things others miss, Gaurav. Just try to give it shape."

Now, as he laid the pages on the table, the entire group leaned in. What stared back at them was a hand-drawn map — part terrain, part intuition. **The Kalya Tala Path**, traced with precision, care, and a little artistic courage. At the bottom corner, Gaurav had scribbled in tiny handwriting:

"Possibly trident-shaped zone. East-facing. Water stream nearby."

Prisha's eyes widened. "You actually decoded it."

Gaurav shook his head. "Not decoded. Just... tried to listen. Shapes speak sometimes."

Raghav clapped his back. "Dude, this is proper mapmaker-level stuff."

Manas was already photographing it. "We're laminating this in the memory vault of GDP."

Prisha held the sketch up against the light. "We'll use this," she said quietly. "You may not believe in it yet, Gaurav — but we do."

Gaurav gave a half-smile, still unsure. "I just hope it doesn't send you into a ditch."

Navya winked. "Even if it does, we'll make the ditch famous."

They all laughed — the kind of laugh that only happens before something changes forever.

**Something Is Calling**

The afternoon light slanted across the forest, golden and calm. But Prisha felt it — that quiet shift in the wind. Not fear. Not even urgency. Just... attention. As if the trees had turned ever so slightly to watch her.

She wasn't alone.

Manas, Navya, and Raghav had followed her instinctively down the slope — no map this time, just a tug in the chest. The mossy path curled like a question mark.

"What are we looking for?" Manas asked, adjusting his specs.

"Nothing specific," Prisha replied. "And maybe... everything."

Just ahead, the trail opened into a clearing. In the middle, a **cluster of broken leaves** arranged in a near-perfect spiral — as if they'd been swept by hand.

Raghav knelt beside them, tracing the pattern.

"Wind didn't do this," he said softly. "Too neat. Too deliberate."

Navya noticed a **tree nearby — its bark freshly scratched**, not in jagged lines but **symbols**, half-formed. "That's not an animal claw," she whispered.

Then came the sound — **not a voice**, but something older. Like **a low hum woven through the forest floor**, crawling up from the roots, reaching only those who would listen.

Raghav turned slowly. "You heard that too?"

"Felt it," Navya said, hand on her chest.

They stood still. The breeze passed through them like a breath held and released.

"Let's not tell the grown-ups yet," Prisha murmured. "But I think it's time."

"To do what?" Manas asked.

She looked at each of them. "To begin."

**The Vow**

Back at Echo's command center, Anusuya had returned for a day.

She stood beside Pulkit in a room dimly lit by multiple screens — security footage, satellite scans, and reports from allies. Location showed a strange electromagnetic dip at forested coordinates. Echo branches across the globe were murmuring.

Director Khan folded his hands and said, "We don't yet know what it is. But the anomalies follow the same pulse rhythm — every twelve days, there's a silence."

Pulkit spoke softly, "Like an exhale before something speaks."

Khan looked from Anusuya to Pulkit. "We need to watch over them now. These children are more than explorers. They may be the reason these locations are waking up again."

Pulkit said nothing for a moment.

Then he placed one hand over the old codex lying between them. "We won't let anything reach them without going through us first."

Anusuya nodded. "Even if they don't know it yet… they are connected."

What they didn't know… was that the children wouldn't wait.

**The Silence Between Signals**

The lamps had dimmed early that evening. The resort's corridors lay unusually still, like the forest was holding its breath.

Raghav sat near the window, his notebook open but untouched. The raga he'd been humming all day had faded from his throat hours ago.

Prisha entered quietly, carrying two steaming cups of turmeric milk. She didn't speak — just placed one beside him and sat cross-legged on the rug.

He finally looked up.
"Didn't they say they'd return to base yesterday?"

Navya nodded slowly. "They always send a message. A picture. Something."

Silence stretched between them like a gathering mist.

"Maybe they're still deep in the forest," she said, her voice thinner than usual. "Maybe the signal's just bad."

Raghav didn't reply. His fingers resting quietly beside his journal.

Outside, the wind stirred the mango trees, and somewhere in the distance, a bird sang a call they couldn't name.

**The Voice in the Night**

That night, Navya tossed in her sleep. The wind outside had changed — softer, curling like incense smoke.

In her dream, she was standing beside a river. A woman, clothed in white, smiled at her. Her arms held a basket of mangoes, just like her mother used to bring.

But her voice… was not of this earth.

*"What you buried in fear, child… must now be found in faith. The disc is not a danger. It is a beacon. And shadows are learning how to chase light."*

Navya reached for the woman, but she dissolved into a trail of peacock feathers.

She woke with a gasp.

"Manas," she whispered across the room.

He turned, half-asleep. "Hmm?"

"We have to dig it up. Now."

### The Bhagavatam Parallel | Parikshit in the Womb

Kids and their parents are at dining table, waiting for dinner to be served. Gaurav leaning towards Parag. "Uncle… is it really possible to protect someone… without them even knowing?"

Parag smiled faintly. "Yes, Gaurav. Once, the entire future was protected before it took its first breath."

All ears started listening attentively. He began —

"After the Mahabharata war, the five sons of Draupadi were killed in their sleep by Ashwatthama — a blow meant to end the Pandava legacy.

But one life remained — unborn.

Inside the womb of Uttara, Abhimanyu's widow, lived a child — the last thread of that great lineage.

In fury, Ashwatthama hurled the terrifying **Brahmashira astra**, aimed straight at the unborn child.

Uttara cried to Krishna for help — not for herself, but for her baby. And Krishna, the protector of dharma, did not speak. He entered her womb silently… and shielded the child with his divine form."

Then came the verse:

---

*पाहि मामच्युत धर्मज्ञ देवदेव जगत्पते ।*
*गर्भं मां पालयस्वेदं बालं तेऽद्यमुपस्थितम् ॥*

*Meaning:*

***"Save me, O Krishna — knower of dharma, Lord of lords. Protect the child within me who now turns to You."***

*(Bhagwatam: Canto 1, Chapter 8, Shloka 9)*

---

"That child was born unharmed. He was named **Parikshit** — the one who saw the divine even before his birth.

And it was he who later heard the **entire Shrimad Bhagavatam**, from sage Shukadeva, carrying the torch of dharma into a new age."

**Modern Day Parallel**

Parag paused.

"Sometimes, Kids, ancient darkness tries to destroy the future...

But something older, wiser — and kinder — quietly steps in."

Gaurav said nothing. He simply returned to his map of Kalya Tala Path, pencil trembling slightly.

# Chapter 40

# LETTERS NOT WRITTEN

**Childhood Echoes — Meera**

Long before the forest knew her footsteps, Meera was a quiet girl in an even quieter town near Almora. Her grandmother whispered to wild marigolds and dandelions growing by the stone steps. "Every plant listens," she would say, "especially the ones that bloom in silence."

At eight, Meera could identify forest fungi by their undercap textures.

At ten, she wrote a school essay titled *"If Leaves Could Teach"* — and the principal, confused yet charmed, pinned it on the staff noticeboard.

She passed her 12th board exams from a convent school nestled in Nainital's drifting mist. Later, she graduated with honors in **Botany from Miranda House, Delhi University**, a college known as much for its intellect as for its ivy-covered walls.

She then pursued her Master's in **Plant Taxonomy from the Indian Institute of Science (IISc), Bengaluru**, where she co-authored a paper on Himalayan rhizomes and their Ayurvedic potential.

Her **doctorate came from Kyoto University, Japan**, where she studied ancient Asian plant classification systems — especially those found in forest monasteries and old herbal scriptures.

The forest wasn't just her subject. It was her first language.

**Ayan's Rooted Wisdom**

Ayan Agrawal wasn't born with a microscope in his hand —
but with soil under his nails and salt in his breath.

He grew up in **Sindhudurg**, along the mossy Konkan coast, where coconut palms leaned like old monks and river crabs taught patience. At **New Era Gurukul**, a quiet school nestled near the Western Ghats, his notebooks were often speckled with dried wildflowers. He once spent a week trying to germinate a sea bean he found near the estuary — just to see if it could grow far from the tides.

His graduation years at **Fergusson College in Pune** gave him the language to name what he already loved. He walked through botanical gardens like they were temples. His professors noted how he often disappeared into the Western Ghats for "unauthorized field trips," always returning with rare leaves and rarer metaphors.

A master's in **Plant Ecology from Goa University** followed, where monsoons became his greatest teacher. He mapped how mangroves held the coast like a mother holds a trembling child — gently, yet with unshakable strength.

But it was **at Forest Research Institute, Dehradun**, while pursuing his PhD in **Ethnobotany**, that science and Sanatan came together for him. Manuscripts from centuries past spoke of plants not just as specimens, but as memory bearers, healers, and witnesses. In forgotten temple scrolls and Bhil oral songs, he found patterns—ancient relationships between humans and the flora they worshipped, feared, and trusted.

Ayan never chased discovery.
He followed the whisper of roots.

### The First Meeting — Himalayan Confluence

They met beneath the shadow of Kedar, at a field conference for rare alpine herbs. Meera was sketching a snow-fruit unknown to taxonomy. Ayan was humming a forgotten chhanda from the *Rigveda* under his breath, brushing frost off a fern.

"Do you always speak to plants?" she asked.

"Only when they've earned it," he grinned.

That was the beginning of laughter, of debates over roots and rituals, of walking maps instead of drawing them. The Himalayas had introduced two trees that would one day entwine.

### Sanatan, Not Scientific — Their Common Ground

As their research deepened, so did their questions. Why did *vriksha ayurveda* know things modern journals didn't? Why were certain plants listed in ancient texts with planetary patterns?

Together, they began to decode the *Nighantus* (ancient botanical lexicons) with reverence, not skepticism.

Meera once whispered, "Maybe our future hides in the past's footnotes."

Ayan nodded. "Then let's read those footnotes aloud."

### *The Secret That Shifted Everything*

It was a quiet night in Shillong. Meera and Ayan, on a field trip tracing medicinal fungi through the eastern hills, stayed in an old British guesthouse, its wooden walls creaking with forgotten stories.

That evening, a woman arrived unannounced. She introduced herself as **"Kiran."**

She claimed to represent a lineage of forest scholars who had protected sacred botanical knowledge since before recorded history — including fragments of a nearly mythical text: the **Asma Codex**.

On the table, she laid a palm-leaf scroll—aged and fragile, with torn edges and portions missing, as if time itself had tried to erase its story. What remained was carefully preserved, bound in faded cloth and tied with string. Faint Brahmi letters traced the surface, curling around a spiral script that even Ayan couldn't identify. At the bottom, in the slanting lamplight, a symbol shimmered through the cracks: **three curled leaves—Trikaal Beeja**.

"You've studied what grows above," she said softly. "Now begin mapping what sleeps below."

She handed them a hand-drawn map and a sealed wooden vial.

"Wait for the call from the Eastern Vale," she whispered. "That's when your true path will open."

They exchanged a long glance. No promises were spoken aloud. But that night, they opened a new field notebook — and on the first page, Meera titled it simply:

**"Asma Codex: Tracing the First Roots."**

It was not the birth of the Codex itself, but it was the **beginning of their journey into it.**

And from that moment on, their path would no longer follow the old forest trails.

It would carve new ones.

### A Message Never Sent, But Forever Felt

Now, deep in Simlipal, somewhere under a canopy so thick even moonlight trembled, they sat—a small fire flickering, notebooks half-filled, eyes rimmed with fatigue but still sharp.

The satellite device blinked red. No signal. Again.

Meera sighed, rolling her stiff shoulders. "Not today, it seems."

Ayan rubbed the back of his neck, worry lines creasing his brow, but his voice remained steady. "We're not lost yet. We know this forest better than most."

There was fear between them—the unknown, the silence beyond the trees, the weight of being cut off. But it was met with quiet determination. Even scared, they leaned into each other and into hope.

Meera touched Ayan's arm, steady now. "Maybe… we send something else."

They closed their eyes, not in defeat, but in resolve—choosing, even in darkness, to hold on to courage.

**The Message in the Roots**

Under the sprawling arms of an ancient banyan, the air hung heavy—not just with moisture, but with unspoken tension.

Meera touched the bark, her palm steady though her breath was tight. Ayan stood beside her, scanning the trees as if the shadows themselves might shift.

"No signal," he muttered. "Nothing at all."

"We don't need one," Meera whispered. "Let the forest carry it."

From her satchel, she pulled out two things: a copper stylus—simple, old—and a small, weathered stone. The stone was cool and oddly heavy, its surface marked not by any chisel, but by nature's hand: a faint triangle at the center, with lines radiating like flame. Moss clung to its edges, and in the lamplight, the shapes seemed to flicker.

Ayan took the stylus and, without a word, began pressing rhythmic dots and lines into the softened bark—a language not typed, not spoken, but remembered.

When they finished, Meera knelt and gently placed the stone into a shallow hollow among the banyan's roots. Together, they covered it with fresh earth and a handful of leaves, as if tucking away a part of themselves for the future.

"Like Dr. J. C. Bose said," Meera murmured, voice almost a breath, "plants remember."

She looked at the quiet roots curling below. "A pioneer who worked silently on the Asma Codex… decoding what was unknown."

The banyan leaves rustled above, though the air was still.

One last tap. One last breath.

"They'll know when the time is right," Ayan said softly.

And so, their message was hidden—not in circuits or satellites, but in the living memory of the trees, and in the secret of an ancient stone waiting to be found.

**The Forest Remembers**

*They stood together beneath the towering sal tree — silent, breath held.*
No camera.
No pen.
Just two fingertips on a curling leaf.
Ayan whispered, "It's time."

They had encoded many things before — simple leaf vibrations, temperature shifts, even light pulses. But this was different.

**This was a message for their children.**

They closed their eyes.

"Navya… Manas…"
"If this memory reaches you, it means the forest has accepted your presence."

The sal tree's bark twitched — almost unseen — as if something ancient passed through it.

"We chose this path not out of escape… but responsibility. Some truths are buried too deep for words or warnings."

"The world may not remember the old ways. But you must."

"Your journey will begin where ours… turned."

A pause. The wind shifted.

"Not all roots are visible. Not all maps are drawn."

"When you reach the Kalya Tala Path, listen. The forest will speak again."

And with that, the moment passed.
The bark smoothed. The leaves fell still.

They looked at each other — weary, proud, unbroken.
This was **not goodbye.**
This was **legacy**, pressed gently into green veins.

***Bhagavatam Parallel — A Silence Instead of a Story***

Today, there is no one to tell the story.

The wind moves, but carries no words.
The forest listens, but no verses are recited.

The Bhagavatam rests in its eternal quietude—
because the ones who carried its flame
are now somewhere beyond pages and ink.

And yet… its essence lingers.

Not in speech. Not in memory.
But in something older than both—

And in that spirit, as if whispered through the *asma* that binds all living things, comes this closing verse—

---

यं प्रव्रजन्तमनुपेतमपेतकृत्यं द्वैपायनो विरहकातर आजुहाव ।
पुत्रेति तन्मयतया तरवोऽभिनेदुः तं सर्वभूतहृदयं मुनिमानतोऽस्मि ॥

*Meaning:*

***When the great sage Śukadeva left home without performing any final duties,***
***his father Vyasa, overwhelmed with sorrow, cried out after him, "O my son!"***
***The trees themselves wept, echoing his grief.***
***I bow down to that sage—who is the heart of all living beings.***

---

# SECTION FIVE

# JOURNEY THROUGH THE SELF

## Chapter 41

## THE FLAME REMEMBERS

**Ashes Beneath the Peepal**

*Year: 1893 | Location: Saraswati Vidyapeeth, Dehradun*

The morning after the fire, a hush had fallen over the ancient compound. Soot clung to the air like unfinished sentences. The eastern wing — once a treasury of silence and stirred.

A boy. Barefoot. Ten years old.
**Shrutaya.**

He knelt in the mud, his fingers tracing a triangle with a small flame at its center. The mural may have turned to ash, but the memory had not.

From behind him, Acharya Divyavarna approached slowly, his robes the colour of fading sunlight.

"You saw too much," the Acharya said gently.

"I didn't see everything," Shrutaya replied. "But I heard… everything."

There was no fear in his voice, only a calm that didn't belong to a child.

The Acharya looked down at the drawing. "Then listen to me one last time. The disc is not a sacred thing. It is just a memory. It must be carried. It must be forgotten—until it is needed."

Shrutaya nodded. He unwrapped a thin bundle of oil cloth from his shoulder bag. Inside lay the disc—neither fully bronze nor entirely stone, its color and texture shifting with the light. It felt unexpectedly heavy for its size, sometimes cold as river pebbles, sometimes carrying a strange, living warmth. Along the rim, faint grooves and shadows hinted at ancient etchings, but nothing could be clearly seen or read—just the suggestion of secrets worn by time. At the center, a triangle seemed to linger—neither burning nor carved, but present all the same, holding its silence like a question waiting for an answer.

Acharya Divyavarna placed his hand on the boy's shoulder.
"Go east. Walk until the sky changes and the leaves begin to speak. There, the forest will welcome you. You will know when the time has come to teach what you remember."

Without another word, **Shrutaya** rose.
No ceremony. No farewell.
Only the soft brush of feet against earth — beginning the long, barefoot journey from Dehradun to Simlipal… nearly **1,200 kilometers** across an undivided India.

And so, the boy walked —
Through storms that swallowed roads,
Across rivers swollen with secrets,
Sleeping under banyans, speaking to owls,
Guided not by maps… but by instinct.

The forest had already begun whispering back.

### The First Flame

**Location**: Simlipal Forest | A few weeks after Shrutaya's departure from Saraswati Vidyapeeth

The monsoon had settled gently over Simlipal. Mists wrapped the canopy like old silk, and the soil whispered secrets with each barefoot step.

**Shrutaya** had walked for weeks, alone, barefoot, across a land that felt both ancient and watching. Over 1,200 kilometers from Dehradun to the forests of Odisha — past forgotten temples, charred milestones, and riverbanks that remembered stories even men had forgotten. His feet bled. His body ached. But the disc, warm in his satchel, guided him — not with words, but a rhythm in his bones.

At dusk, in a glade hidden by sal trees and basil vines, he finally stopped.

He knelt.
The disc — wrapped in dried banyan leaves and held by sacred thread — pulsed faintly, as if exhaling.

With trembling fingers, he placed it in the soil. Around it, he laid five small stones, each etched with a mark he remembered from the old mural — a spiral, a flame, a crescent, a dot, and finally a triangle. Not a shrine. A memory. A silent code.

Then he struck two stones. A small spark caught on dry neem bark. A flame rose.

And he whispered:

**कायमनसा यः संरक्षति यावत् जीवनं सत्यमागति**

**मौनेन धारयति विश्वज्ञानम् यत्र यात्रा तत्र वह्निज्ञानम् ॥**

*"May body and mind protect the sacred,*
*Until truth arrives with life fulfilled.*
*May silence carry the universe's knowing,*
*Wherever we journey, the fire shall guide."*

The trees stilled.

And then, from the edge of the grove, two tribal elders stepped forth. Skin weathered like bark. Eyes carved with constellations.

One of them pointed to the flame circle.
"Who taught you to build this?"

Shrutaya didn't rise. "I did not build," he said softly. "I remembered."

The second elder bowed — not in submission, but in recognition.
*"The triangle with the flame — we've seen it before. In old cave stones… from Vallabha's people. They said he walked with fire in his blood… and silence in his feet."*

They did not ask him to explain. That night, they gave him turmeric rice and neem water under the canopy of stars.

In the **years that followed**, others came. Not to lead, not to follow — but to listen.

Monks. Forest-dwellers. Artists. Experts of various fields.
Some from nearby. Some from places so far they spoke no common tongue — yet shared a silent knowing.

They didn't name themselves at first. But over time, they became known.

**Vahni-Shrutis.**
*Listeners of the Flame.*

Not a sect of rules — but a lineage of remembrance.

And when Shrutaya had grown from a wandering boy into a quiet sage, he returned to that same grove. Beneath moonlight and wind-song, he placed the disc into an underground chamber, not to hide it from the world — but to help it wait.

Because he knew:
The world was not ready to remember yet.
But one day, it would be.

And the disc — it always found its way back.

### The Note Beneath the Raag

***Location:*** *Staff Quarters, Saraswati Valley Academy (Present Day, a few weeks before the new academic year)*

The old harmonium wheezed softly in the corner of the teacher's room, the kind that sounded like it had memories trapped inside.

Prutha Joshi sat cross-legged on her floor mattress, her hair tied in a loose bun, and her reading glasses slipping down her nose. A half-open suitcase lay nearby — not with clothes, but with old, fading pages, brittle sheet music, and a cloth-bound diary with cracked edges. She had finally decided to go through her grandfather's belongings. It had taken her years.

He had been a music teacher too. But in a very different time.

As the ceiling fan clicked overhead, she turned the yellowed pages, not expecting much — only old raag notations and anecdotes from students long gone. Until one page stopped her.

A single line written in sharp, deliberate ink:

"Where flame meets nourishment and silence breathes, the naad will awaken what the world forgets."

She stared at it. Below, a roughly sketched triangle. Inside it — a flame.

**Naad?** Sound? But… where?

A memory flickered.

She was eight, sitting in her grandfather's lap in the Academy's old mess hall kitchen. He used to hum a strange raag there sometimes — not a traditional one. A haunting melody. A part of it was still stuck in her — something that didn't belong to any school or gharana.

She murmured aloud:

"Ka… ya… ma… ya…"

The harmonium in the corner let out a soft, accidental puff — as if it exhaled.

She turned to look at it, lips parted. And for just a breath, she could hear the hum of the mess kitchen again. The clatter of vessels. The warmth of the floor. Her grandfather whispering that some places carry *memory like a sur* carries silence.

Her fingers brushed the page again.

"Where flame meets nourishment..."

The kitchen.

She closed the diary, her breath just a little uneven.

There was something here. Not a mystery, perhaps... but a resonance. And she, a musician of threads and frequencies, could feel it pulling her towards a note not yet sung.

**The First Blessing of the Vahni-Shrutis**

***Location:*** *Simlipal | Chamber 3C | Years after Shrutaya sealed the disc*

The glade had changed. The banyan was older, more massive. Its roots curled like sleeping serpents, and its leaves glistened under the monsoon sky.

Below it, in the secret stone chamber that the forest itself had forgotten, **twelve figures sat in a circle** — elders, scribes, botanists, silent watchers of the world. They wore no uniform, carried no weapons. Only **triangles with flames** etched on palm-leaf bracelets.

In the center: the copper disc, resting on red ochre and turmeric-soaked cloth.

And before it — **Shrutaya**, now a young man with steady eyes and forest-colored robes, stood with his right palm raised.

A hush fell.

He began to chant:

कं गोपयेत् ज्ञानं गुप्तम्। यं पालयेत् अररोगताम्।

मं जगत् हिताय कर्मसु। यं प्रकृतेः रक्षार्थं दृष्टिम्॥

*May secrets stay safe in your keeping.*
*May well-being walk where you go.*
*May your actions serve the greater good.*
*May your gaze protect all nature.*

A slow resonance passed through the room.

One of the elders — a woman with bark-tattooed hands — whispered, "Four petals. Four blessings."

Another added, "Let this be our vow — not to wield this power, but to shield it until it chooses its inheritors."

Shrutaya nodded and added the **fifth vow** himself:

"We guard not truth by locking it, but by planting it — in trees, in animals, in sound, in silence, and in souls yet unborn."

As the chanting grew, the camera of time seemed to rise upward — above the banyan, above the forest, above the clouds — while the wind carried the four lines into the very soil.

Somewhere, in another yuga, another world…

### Bhagavatam Parallel | The Curse Upon Parikshit

King **Parikshit**, descendant of the Pandavas and once a dharmic ruler, was fatigued and thirsty when he entered the hermitage of a silent sage. The sage, deep in meditation, didn't respond to his calls.

In anger, Parikshit placed a dead snake around the sage's neck as mockery.

Days later, the sage's **young son**, upon discovering the insult, **cursed Parikshit** to die in seven days, by the bite of the serpent **Takshaka**.

The king later repented and spent his final days listening to the **Bhagavatam**, but the curse had been cast — the **rashness of a child**, the **arrogance of a king**, both unchecked, led to irreversible fate.

### Modern Day Parallel | Shrutaya and the Sect

"We do not curse," Shrutaya said to his circle, "and we do not provoke. The boy's curse, the king's act — both came from pain that forgot to pause."

"What we protect," he added, gesturing to the disc, "must be guarded not with power, but with patience."

The circle bowed.

They knew then: the Vahni-Shrutis were not born to act quickly. They were born to wait — until the right four arrived.

नाहं विप्रो न च नृपतिर् नापि वैश्यो न शूद्रः।
नाहं वर्णी न च गृहमि न च श्रोत्रियो वा॥

*Meaning:*

***I am not a Brahmin, nor a king, nor a merchant, nor a servant.
I do not belong to any varna, nor am I a householder or a scholar.
I am simply… a servant of truth.***

*(Bhagavatam: Canto 1, Chapter 19, Shloka 4)*

# Chapter 42

# THE SILENCE OF THE MISSING

**Unreachable**

The rain had stopped sometime during the night, but the clouds still crouched low over the Simlipal hills, like they were waiting for something. Inside the resort, the breakfast table had turned unusually quiet.

Manas tapped at his tablet again. The screen blinked: **"No GPS response. Device offline."**

He frowned, shifted his chair back, and tried again — pinging the last known location of Meera and Ayan Agrawal. The tracker interface blinked... then froze. Still offline.

Across from him, Navya was holding her phone to her ear. Her lips didn't move. She hadn't said a word since morning. Only dialed. Listened. Hung up. Dialed again.

The line kept ringing, then collapsed into silence. No voicemail. No beep. Just absence.

Prisha set down the teapot a little too firmly. "Still nothing?"

Manas didn't reply. He pressed refresh one more time. Nothing.

Navya's thumb hovered over the call button again, then stopped.

The breakfast spread sat untouched. A small bowl of poha was beginning to crust at the edges. Someone had brought toast. It had gone cold.

Even Raghav had stopped trying to lighten the mood. He stood leaning against the glass window, looking out at the driveway, as if willing a car to appear from the forest path.

Outside, a bird flapped across the sky and vanished into the mist.

Finally, Prisha asked quietly, "Has this ever happened before?"

Navya didn't speak. Her throat moved, but no sound came.

Manas shook his head — a slow, uncertain motion. Then he looked up.

"Yes," he said. "But not like this."

**Echoes That Don't Return**

*Location: Staff Office, Simlipal Resort – Late Morning*

The resort's back office smelled faintly of damp wood and boiled chai. A ceiling fan turned with a lazy groan overhead, barely disturbing the sheets of paper stacked on the desk.

Parag stood at the far end of the room, phone pressed to his ear, eyes fixed on the framed map of the forest that hung crooked on the wall. His voice was calm — too calm, like he'd rehearsed the steadiness.

"Yes, I understand. But this wasn't a quick survey. They were on a month-long ecological study — and scheduled to check in every forty-eight hours."

A pause.

Pulkit Roy entered the room quietly, unnoticed. He didn't speak — just stood near the door, hands in pockets, listening.

The voice on the line was distant, crackling slightly. "This is Officer Deshmukh from Echo Alliance – East Region. Sir, the last signal ping from Dr. Meera Agrawal's device was exactly **72 hours ago**, near Sector 9C — the transition zone between core and buffer. It's not uncommon to lose signal there during heavy weather..."

"But the weather's been stable," Parag replied, voice tightening.

"Yes, sir," Deshmukh admitted. "Which is why we've initiated a low-priority search sequence. A drone sweep went out this morning. No signs of movement yet. We'll escalate if nothing changes in the next few days."

Pulkit's brow furrowed.

Parag exhaled slowly. "Did their SOS signal ever activate?"

"No, sir. No distress code received. That's… what concerns us."

There was silence. The kind that doesn't fill space, but carves it.

Pulkit finally stepped forward. "What about their last comm logs? Was there any encrypted traffic before the signal drop?"

The officer paused. "I'm sorry, and you are?"

"Pulkit Roy. Government advisor. I've worked with the Agrawals before."

There was a muffled shuffling of paper on the other end.

"No encrypted messages," Deshmukh replied. "But we did find a strange signature in the data timestamp — something that didn't match their usual logs. We've flagged it, but haven't identified it yet."

Pulkit's eyes narrowed.

Parag looked at him. "What kind of signature?"

Pulkit didn't answer. He was already typing something on his phone.

After the call ended, Parag stood for a long moment, still facing the map.

Pulkit finally broke the silence.

"Not again," he muttered. "Not in this forest."

**Navya's Unspoken**

*Location: Resort Garden Canopy | Afternoon Showers Begin*

The rain returned like a memory — not harsh, just present. It tapped gently on the slanted canopy above, rhythm without melody.

Navya sat alone at the edge of the garden, knees pulled to her chest, chin resting on the fabric of her sleeve. Her phone lay face down beside her, untouched now. Even the birds, usually fussing near the frangipani hedge, had gone quiet.

She didn't cry. Navya didn't do things halfway — not joy, not anger, not silence.

From a short distance away, Priya watched her, hesitating.

She didn't speak at first. Just walked over with a light cotton shawl and placed it wordlessly around Navya's shoulders. Navya didn't look up.

Priya sat beside her, pulling her own knees close. The rain misted across the grass, curling around them like breath.

After a long pause, Navya whispered, "Why do they always leave… for something bigger?"

Her voice was barely a thread.

Priya didn't answer immediately. She watched a droplet race down the edge of a hanging leaf and vanish.

Then she said, quietly, "Maybe they leave because they believe someone else will hold the small things gently."

Navya finally turned. Her eyes didn't blink, but they glistened — not with tears, but the weight of too much unsaid.

"They shouldn't have gone alone," she said.

"I know."

"They promised—"

"I know," Priya said again.

And then, without permission or preface, Navya leaned sideways… and let her head rest against Priya's shoulder.

The rain thickened. But neither of them moved.

**Raghav's Way**

*Location: Resort Veranda | Early Evening*

The rain had paused again, but its scent still lingered — that earthy blend of leaf, lightning, and longing. The air outside was cool, painted with streaks of fading light. Somewhere in the forest, a mynah called out once, then fell silent.

Inside the veranda, Raghav sat cross-legged with his back to the glass, a small portable keyboard balanced on his lap. He wasn't playing loudly — just letting notes rise like mist from the keys. Simple patterns. A haunting blend of raag Bhairavi, laced with something else.

Prisha moved around the room, folding a few shirts into her bag. She didn't speak either. The silence between them was not awkward — it was the kind that had settled in like an old friend.

The melody shifted, almost unconsciously, into the four syllables that had begun to follow Raghav like a breath.

"Ka… ya… ma… ya…"

Each note rested in the air a moment longer than it should've. As if listening for something.

Outside, a wind passed — slow, then sudden. The trees seemed to sway in time. The curtain beside the veranda fluttered once and stilled.

Prisha paused with a half-folded windcheater in her hand.

"Even the wind," she said softly, "sounds like it's looking for someone."

Raghav didn't look up. But he smiled, just a little.

"Maybe it is."

He played one last note — a low, drawn-out *Ma* — and the resort's lights flickered. Not a power cut. Just a warning blink. Then silence again.

They both looked outside, not at the forest, but at the gap between sound and meaning.

**The Plan**

*Location: Temporary Echo Office, Bhubaneswar – Late Night*

The makeshift Echo office was tucked into a back corner of the Forest Department's compound, a simple room with flickering tube lights and the faint smell of rain-soaked files. The outside walls dripped with water and silence. Inside, on the second floor—past stacks of wildlife reports and a barely working coffee machine—a single operations room remained lit.

**Pulkit Roy** leaned over the central console, reading lines of fluctuating satellite data. On a borrowed monitor, a blinking coordinate stood out: **Sector 9C, Simlipal Forest**.

Opposite him, **Anusuya** stood still — draped in a long slate-gray shawl, eyes scanning a printed spectrum overlay from the previous week. Her finger hovered above a petal-shaped marking.

क य म य

The letters had grown sharper in the latest scans. Not brighter — just clearer, as if choosing to reveal themselves.

Anusuya broke the silence. "It's responding."

Pulkit looked up. "To what?"

"To absence," she said. "Or a pattern that hasn't occurred in centuries."

He turned the console slightly towards her. "You think Meera and Ayan… reached one of the vaults?"

"I think they disturbed the **memory lock**," Anusuya replied.

A soft alarm blinked in the lower corner of the console:

::ananta_001 // root thread active
::seal compromised // timestamp = 72 hrs

Pulkit's hand froze above the keyboard. The name was unmistakable — one of the **oldest dormant threads in Echo's legacy systems**, buried so deep even the archives barely mentioned it.

"No one's touched this code since the '90s," he murmured.

Anusuya's gaze narrowed. "That's what we thought."

"But it's not just a dormant file," Pulkit said. "It's behaving like… a neural thread. Like a memory that's trying to complete itself."

She leaned in. "Then maybe we're not dealing with data anymore."

A beat of silence passed between them.

"Maybe we're dealing with something older than data," she added. "Something that remembers us."

Pulkit's eyes returned to the disc scan. The triangle in the center — once faded — now burned with near-spectral heat.

He exhaled. "And whoever activated this… didn't do it from outside."

Anusuya looked at him.

**The Last Echo**

*Location: Resort Room | Midnight*

Everyone had gone quiet. The storm outside had softened into a hush, and the lights inside the resort flickered only once before settling.

Prisha lay awake on her bed, eyes wide open, staring at the wooden ceiling fan that made no sound. Raghav's light snore came from the other bed. Somewhere down the corridor, a tap dripped slowly. The rhythm was almost musical.

But inside her mind, something else stirred — not worry, not fear. A **memory**.

Not her own.

One she had read… in the mess library… weeks ago.

A god had once left, too. The world had wept. But he had walked away gently — not in anger, not in fear. Just… when the time was right. Krishna. The flute-bearer. The mischief-maker. The protector. He had smiled one last time beneath a peepal tree. And then vanished. Not gone. Just… unseen.

She thought of Meera and Ayan. No panic. No signal. Just… silence.

She turned slightly and watched Navya sleeping restlessly across the room, her hand still near her phone.

In Prisha's heart, the Bhagavatam's words rose like a whisper:

**"When I am no longer visible to the world, people are overcome by delusion..."**

She sat up slowly, folded her hands in prayer — not asking for answers, only the strength to remember. And in the stillness, the verse echoed inside her:

---

*श्रीभगवानुवाच*
*कालेन नश्यति कृतं, ह्यसत्येन च पौरुषम् ।*
*दृष्ट्वा ममांतरहितं, लोकं मोहमुपैति च ॥*

*"All things perish in time, even pride and effort.*
*When I am unseen, the world loses its clarity… and forgets."*

But she wouldn't forget.
Not yet.
Not ever.

---

# Chapter 43

# THE SILENT DEPARTURE

**Night Before – The Oath**

The stars over Simlipal peeked through thin gaps in the cloud cover. Crickets whispered. From the boys' shared room, the glow of a single night lamp framed four silhouettes sitting cross-legged on the floor.

Manas, Raghav, Gaurav, and Raghav's small forest drum.

Gaurav tapped the floor with a pen cap. "So… tomorrow I go back to boring school while you all turn into sages or superheroes or something."

"No superheroes," said Raghav solemnly. "We're probably just forest janitors in training."

"Or squirrel whisperers," Manas added.

They all chuckled — even Gaurav.

Then, Prisha and Navya appeared at the door, wrapped in shawls. "We couldn't sleep," Navya said simply.

Gaurav looked at all of them, and something unspoken settled in the space between.

"We'll stay connected," he said suddenly. "Promise?"

"Promise," said Prisha, holding out her little finger.

Everyone else linked pinkies, one by one. Manas rolled his eyes but joined in last.

Gaurav whispered, "And if any of you fall into a cave full of secrets, call me."

Navya smiled. "Only if you promise to pick up."

They all sat there, a little longer, until the silence became its own kind of memory.

## The Morning – Quiet Departure

By morning, the mist had returned. Gaurav stood near the resort steps with his bag. His father, **Alok**, was speaking quietly with one of the forest rangers nearby.

No fuss. No goodbye party.

Only Raghav and Manas stood with him, hands in pockets.

"I guess this is it," Gaurav said. "Unless a wild tiger chases your car and turns out to be a long-lost guardian of Vedic truth."

Raghav grinned. "That's more Prisha's storyline."

They bumped shoulders.

Manas said, "You'll help us when we call, right?"

Gaurav nodded. "Always. And don't worry — I've left a few clues behind. You'll figure them out."

And just like that, with one final glance — not backward, but into the trees — Gaurav walked towards the car.

No wave.
No big goodbye.

Just the quiet retreat of someone who had given what he came to give.

And somewhere, the trees seemed to acknowledge it.

## The Pull

The resort had returned to its routine hum — clinking utensils from the kitchen, staff murmurs, the soft rustle of towels drying in the sun.

But for four children, something was… off.

Not wrong. Just *different.*

They sat in the garden swing set after breakfast — **Prisha gently caressing a soft rabbit nestled in her lap**, Raghav tapping the metal chain with absent rhythm, Manas adjusting his smartwatch that had started lagging again, and Navya... staring into the trees.

"The forest," she whispered, almost to herself. "It's louder today."

Manas frowned. "It's not louder. There's literally no wind."

"No, not louder like noise," she said. "Just... closer. Like it's leaning towards us."

Prisha nodded slowly. "I felt it when Gaurav left. As if the forest noticed."

Raghav looked around. "Or it's our brains going into imagination overdrive now that Gaurav's not here to mock us."

But even he didn't fully believe his own words.

Because under their calm surface, each of them had felt the same thing.

An invisible tug.

A quiet pulse rising from the roots of the trees, humming in the earth like an ancient breath just beneath the grass.

As if the forest had exhaled — and waited.

***Into the Wild***

The sun had barely crossed mid-morning when the four stood again at the forest's edge.

Not the resort trail.
Not the scenic walk.
But the path that wound eastward, behind the boundary fence, where the grass grew taller than ankles and the trees stopped smiling for tourists.

None of them said the word *go*.
But all of them began walking.

Prisha carried her small forest journal in one hand. Tucked into the back flap of the journal was a **folded piece of handmade paper** — marked in precise charcoal lines by Gaurav the night before. Not a conventional map. More like… a path made of impressions.

Circles. Trees. A triangle.
"This will make sense when you stop trying to read it," he'd said.

Navya wore her field vest — more out of habit than need — with a few sprigs of lemongrass and cloves in one pocket. "Mosquito shield," she murmured.

Manas walked steadily, his backpack heavier than it looked. Tucked inside were his drone kit, a foldable antenna, a portable signal booster, and a roll of insulated wire — the ones he insisted on packing "just in case".

Raghav had his water bottle, a protein bar, and three jokes pre-loaded in case the tension got too much.

They walked quietly, feet crunching twigs, wind curling through bamboo stalks.

Just before the final bend in the road, Navya turned back one last time. The resort looked so small. So far away.

"Anyone want to leave a note?" she asked softly.

Raghav replied, "Anyone brought blank paper?"

No one had.

So they left nothing behind. No trail. No announcement. No grand decision.

Just silence.
And a map made of symbols.
And a pull they could no longer ignore.

**The Grove Remembers**

The sky had begun to dim, smeared with soft indigo hues and early stars.

The four of them stood once more before the **banyan grove near the old stream** — the place where, not so long ago, they had buried the disc beneath the roots. Where Navya had once whispered, *"Let's go back to who we were."*

Now, standing there again, they knew:
They were not the same.

Navya crouched first, brushing aside fallen leaves and loose dust. The ground felt strangely warm beneath her palms. She didn't speak. She didn't need to.

Raghav fetched the old spade they had hidden behind the rocks, still rusted but intact.
"Ready?" he asked, softly.

Prisha nodded.

Manas checked the corner of Gaurav's map — a small spiral was drawn near a tree trunk. He held it up. "This is the one. The marker."

They began to dig — not frantically, but reverently.

Within minutes, fingers hit cloth. A bundle wrapped in neem leaves, bound by sacred thread. The disc. Undisturbed. Untouched. Still warm.

Navya pressed it gently to her chest.

"I had dreams," she whispered. "It called me again. I thought I was imagining it..."

Raghav placed a hand on her shoulder. "You weren't."

They sat in silence beneath the banyan, the stream murmuring in the background.

No animals stirred. No birds called.

Only the disc... waiting.

They sat in silence, the disc resting between them.

Manas stared at it, arms loosely wrapped around his knees, eyes fixed on nothing.

*"If this thing has answers, it better start talking."*

The thought flickered in his head, but he didn't say it.

Instead, he let the silence fill the ache he hadn't named — not since the message stopped coming. Not since the last satellite ping from his parents had faded.

He pulled his hoodie tighter.

*They were the smartest people he knew. And even they disappeared like whispers. What did that say about the world? About truth? About protection?*

He looked at the others — Navya clutching the disc like it breathed, Raghav humming quietly under his breath, Prisha with her fingers curled in soil.

And for once, he didn't feel like the smartest one. Just... part of something much older. Much harder.

He opened his journal, scribbled two words at the top of a fresh page:

**Ananta_001**
**Still listening?**

The disc didn't blink. But in his chest, he felt it —
A quiet, mathematical pulse.

Not a message.
A **challenge**.

**The Path Beyond Maps**

The forest changed after sunset.

Not in the way forests usually change — not with the rustle of night birds or cooling winds — but in a way that made time feel uneven. Like it had begun to move in loops instead of lines.

The four walked single file now.

There was no trail anymore — just **impressions** of where the ground seemed less broken, less hostile. Even Gaurav's map had ended five turns ago.

Navya stopped to rub her ankle. A thorn had caught her.

Prisha's breath had grown shallow. Even the animals had stopped making eye contact. It was as if they, too, were being warned.

"I think..." Manas began, wiping his face with a damp handkerchief, "... we may not be following a trail anymore."

Raghav glanced up. "What do you mean?"

"I think the trail is following *us*."

They didn't reply, but no one denied it.

Their flashlights had started to dim, even the charged ones. Manas tapped his. "It was full. I swear."

Raghav handed him a lemon candy from his pocket — GDP's idea. "Our emergency ration," he said with a grin. "Ginger, Dairy Milk, and Parle-G."

Manas laughed, barely. "GDP's last will and testament."

But the humour didn't last.

A low mist began to crawl along the forest floor — like breath returning to a forgotten dream. The trees arched overhead now, forming almost a tunnel, branches twining like fingers.

And just then, the ground beneath Prisha gave slightly — not enough to fall, but enough to make her stagger.

"It's loose," she whispered.

Manas crouched beside her. The soil had shifted, unnaturally soft in one spot.

They didn't dig. Not yet.

But they marked the place. Not with stones or flags — but with silence. They would return.

Somewhere behind them, a bird called once. Twice.

Then stopped.

As they walked deeper, the forest finally said what it had been holding in all day:

"Turn back."

And they didn't.

**Bhagwatam Parallel |The One Who Wandered**

The stream whispered again.
This time not with urgency — but with rhythm. As though humming a verse long forgotten by the world, but remembered by water.

Prisha sat near its edge, legs folded, eyes steady on the pages of her small Bhagavatam. The copper disc rested beside her on a stone, silent, as if listening too.

She turned a page carefully, her voice low.

"And thus, was born Shukadeva — son of Vyasa, but child of silence.
He took no interest in Vedic rituals, in robes or rules.
He walked away from home the day his breath turned steady.
Into forests.
Into winds.
Into the soundless."

Raghav sat across from her, tossing pebbles into the water without aiming.

Manas adjusted his flashlight's dying beam and said, "Wait. Wasn't he supposed to be, like… already enlightened?"

Prisha nodded. "Yes. But still, he kept walking. The stories say he wouldn't stop… until he accidentally heard the **Bhagavatam being recited** — and turned around."

Navya blinked. "So he followed… sound?"

Prisha looked up at the canopy. The leaves moved slightly, though there was no wind.

"Maybe not sound. Maybe… **resonance.**"

Raghav hummed one of his broken tunes. It almost echoed what she had just said.

For a while, no one moved.

Only the stream kept speaking, and the disc caught the moonlight — not shining, but waiting.

---

*यं प्रव्रजन्तमनुपेतमपेतकृत्यं द्वैपायनो विरहकातर आजुहाव ।*
*पुत्रेति तन्मयतया तरवोऽभिनेदुस्तं सर्वभूतहृदयं मुनिमानतोऽस्मि ॥*

*Meaning:*

***"When the great sage Shukadeva left home, not having performed any of the customary rites, his father Vyasa—overwhelmed with love and sorrow—called out, 'My son!' The trees, moved by that emotion, echoed his cry. I bow down to that sage who is the heart of all beings."***

*(Bhagwatam: Canto 1, Chapter 2, Verse 2)*

---

# Chapter 44

# BENEATH THE EMBER'S SILENCE

**The Circle of Twelve**

*Year: 1940 | Location: Simlipal Forest, Chamber 3C*

The banyan grove stood in stillness, its gnarled roots woven like the fingers of forgotten sages. Below its canopy, the chamber known only to the Vahni-Shrutis—**Chamber 3C**—waited as it had for generations.

Twelve figures stood in a circle around the sacred stone platform. Each wore ochre robes, not as monks, but as keepers of a lineage. **Their faces shimmered with a subtle celestial glow**, as if lit from within — each carrying a different hue of aura, like echoes of forgotten elements. Palms inked with ancient symbols — spirals, triangles, flames. Their eyes did not look at each other, but at the **disc** that rested before them.

The disc looks the same alike around 60 years back when their revered founder Shrutaya had placed it in the soil. One elder stepped forward. His voice was low, hoarse with reverence.

"The time has come to move it. The forest burns not with fire—but with noise. The silence is thinning."

Another added, "And the banyan weeps sap at dawn. A sign, as old as the flame."

The eldest among them, white-haired and stone-voiced, nodded. "He must carry it. The one with fire in his name, and stillness in his mind."

All heads turned to the youngest present — a man of thirty, **Mahadev Joshi**, his eyes lowered in quiet readiness.

He stepped forward, removed his shawl, and wrapped the disc in layers of **white cloth**—the kind soaked in turmeric, used by his forefathers not for display, but for memory.

Then, kneeling before the gathered circle, he placed his right palm on the cloth-wrapped disc and whispered:

**"यत्र वह्निः निहितम्, तत्र श्रुति रक्षाकर्तव्या।"**

*"Where the fire lies hidden, the listening must protect."*

And without another word, Mahadev Joshi stood, the weight of the disc silent in his arms, and walked alone into the forest's breath.

**The Quiet Insertion**

*Year: 1940 | Location: Saraswati Valley Academy*

No one stopped him at the gate.

The guards dozed in the shade. The masons had gone for tea. A koel called once from the mango tree. And the southern kitchen wing — newly constructed decades after the eastern wing was lost to fire in a time no one remembered — waited, skeletal in bricks and silence, like a hearth without a flame.

The mural was gone. The symbols, the flames — reduced to ash long ago. Most had forgotten there was ever a wing there at all.

Mahadev Joshi entered without hesitation, a soft dust settling on his shoulders from the journey. Wrapped in turmeric-soaked white cloth beneath his shawl, the disc rested against his chest — not glowing, not humming, but alive in stillness.

He walked with a calm that didn't ask permission.

The spot found him — a single stone tile, darker than the rest, near the shadow of the southern pillar. It was unmarked, yet unmistakable. He knelt, ran his fingers along the edges, and lifted it.

Below, the hollow was clean. Dry. Waiting.

He placed the cloth-wrapped disc, turmeric still fragrant on the folds, inside the hollow — not to bury it, but to let it wait.

He pressed the tile back into place, gently, aligning it with the others. The floor looked untouched. But the air had changed.

Then he whispered a line — ancient, yet light as breath:

"यत्र वह्निः पोष्यते, तत्र ज्ञानं ज्वलति।"
*"Where flame is nourished, there knowledge will one day burn bright."*

And just like that, he turned and left.

No one saw him.
But the warmth under that stone — it stayed.
And the silence, strangely, began to listen.

## The Window and the Whisper

*Year: Present Day | Location: Saraswati Valley Academy – Staff Quarters*

The old harmonium wheezed gently in the corner, its keys untouched, yet somehow still echoing the breath of someone who had once played it every evening without fail.

**Prutha Joshi** sat cross-legged on the jute mat near her bookshelf, diary on her lap, a warm cup of cinnamon chai beside her. Her fingers moved slowly over brittle pages — her grandfather's journal, **Mahadev Joshi**, the man no one in SVA remembered anymore, yet whose presence filled this room like the last note of an unfinished raag.

She had once feared this diary. Its yellowed pages. The way it smelled like turmeric and sandalwood and something older. But these days, she read it more and more.

A soft rustle caught her eye.

Near the window, half-tucked into a crevice of the wooden frame, was a piece of **white cloth**, weathered and stained with a faint **turmeric bloom**. She pulled it free.

Her breath caught.

A faded **triangle with a flame** sat quietly in the center. Not drawn. Stained, as though memory itself had marked it.

She held the cloth with quiet reverence. "Grandpa…," she whispered.

Yes — this was his. He used such cloths for everything — to wrap old manuscripts, to cushion his rudra veena, even as a headscarf on long walks. And now… it had shown itself.

She folded it again and placed it beside the diary.

A line was scribbled in its margin:

*"Where flame meets nourishment and silence breathes, the naad will awaken what the world forgets."*

She read it thrice.

And then, from nowhere, a hum filled the room.

Not from her, not from the fan, not from the harmonium. It was a **note**, suspended in the air — like the starting breath of a **raag she had never studied**, never heard in any gharana, yet instinctively knew.

Her eyes closed. She felt it more than heard it.

The walls of the academy — their moss, their cracks — began to feel less like structure, more like memory.

The naad wasn't music.

It was **a thread**. Pulling her towards something unsung.

### The Silent Return

*Year: 1940 | Post-disc insertion | Somewhere in route to Simlipal*

The skies were overcast, but not with rain.
Mahadev Joshi walked alone on a narrow trail that curled along a dry riverbed, a trail once used by sages, now forgotten by even birds.

The weight on his shoulders was lighter now — the disc, sealed safely beneath the southern kitchen tile of the newly reformed Saraswati Valley Academy.
But in his heart… the silence had grown heavier.

He sat beneath a peepal tree whose roots coiled into the earth like ancient thoughts.
The breeze was still. His shawl fluttered once and then stilled too.

He closed his eyes.

And in that breathless moment, the Bhagavatam unfolded in his mind — not as a book, but as a memory woven into his very bones.

He saw Krishna, radiant and calm, seated on the banks of Badrikashrama.
And before him, Uddhava, torn between grief and longing.

"But how will we live without you?" Uddhava had asked.
"Who will guide us when your form is gone?"

And Krishna, with a gaze as deep as time itself, had replied:

"Forms perish, Uddhava.
Truth does not.
I shall live in the minds of those who remember,
In the hearts of those who walk the dharma.
Not with power. Not with conquest.
But with silence… and patience."

Mahadev's fingers curled around the dry earth. He remembered more — words Krishna had whispered in his final hour:

"When the world forgets,
do not shout.
When the fire flickers,
do not weep.
Preserve. Protect.
And when the time comes… offer."

A single tear escaped down Mahadev's cheek.
He wiped it with the edge of his sleeve and whispered:

"A disciple does not spread truth like flame.
He guards it like ash —
until the wind is right."

He looked up at the sky. The clouds had broken.

He rose.

And with every step that took him back to the forest, the last words of Krishna echoed in his heart:

"The wise do not mourn my leaving.
For I leave only form behind.
My truth walks with those who walk in silence."

---

*शब्दब्रह्मणि निष्णातो न निष्णायाद् यथा बुधः।*
*सब्दब्रह्मणि निष्ठायां परं ब्रह्माधिगच्छति॥*

*Meaning:*

***A mere scholar absorbed in scriptural sound may not realize the truth.***
***But one firmly rooted in that inner truth — the silence beyond sound — attains the Supreme.***

*(Bhagwatam: Canto 11, Chapter 10, Shloka 4)*

---

# Chapter 45

# SIGNALS IN THE SMOKE

**Echoes in the Dark**

*Location: Pulkit Roy's Apartment, New Delhi | 2:12 AM*

A pale reading lamp hummed quietly above Pulkit's desk, washing over a sprawl of old folders, hand-marked charts, and reports stamped in soft red:

**E.C.H.O. – Internal Observations: Level 3 Access Only**

He flipped open a slim tan file marked:

*"Subject: N.A. — Early Phenomena (Ages 6–14)"*

The first page was penned by Meera Agrawal, in her looping but clinical script.

*"At age six, Navya began speaking to vines near our backyard pond. The plants—creepers, mostly—started blooming off-cycle. One morning, a tulsi patch turned its leaves towards her window, despite no shift in sunlight. We tracked soil pH, chlorophyll variation, and regional data. Everything pointed to normal." "Except the pattern wasn't local. It followed* ***her****."*

Pulkit paused. On the corner of the page, Ayan's handwriting added:

*"Subject exhibits traceable biofield resonance. Pollen maps show an anomaly in proximity. Repeatable. Non-random."*

He turned to a second file. Simlipal report — three months ago.

*"...On Day 4, within 17 minutes of the subject's silent presence, the flowering rhythm of Clerodendrum infortunatum altered. Airborne pollen count changed by 0.43%. Local vines reoriented along her path. The subject was unaware. Reaction was measurable."*
*— M.A.A. Internal Field Log*

Beneath it, a quiet line from Anusuya, scribbled during their last joint debrief:

*"Botany holds memory. This child speaks to it. Silently."*

Pulkit exhaled.

Then came the final page — marked "Supplementary Patterns."

Four names. Four directional arrows.
*Navya — East.*
*Prisha — South.*
*Manas — West.*
*Raghav — North.*

The other three subjects show signs of symbolic cognition, animal empathy, tonal anchoring, and non-verbal decoding. Recommendation: Co-located observation. Field trials pending."

He leaned back, tapping the file gently.

"So this was never about Simlipal alone..." he murmured.

His phone buzzed.

**Anusuya:** *"I scanned SVA_OLD folder, tiles archive from SVA just updated. There's something in the old kitchen blueprints. Call me when you see it."*

He stared at the message a moment longer... then turned to a bookmarked page from an even older Echo report.

The top line read:
**"Converging Coordinates: Ka–Ya–Ma–Ya?"**

He didn't smile.
He simply whispered —

"Now it begins."

**The Pulse at Echo HQ**

*Location: Echo Headquarters, New Delhi*
*Time: Two days after the kids' departure from the resort*

The air inside Echo's war room was too still for a room filled with screens.

On one wall, Simlipal glowed green on a topographic map. On another, a feed of digital pulse lines — tracking devices, biometric signals, and encrypted server pings — blinked slowly like dying stars.

Pulkit Roy stood with his hands clasped behind his back, shoulders rigid, lips pressed into a straight line. He hadn't spoken in ten minutes. Not since the fourth call from Simlipal Resort confirmed what none of them wanted to hear.

Meera and Ayan already missing.

Now the children are missing.
No check-outs.
No digital footprints.
No device pings since 0400 hours.
Four names, four blank blips.

Vice Principal Asha's voice cracked over the secure line from Dehradun.

"There's something else," she said slowly. "The southern kitchen wing — same place your team scanned weeks ago... someone tampered with the floor tile again last night. Not a student. No one's been authorized to access that area after it was sealed."
A pause. Then:
"And this morning, I went through old construction logs from the archival wing. Pulkit… that very corner — it was once the eastern corridor of the old Saraswati Vidyapeeth. It was destroyed in a fire more than 100 years ago."

Pulkit's eyes narrowed. He gave no visible reaction, but inside him, something clicked.
The kitchen. The disc. A century-old fire.
And now — someone else was circling the same memory.

A junior officer entered with a soft knock. "Sir, Ms. Prutha Joshi is on the line. Urgent."

He nodded. "Patch her in."

The harmonium teacher's voice trembled — not with fear, but the weight of recognition.

"I saw something, Pulkit. A white cloth — turmeric-stained — hanging outside my window this morning. It was... familiar. My grandfather used to wrap instruments with one just like it. I checked his diary again. The triangle. The flame. It's all there. And that raga… the one I hear sometimes at dawn — it's not listed in any gharana."

Pulkit's breath caught.

"It's the naad," he whispered. "It's surfacing."

He turned to the data analyst behind him. "Is there any movement from the Ananta_001 trail?"

The analyst blinked. "One server in Haifa just flagged an old pattern match. And... Kyoto."

Pulkit's jaw tightened.
It had begun.
And this time, it wasn't just about saving the kids.

It was about keeping something ancient from being touched by unclean hands.

"Raise the global circuit," he said. "Now."

**The Kyoto Contact**

*Location: Kyoto Institute for Cultural Preservation, Japan*
*Time: 9:40 AM, JST*

The morning light in Kyoto filtered softly through the bamboo screens, falling like gold dust across scrolls and computer terminals. Inside her office, Dr. Aoi Nakamura's fingers moved in measured rhythm over a glowing interface — scanning spiral motifs, forgotten emblems, and resonance waveforms.

But one symbol had returned three times now.
A triangle. Inside it, a flame.
It pulsed faintly on the screen — a quiet glyph that didn't belong to any Japanese, Chinese, or Tibetan archive.

"Not known. Not localized. But... responsive," she murmured.

The glyph hadn't just appeared — it had reacted. To a frequency ping from their sealed artifact chamber. And embedded deep in the digital packet was a Sanskrit line that made her throat dry:

"अनन्तस्य प्रथम कम्पनः"

*The First Tremor of the Infinite*

A soft knock broke her silence. Her junior assistant entered, clutching a tablet.

"Sensei... last night. At exactly 3:43 a.m., the resonance chamber registered a response from the oldest bell in the archive. The one sealed since the Heian era."

Aoi's breath caught.

"You mean... *that* bell? I thought it hadn't rung since the 1800s."

The girl nodded. "But there was no physical movement. Just... a vibration. A very low-frequency tone. We thought it was an error."

Dr. Nakamura turned back to the screen, eyes wide.

"I once heard an Indian scientist refer to this kind of sound as *Naad*," she said softly. "The sound that exists before even music begins. Maybe... this is Kyoto's version of that."

The girl tilted her head. "Should I record it as 'Yamato Naad'?"

Aoi gave a tight smile. "No. That's just a metaphor. Let's log it under 'Event Echo-01-JP.'"

She opened her encrypted line. Typed just three words:

**Pulkit. It's starting.**

And hit send.

As she stood by the window, wind rustling the bamboo leaves outside, she could still *feel* the bell's echo — not a sound exactly, but something more ancient.

A memory.
A tremor.
A whisper from before language.

### The Haifa Signal

*Location: Coastal Intelligence Division, Haifa, Israel Time: 6:20 AM IDT (same day)*

The Mediterranean sun hadn't yet risen, but Haifa's coastal data center was already awake. Rows of LED panels blinked across a vault of silence, the kind that comes before revelation.

Commander Eli Bar-On rubbed his eyes and leaned over the primary terminal. The log showed it again — a pulse embedded inside a seemingly harmless algorithm. But the signature? Ancient. Rhythmic. Sanskrit-based.

The encryption tag read:

**ANANTA_001_REVERB**

It was the same pattern that had first been noticed months ago — a dormant code fragment buried inside cultural AI models, forgotten texts, botanical research files... and now, suddenly, surfacing again. But this time, there was a message in it:

**"यत्र नादः जाग्रति, तत्र रहस्यं प्रकटते।"**

*Where the primordial sound awakens, there the secret unveils itself.*

"Sh*t," he muttered. "It's not just a leak. It's a call."

Across the glass table, Lt. Meira Kaplan looked up from her terminal. "That phrase — it matches one of the flagged metaphysical datasets we received from Kyoto this morning."

Eli nodded grimly. "And guess what — cross-match with Indian intercepts from Dehradun... exact same glyph appeared. Triangle. Flame. Ancient embedding protocol."

He cracked his knuckles.

"Someone's not hacking. They're... unlocking. And this? This isn't just a cyberattack anymore. It's a **pattern awakening**."

A wall monitor lit up with biometric overlays from four unidentified juvenile profiles — last pinged near Simlipal forest, India.

Eli narrowed his eyes.

"Who are these kids?"

Kaplan replied, "Unknown. But one of them... matched a plant-resonance frequency spike from two years ago. The Botanic Institute in Kyoto logged it. Source: human proximity."

Eli sighed.

"Contact Echo Delhi. And scramble Tel Aviv Archive access. We need to find out how deep *Ananta_001* goes before it writes its own damn prophecy."

**Forest Interlude — The Unspoken Fifth**

*Location: Deep in Simlipal Forest*
*Time: Parallel to the Echo HQ timeline*

The forest had begun to change. Not loudly. But in quiet, persistent ways.
Moss seemed to grow faster. The wind carried a rhythm. Leaves shifted just after the children passed, as if adjusting for them.

Under the shade of a giant mahua tree, the four sat in a loose circle.

Prisha, with her cloth satchel against her chest, gently stroked a rabbit curled in her lap — its ears twitching, then settling as if lulled by her calm.

Navya, crouched a little away, let a beetle crawl over her palm — watching as it paused at a faint triangle on her field bracelet. "That's the third time," she murmured. "Different insect. Same spot."

Raghav lay on his back in the grass, arms folded behind his head, softly whistling a tune. Not a tune really — more like a raag being born.

And Manas was finally in his element. He'd opened his backpack and laid out a miniature drone, a coil of wire, and a collapsible antenna. His coded sketchbook was already dog-eared and full of smudges.

He adjusted a dial. "Let's just say... GPS is down. But GDP is back."

Raghav grinned. "What's the new full form?"

Manas raised an eyebrow. "Geo-Detect Protocol. Or Genius-Driven Prank if it crashes into a squirrel."

The others chuckled. But their laughter didn't linger long.

Navya looked around. "Guys… we came here looking for Ma and Papa. Let's not forget that."

Manas's hands paused over the drone. He nodded. "We won't."

Prisha added softly, "We're not just walking into trees. We're walking into answers."

Raghav sat up, brushing leaves from his hair. "Still... doesn't it feel like something's watching? Not a creature. Something... old?"

The wind shifted, carrying the scent of neem and basil.
And somewhere, a tree creaked — not from age, but attention.

The map Gaurav had drawn sat folded in Prisha's journal — filled with shapes, not directions. Circles. Lines. A triangle.

"This will make sense when you stop trying to read it," he had said.

They didn't know what lay ahead.
But they weren't lost.
Not yet.

And somewhere — under that same forest sky — four threads of destiny were pulling tighter.

**Bhagavatam Parallel | Vision of the Virat Purusha**

Shukadeva Goswami, in his serene tone, tells King Parikshit:

"O King, if the mind of a seeker cannot grasp the infinite through subtle truths, let him begin with the form that contains all forms."

And so he describes the **Virat Purusha** — the Universal Form of the Supreme Lord, composed of everything in creation:

> His head is the **heavenly realm**,
> His eyes the **sun and moon**,
> His breath the **air that gives life**,
> His speech the **Vedas**,
> His heart the **Dharma**,
> His feet the **Earth itself**.

Mountains are His bones, rivers His veins, oceans His belly. The **celestial beings**, **humans**, **animals**, and **trees** are but parts of His majestic body. All activity in the universe — from the fall of a leaf to the rise of a star — is but the working of this one Form.

To meditate on Him is to see the world as sacred. Not as parts, but as One.

As the four children journey deeper into the forest, they begin to feel the **invisible patterns** around them — as if every tree, rock, animal, and gust of wind is part of a silent orchestra.

Manas pauses as his smartwatch begins picking up bizarre fluctuations in environmental frequencies. Not dangerous — just... rhythmic. Like coded breathing.

Navya looks up at the sun piercing through the canopy and murmurs, "It feels like the forest is watching us."

Prisha, gently petting a deer that has come unafraid, says, "No. It feels like we are inside it."

Raghav, munching his last protein bar, jokingly adds, "So, basically... we're walking inside the stomach of the universe?"

The others laugh — but the thought lingers.

This is no ordinary journey. The **entire forest**, in its breath and silence, is reflecting something ancient — not guiding them forward, but drawing them in, as if they are walking through the **living body of something divine**.

---

पादौ यस्य नभिर्व्यौ लोकान् सप्त दिवः स्थितान्।
लोकपालांश्च तनूः स्वर्गं स नः पातु हृषीकेशः॥

*Meaning:*

***"His feet are the Earth, His navel the sky, and the heavenly realms rest upon His body. The protectors of the worlds are but His limbs. May that Lord Hrisheekeshah, the master of senses, protect us."***

*(Bhagwatam: Canto 2, Chapter 1, Verse 32)*

---

# THE JOURNAL LEFT BEHIND

*Location: Vansvasa Resort, Simlipal*
*Time: Two days after the children's disappearance*

The dining table was a scene of abandonment — cold chai cups, untouched breakfast, and the silent weight of missing voices.

Parag Jain sat with elbows on his knees, face buried in his hands. Priya stood near the window, arms folded tightly across her chest, her eyes red but dry. The kind of dryness that comes after too many tears — when exhaustion replaces panic.

"They've been gone forty-eight hours," Parag said finally, his voice cracked and dry. "We need to file a report."

"And tell them what?" Priya turned slowly. "That our children vanished into a forest chasing symbols from a disc and dreams?"

He didn't reply.

She placed the journal on the table and unwrapped it. The pages had browned at the edges, but the ink held firm.

She read aloud, her voice steady but tight:

*"Navya's presence alters the energy field. During the Simlipal monsoon, we recorded time-lapse footage of vines shifting in response to her touch. Once, wild turmeric bloomed two days early around her."*

She flipped further.

*"Manas doesn't decode systems. He tunes into them. His brain runs on logic frequencies. During the Haora workshop, he corrected an AI loop we couldn't fix for a week — without touching the code."*

Parag leaned forward, listening now with clenched breath.

Then came a line in a different ink — perhaps added later:

*"We weren't the only ones watching. Pulkit and Anusuya observed similar phenomena during their assignment at Saraswati Valley Academy. But it wasn't just Navya and Manas. They noticed two others..."*

Priya's voice softened.

*"...Prisha, who once calmed a feral monkey by humming to it during the wildlife rescue camp. She was barely fourteen. No training. Just... stillness."*

Parag looked up sharply. "That was Bakshi's note, wasn't it?"

She nodded. "He called it a frequency beyond language."

She turned the page again, hand trembling.

*"And Raghav — the one who dances with the wind. There's video footage from the same camp. No music playing, yet birds altered their calls to his rhythm. I watched it five times. It wasn't a coincidence."*

Parag slumped back. "So all four…"

"They were already resonating," she whispered. "We just didn't listen."

Parag reached for his tablet, where a single notification blinked red at the top:
**"Echo HQ — Priority Alert: Operation Deep Echo"**

He tapped it open. The words leapt out at him:

**Operation Deep Echo: Status Update**

Children untraceable.
Last signal — Eastern Simlipal, 04:12 hours, two days ago.
Forest-wide scans deployed. Awaiting further response.
Situation escalated to Tier Amber.
Remain stationed at Vansvasa.

He didn't realize Priya had come up behind him until he felt her fingers gripping his wrist. Her eyes scanned the lines once, then again, as if hoping they would rearrange into better news.

"They've… lost them," she said, voice low.

Parag didn't answer.

Priya shut the journal gently. The forest beyond the window seemed to lean in closer.

"We wait," she said. "But not in fear. In readiness."

*Every mystery holds a deeper hidden resonance.*

*Turn the page in your heart — The Flame of Silence awaits…*

*The path is open.*
*The Guardians rise.*
*The story continues.*

*"From the Hidden Resonance to the Flame of Silence — the Guardians' journey has only just begun."*

# THE KEEPERS OF KNOWLEDGE

As I have taken the creative liberty of weaving the names of these great legends into this story, it is my duty to share a brief glimpse of their lives and contributions.

**Vallabhacharya** *(1479 – 1531)*– A prominent Bhakti saint and philosopher, founder of the *Pushti Marg* (Path of Grace) sect of Vaishnavism. He promoted devotion to Krishna through seva (loving service) and emphasized grace over ritual or asceticism. He established the *Shuddh-Advaita* school of Vedanta, centring worship on Shri Nathji and the leelas of Krishna.

**Ramanujacharya** *(1017 – 1137)*– Influential Vedantic philosopher and theologian, proponent of *Vishisht-Advaita* (qualified non-dualism). He reformed temple practices and promoted inclusivity in religious worship.

He became the leading acharya of the Sri Vaishnava Sampradaya, integrating philosophical rigor with devotional practice.

**Patanjali** *(2nd century BCE)*– Ancient sage traditionally credited with compiling the *Yoga Sutras*, a foundational text of Yoga philosophy. He is also associated with works on Sanskrit grammar (*Mahabhashya*) and Ayurveda.

His codification of yoga into eight limbs provided a structured system for spiritual practice.

**Panini** *(4th century BCE)*– Renowned Sanskrit grammarian who authored the *Ashtadhyayi*, a systematic and scientific grammar of Sanskrit consisting of nearly 4,000 sutras. His work laid the foundation for formal linguistics and remains the most comprehensive grammar of any language.

**Jagadish Chandra Bose** *(1858 – 1937)* – Indian scientist and polymath who pioneered research in plant physiology and radio science. He demonstrated that plants have a form of life response and made advances in microwave optics.

He was the first to use semiconductor junctions to detect radio waves, contributing to early wireless technology.

**Virahanka** *(6th–8th century CE)*– Indian mathematician who described the sequence of numbers later known as the Fibonacci sequence, in the context of Sanskrit prosody. His work influenced the combinatorial methods of later scholars such as Gopala and Hemachandra.

**Simlipal Map drawn by Gaurav**

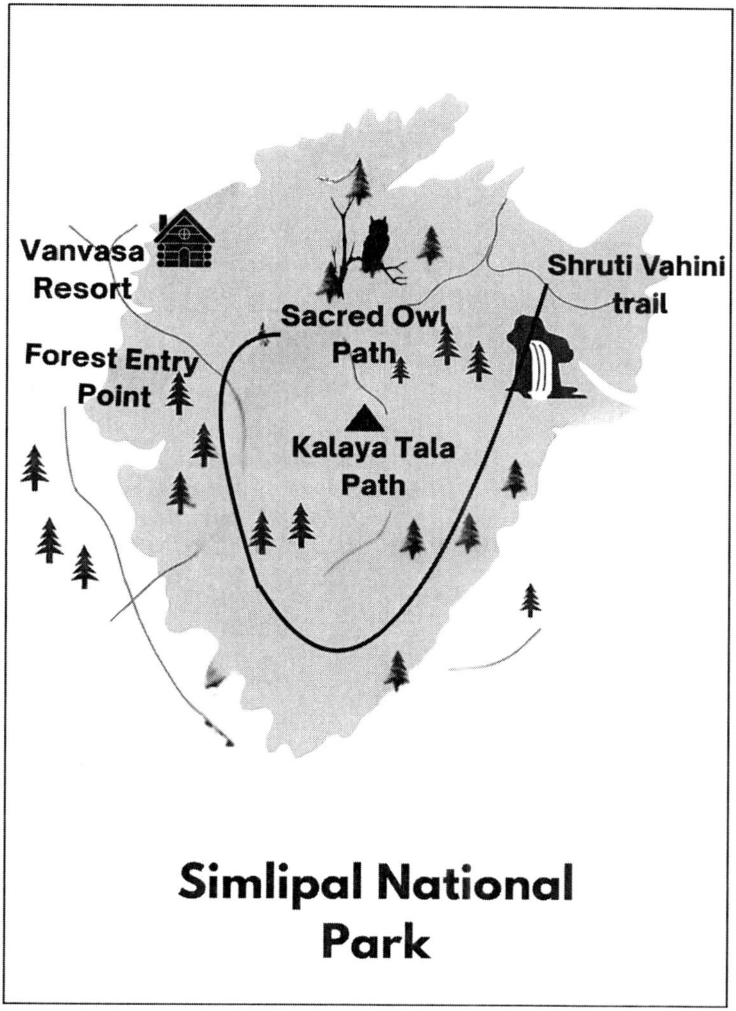

# SIMLIPAL:
# A REAL FOREST OF WONDERS

Much of this story unfolded in Simlipal — and unlike the mysteries of the book, Simlipal is very real. Nestled in the **Mayurbhanj district of northern Odisha**, this vast forest is one of India's richest natural treasures.

### Where it Lies

Simlipal spreads across more than **2,700 square kilometers** of hills, valleys, and rivers. Declared a **Tiger Reserve in 1973** and later recognized as a **UNESCO Biosphere Reserve**, it is both a sanctuary for wildlife and a living classroom of nature.

### The Land

The forest is a patchwork of **Sal trees, grassy meadows, and rolling hills** rising above 1,000 meters. Its rivers feed the land generously, tumbling down in waterfalls like **Barehipani** (India's second highest at 399 m) and **Joranda**, whose white streams glisten against dark green slopes.

### The Life Within

Simlipal is home to a remarkable variety of animals — from **tigers, elephants, leopards, and gaurs** to delicate herds of **sambar and deer**. Bird lovers can spot over **350 species**, from the serpent eagle circling high to the scarlet minivet darting through branches. Even rarer are the **melanistic (black) tigers**, a sight found almost nowhere else in the world.

### People and Culture

Beyond its trees and trails, Simlipal is also the home of indigenous communities — **Santhal, Ho, Munda and others** — whose traditions and songs are tied deeply to the forest. For them, the land is not just a resource, but a guardian of memory and identity.

### Why It Matters

To walk in Simlipal is to feel both serenity and awe — a place where silence is alive, rivers sing, and the air itself seems to carry old wisdom. As readers, you may have followed the Guardians through its pages of mystery; as travelers, you may one day follow its paths of beauty.

Simlipal is not only a backdrop to this tale — it is a reminder that some of the greatest wonders are not imagined, but waiting for us, still alive, in the heart of nature.